midnight in the chapel of love

matthew r. davis

ISBN: 978-1-950305-58-2 (sc)
ISBN: 978-1-950305-59-9 (ebook)
Library of Congress Control Number: 2020937698

First printing edition: January 29, 2021
Published by JournalStone Publishing in the United States of America.
Cover Design and Layout: Don Noble
Edited by Sean Leonard
Proofreading and Interior Layout by Scarlett R. Algee

JournalStone Publishing
3205 Sassafras Trail
Carbondale, Illinois 62901

JournalStone books may be ordered through booksellers or by contacting:
JournalStone | www.journalstone.com

In loving memory of my aunt, Margaret Pasche (1935-2015)

midnight in the chapel of love

destruction makes the world burn brighter

BILLY ROSS JR. HAD GROWN up hard with nothing but a bad reputation and a chip on his shoulder, both handed down by his deadbeat father, but now he had everything he'd ever wanted: the car, the girl, and the gun.

The wind streaming through the open window of the stolen FB Special was warm even this early in the morning, and the summer sun hovered low over the horizon ahead as if beckoning them home. He knew they'd never make it, but this ride was worth any price. And if he needed a reminder of freedom's cost, he had only to glance down at the .223 calibre rifle leaning against the vinyl bench seat by his thigh…or across to his passenger, the only thing he'd found in eighteen hardscrabble years that made life bearable.

Poppy Diamantopoulos rode beside him like teenage royalty, resplendent in her navy polka-dot baby doll dress, long strands of liquorice-black hair dancing on the wind as she tuned the FB's Air Chief radio into a hissy rendition of "Poison Ivy". Her heart sustained him; he had been and would be nothing without her love. Just the sound of her voice was enough to send a pulse of passion up his spine—whether whooping in delight at a favourite song, panting devotion into his ear as he rode her hard to heaven, or passing cold judgement on the world that had tried to keep them apart. Poppy was his bride in all but law, his accomplice and lover and completion in all senses. Barely two months had passed since her fifteenth birthday, and barely two days since they'd begun their hot red honeymoon. In the last forty-eight hours, they had killed nine people.

Poppy sang along to "Poison Ivy" with relish, curling bare legs beneath her on the bench seat, and asked one of her favourite questions: "Is this song about me, Billy?"

He smiled and gave his standard response. "All the songs are about you, baby."

She laughed high and fast, pleased. "I'd like to be a pop singer. And you're handsome enough to be on *Teen Scene* and *Kommotion*. Hey, maybe we could cut a record, Billy! All the famous people do one."

And sure enough, they were that now; Billy had heard the news reports over the wireless, seen their photographs in the papers. "Strewth, wouldn't *that* be a thing? Nah, not with my ugly mug. And we're the wrong kinda famous, Pops."

He pictured them pulling up in the next town like Hollywood celebrities, greeted by the same crowd who'd turned out for The Beatles six months ago. Billy had seen reports on a mate's television and marvelled at the spectacle—he'd never seen so many people in one place, never witnessed such uncurbed passion. Those girls looked terrified and terrifying, blissfully hysterical—if they'd managed to get their hands on the Fab Four, the poor bastards would have been torn limb from limb. In his head, those girls now screamed for him, their desire as savage as it was sexual, longing for his love even as they bayed for his blood.

"That's too bad, Billy. And I think you're more handsome than all the Beatles put together."

But his love belonged to one girl only, now and forever. How could it be otherwise when she could pluck thoughts out of his head like that?

"Thanks, sweetheart." He knew he wasn't much to look at, really—thick jaw, sullen eyes, lopsided mouth—but Poppy would never believe that. And Christ, she was a stunner: wide eyes that burned like brown suns, a strong nose that softened and improved upon her dad's hawk-beak, lips of the softest velvet and sweetest promises. "You're the most beautiful girl I ever saw."

She threw him a dazzling smile and propped her head up on one hand as she sprawled against the bench seat, long locks spilling through her fingers, a certain promise made by those shining eyes and parted lips. God, she was all he could ever wish for…and to think, the world had tried to keep them apart.

Growing up poor and without prospects, Billy had quickly come to see that his place in Waterwich was a lowly one, and for years he'd even accepted that—dropping out of school because they said he'd never be smart, starting at the garage because they said he'd never do any better. And in idle moments he had sometimes dreamed of turning on those who considered themselves above him, their scornful mutters turning to blood in their mouths as he fell upon them. These thoughts had passed when he'd met Poppy, the optimism of young love throwing shade on anything outside of it—only to return with a vengeance when the world had tried to keep him from her. And eventually, dreading the outcome but seeing no other way, Billy had acquiesced to his violent urges and become a killer.

But the reality of murder was so much less than he'd expected; he might as well have been slaughtering pigs on Dad's farm. He'd pulled the trigger on the .223 and watched Mr. Diamantopoulos go down with one eye burst into a wet red rose, forty years rich with memory and experience ended in an instant—and in the soil of his soul, where he'd expected regret to bloom, there was only a blank plot where a noxious weed had been pulled. Billy had shrugged off the deed like nothing at all as he turned and lined up the rifle sight on the face of Dion, Poppy's older brother. The boy had just enough time to piss himself and beg, and he'd been trying to grow a moustache that only made him look more like a child, but the rifle barked and the boy fell and Billy's second kill carried no more weight than the first.

Maybe he'd been taking the whole thing too seriously. For her part, Poppy had not merely accepted but had embraced the carnage he'd wrought upon her family. Once freed from her locked room she'd turned on them with savage glee, holding her screaming mother long enough for Billy to silence her with Dad's old service bayonet. Christ, she'd even taken the blade off him to slaughter her hated little sister, and Billy had thought that would get to him if anything would. But he'd felt nothing, just a kind of dull hum like a television set warming up, until Poppy had wrapped him in a wet red embrace and kissed him with a fierceness born of fire. She was the only thing that could make him feel now.

For Billy, murder wasn't exhilarating, carnal, or freeing; it just *was.* People had to die—that was simply the way the world worked. Some things were fixed, immutable, a natural law. For example, he and Poppy *had* to be together—this had been promised, proven to them in no uncertain terms. Their love was pure and true as tempered steel, tested and triumphant.

And now, just to remind him of this truth, Billy Thorpe and the Aztecs turned the airwaves over to The Dixie Cups. Poppy gave a cry of delight and turned a knowing look on him. He smiled back, ignoring the open road for a moment, and touched rough fingers to her lips. She sent them back with a kiss, then began to sing along with the refrain—and the song, of course, was "Chapel of Love".

In Waterwich, people in need of reassurance or redemption went to church. Those who sought a different kind of communion went looking for the Chapel.

Billy could feel the heat of her eyes as he drove and smiled just to know that she was looking. Hers was the only gaze on him; the fields to either side of the road were flat and lifeless, offering up only the odd curious crow or apathetic cow. They were many miles from Waterwich now, deep into the South Australian countryside, with an occasional farm the only sign of human habitation between tiny towns that looked deserted when they blew through. Perhaps the locals had been listening to the wireless, heard about the killer kids on the lam, and locked themselves in for the duration. Good. Billy had no particular desire to spill blood, but everyone in the country was against him now, would come between he and Poppy—and that couldn't be allowed.

A road sign flashed by, announcing that the next town was three miles away. Billy checked the fuel gauge, figured they'd be okay for a little longer—best not to stop in populated areas. They could always drop in on a farm and steal some petrol if need be, along with food, cigarettes, and other supplies. They probably wouldn't even need to kill the occupants to get their way, but Poppy might insist upon it. Unlike Billy, she seemed to have taken a shine to murder. Some people were just naturals.

And then there were people like his dad. Billy Ross Sr. had met his wife after returning from duty in North Africa, so neither she nor his son knew what he'd been like before the war. But the man who came back was quiet, haunted, quick to anger and prone to follow it up with a guilt chaser. He must have seen death up close and ugly, smelled its breath on his face, maybe even passed it on to a Kraut or two, and this experience had broken him; nearly twenty years on from the war's end, Billy's father was little more than the stench of cheap booze and stale failures. And yet Billy himself had killed—men, women, even children and old ladies—and was no worse off for the experience. He'd always known he was better than that miserable old bastard, but it was deeply satisfying to have that belief confirmed. It was clear from his name on down that William Ross Junior was supposed to be a shadow of his progenitor, but history would remember otherwise.

A stand of gum trees loomed ahead on either side of the road where it curved around and out of sight. Billy cast another glance across at Poppy, his eyes following the smooth olive curves of her legs up to where they disappeared under the hem of her dress, and she giggled and stuck out her tongue before looking away. Then she tensed and her feet came flying down to stamp on an invisible brake pedal.

"*Billy*!"

He cut his eyes back to the road and saw what the bend had been hiding. The paddock fences on either side had been breached, allowing a large flock of Merino sheep to spill through—and now they milled about all across the road, watching stupidly as the FB arrowed toward them at fifty miles an hour. Billy's heart leaped into his throat, choking a shocked curse as he shoved his foot down on the brake. Poppy cried out and slammed against the dash, her hands keeping her from injury in lieu of the seatbelt she never bothered to use, and the car screeched to a halt on the bitumen with a good twenty yards to spare. The engine thumped and fell still like a charging beast shot dead at full gallop.

"You okay, love? Poppy?"

"I'm fine," she moaned, scrambling back onto the bench seat.

"Right, then." Billy pulled out the parking brake and frowned forward at the blocked road. "Well, bugger me."

"Damn it! Those bloody fucking sheep!" Poppy, raised to be a good girl by God-fearing Greek Orthodox parents, had taken to swearing with a naïve relish. "What are we going to do?"

"Well, we can't drive through 'em, Pops."

"I'll make them move." Poppy grabbed his old man's bayonet off the floor and shot him a dark grin. "I always hated sheep."

"Nah, I'll take care of this." Billy hefted the .223 and opened the driver's door. A warning shot ought to scare them off, or failing that, they could just get back in the car and nudge their way through the fleecy beggars.

They left the FB and convened before its bonnet, surveying the flock scattered across the road before them. The sheep were dense, standing at least ten deep, and looked a little spooked. Already wired from having to be constantly on guard, Billy felt a flicker of unease. He glanced behind to see if anyone was cutting them off, but the Holden's tail fins pointed back to an empty road. Facing forward, he peered into the thick stands of gum trees to either side of the road and caught a flash of light that might have been the morning sun glancing off metal.

"Get back in the car," he said, taking a step in Poppy's direction. But her eyes were still fixed on the road ahead, and now they shot wide.

"Oh, fuck," she said.

Amongst the sheep, shadows were rising on two feet. *Men.* At least half a dozen of them, aiming down the long barrels of police-issued rifles as they came up. Billy sucked in a breath and reflexively lifted his own gun, but then a stentorian voice barked a word in the near distance and a string of firecrackers went off. Billy flinched, turning to scream at Poppy.

She was raising the bayonet, her delicate little mouth gaping open, shock and confusion bringing out the child in her. Before Billy could even think of going to her, that baby doll dress puffed out in one, two, three places and fresh crimson carnations blossomed through the navy cotton, ragged and irregular where the polka dots were uniformly round. Poppy flinched backwards, her face dull with shock, and Billy barely felt a bullet take off the tip of his thumb as he watched his lover's final spasmodic dance. A terrible scream filled his head at the sight of her blood flying free, the sound of his world ending, and he welcomed the steel fists that slammed into his own body and stole his breath. His knees crumpled beneath the blows, and the last he saw of Poppy before she spun out of sight was a flap of her skull lifting away on a burst of violent vermilion. It was that, not the sudden impact of bitumen, that hit him hardest, left him dazed and staring up into the bright void.

The sky was so blue.

Billy squirmed on the road, laid open by at least four bullets, moaning in agony and loss and denial. Here it was, the end, just the way he'd known it would be ever since he'd driven out to Poppy's farm with the gun and blade on the seat beside him—but it was too soon, *too soon.* They would never have had the chance to find their own place in the world, raise children, grow old—he'd accepted that—but so fast? *Two days.* They'd been promised forever together, but neither could have guessed just how short forever could be.

He reached out with his right hand as brisk footsteps slapped against the bitumen, as orders were rapped out and sheep protested at the commotion. He needed Poppy's fingers in his one last time. That grip had saved his life once before, kept him sane, kept him here. Consciousness began to roll away from him, and Billy felt dark waters once again closing over his head. Another test. He just had to hold on, prove his love, but this time he couldn't find her hand, and this time, when he was pulled down into the depthless dark, he went alone.

from the edge of the deep green sea

JONNY WOKE SO FAST HE might never have been asleep. One moment he was dead to the world, the next he was wide awake and staring up at the pale ceiling, the sheet thrown half-off him in the summer heat and Sloane's hand warm and moist as it lay clutched in his own. He'd already forgotten the dream that had ejected him from slumber, but he instinctively knew who must have haunted that vision.

Dad.

He groped on the nightstand with his free hand until he found his phone and squinted at the display: *05:03 Thu. 10 Dec.* He let out a hiss of frustration like air escaping a deflating tire—he'd gone to bed at 1 AM, and only then because a few rums had brought on the necessary malaise. Consciousness had returned too soon, and he had the feeling it was here to stay.

Great. Work is going to be a blast today.

He didn't have to be at the Hamburger Hilton until 10:30, but after just four hours' sleep the kitchen might as well be a prison yard. He enjoyed the work and liked his team, but as he moved further into his thirties Jonny found himself treasuring his sleep more and more. Without at least five hours he would feel dazed and dirty and out of sorts all day, and that was bound to come out in his attitude.

Lucky I've already got a good excuse.

Ah, yes. Back to that. Guilt, shame, regret.

Jonny sighed and kicked the sheet the rest of the way off. He noticed he was three-quarters hard, which probably had less to do with the heat of Sloane's hand in his and more with the three glasses of rum he'd drunk before bed. He glanced over, decided she was too deeply asleep to bother, and gently prised his fingers free. Patting her hand, he rolled off the bed and stumbled out of their bedroom.

The bathroom light was painfully bright, its sterile whiteness adding to the surreal nature of this too-early morning. Jonny pissed, flushed, washed up, then padded out into the living room. The bottle of Oakheart was where he'd left it on the dining table, attended by a finger-smeared glass. Why not? It had worked a few hours ago, and in any case, they lived close enough to town that he usually biked or bussed in to work. With a lassitude he hoped to encourage, Jonny slumped naked into his chair and poured himself a glass of rum.

He wasn't much of a drinker these days; he'd probably consumed more alcohol in the past week than in the last three months. But what the fuck, right? Your father only died once.

Of course, that wasn't the worst of it. Everyone's parents died eventually, and no-one was ever really ready for it. But Jonny hadn't spoken to his dad for two months, hadn't seen the man in the flesh for six, and hadn't been back to Waterwich even once in the past fifteen years. That was due to change, of course, because the funeral was on Saturday—and where else would it be held but the small country town where Alan Trotter had been born, spawned, and finally died?

Jonny took a slug of rum and winced. He wasn't looking forward to the trip. He'd never quite felt at home in Waterwich, and a decade and a half of city living had relieved him of any latent rurality he'd once possessed. He'd left his old self there to rot, forgotten by him even as it was all that was remembered by those who had stayed behind, and he'd left his old pains and secrets and griefs there too. But therein lay the rub—you could run from yourself all you liked, but when you finally turned to make sure you'd made a clean break, you'd always find the ghost of your past standing at your heels, holding all those humiliations and heartbreaks in its arms like wounded pets in need of close attention. And maybe you owed it to yourself to take a look, for old times' sake. And sometimes that was like accepting a truth you'd always found too big to handle—a responsibility, a death.

Going home was the last thing Jonny wanted to do—his heart lay here in Adelaide with Sloane and dreams of a bright future, not back there with distrusted memories of a dead past. But his father was going into the ground, and he owed the man too much to not be there. Despite the troubles that had ultimately kept them apart, this was the humble god who'd created him, raised him, taught and praised him. So Jonny was going to Waterwich on Saturday, and he was going to watch as his father was buried, and hopefully everything else he'd left behind in that place would be laid to rest, too.

Jonny had another sip of rum and glanced at the pile of mail on the kitchen table. On top was the funeral announcement Mick Oliver had sent him—everywhere he looked now he saw the past glaring back at him, inescapable. He cut his eyes away across the room, and that was when he noticed the small black object on the floor just inside the apartment's front door.

He froze, glass halfway to the table. For a moment, he assumed a paperback had slipped out of Sloane's overstuffed shelves and tumbled to the floor, but no book was that thin.

Of course. The tenth of December.

With his father's death weighing on his mind, he'd forgotten what else the past could throw up. But now that he was looking at it, he realised he wasn't surprised, not really. Somewhere in the depths of his heart, he'd been expecting this.

Jonny put down his glass and strode to the door, bending to pick up the black envelope that had been pushed beneath it. It hadn't been there when he'd retired to bed four hours ago, so how long had it been awaiting his notice? Before he could think twice, he opened the door and pushed his head out into the corridor.

The other doors on this level stared back at him, poker-faced. The clean white floor of the hallway bore no tracks to show that anyone had walked across its back. The only sound was the quiet hum of fluorescent lights, and beyond that, the repetitive song of early birds. The apartment complex gave off a barren vibe, a movie set that had been closed down and abandoned for the night.

What did you expect?

Jonny remembered he was naked and closed the door before one of his neighbours popped out for a pre-dawn jog. He held the envelope like a dangerous object as he crossed back to the table and slumped in his seat, staring dully at this mysterious missive.

It looked just like the last two. The envelope was smaller than standard, a size often used for greetings or invitations, and the lack of an address or stamp confirmed that it had been hand-delivered. Its blank black face gave no clue to its contents other than the single silver-ink letter penned neatly in the centre: *J*. He turned it over—no return address, of course—and peeled open its flap with a careful fingernail. The plain white card within, like the others before it, bore nothing but a brief felt-tip message in an all-too-familiar hand:

You know where to find me.

Jonny closed the envelope, and it rasped against one cheek as he dropped his face into his hands. The paper bore a faint scent, one he remembered from long ago, and the weight of the past doubled as it bore down on his sorry head. Flashes of memory danced across his mind, some beautiful, some terrible, and he felt himself falling into a deep green sea that had once held all the promise his young mind could imagine. Once it had been so warm, welcoming; now it was cold and judgemental and unforgiving.

He sat up with a jerk and dropped the envelope on the table, staring at it like it had bitten him. A quiet shuffle came from the bedroom, a body turning over, and he turned to watch the hall until he was sure Sloane was merely rolling over in her sleep. After a minute, he relaxed and reached for his glass. The envelope sat there and continued to exist, a bombshell in black, and his free hand reached out to trace its edges. He didn't speak until he'd finished the rum and its cosy heat had failed to chase away the fresh chill in his heart.

"Jessica," he whispered.

the last day of summer

"EVER WONDER WHERE IT ALL goes?"

Jonno was so lost in the gentle rush of the creek that it took him a moment to realise someone had spoken and another to understand that they were addressing him.

Glancing up and to his left, he winced as the afternoon sun glared back and blinded him. Raising one hand to shield his eyes, he could see only a silhouette in the low branches of a nearby tree, backlit hair dancing in the gentle breeze.

"What's that?" Jonno stepped backwards up the bank until another eucalyptus blocked the sun, but then his foot slipped and dumped him on his rump in the grass. "Bugger!"

The girl in the tree barked out a single stab of laughter. She was new in town and new at his school—he'd seen her slipping into the back row of his classes, where she gave off the kind of don't-fuck-with-me vibe usually reserved for the first day of jail. There was no mistaking her for anyone else; none of the girls he knew wore long bottle-black hair, or had a ring through their eyebrow, or would even think about wearing a T-shirt with ZERO stamped across the chest in silver. She was sitting cross-legged on a stout branch about a metre above the bank, thick-soled boots peeping out from beneath the hem of her long black skirt, one hand dangling down to tap cigarette ash on the earth as if she hoped to seed future fires.

"Er, hi." Jonno clambered to his feet, covering his embarrassment with a laugh. "Sorry, what was that?"

"The water. Ever wonder where it all ends up?"

"The sea, I suppose. How, er, how long have you been sitting there?"

"Long enough to get curious. You've been staring at the water for, like, five minutes."

Had it really been that long? "Right. Yeah, I do that sometimes."

"Why?"

Her bluntness was refreshing, and for a moment Jonno thought he might actually tell her. The notion startled him into a silence that stretched out to awkward lengths. In the end, he settled for clearing his throat.

"I've seen you around at school," the girl stated, taking the hint. "You're Jonno, right?"

"Yeah."

"That's such a bogan name."

"Well, it's Jonathan, but people started calling me Jonno years ago and it stuck."

"Doesn't it just." The girl butted out her smoke on the trunk of the tree, popped it into an empty cigarette pack and the pack into her black canvas satchel, then slipped from the branch and trudged across the bank toward him. "But if people start calling me Jesso, there's going to be trouble."

"Oh, yeah. You're Jessica, right?"

She extended a hand and grasped his in greeting, her fingers cool and firm as the rings that adorned them. Jessica was blessed with full lips and matching hips, her skin pale as milk in contrast with the ebony of her clothes and hair. Her eyes were a deep and fascinating green beneath heavy lids that made her look sleepy, sultry, stoned; pencil-darkened brows rose above them in sardonic arches, as if the wind had changed and caught her in a moment of cynical amusement.

"Grzelak."

"Bless you."

"Ha ha. It's Polish. And a word to the wise: *never* make fun of a Polish chick."

"Fair enough. Well, I'm a Trotter. That's English, I guess."

"Trotter! And you were laughing at *my* name, little piggy?"

Jonno frowned at old memories of playground taunts and spoke without thinking. "Grzelak isn't a name, it's a bad *Scrabble* draw."

She watched him with narrowed eyes, and for a moment Jonno worried that he'd pushed back too hard. Then the shadow of a smile crossed her face.

"Cheeky fucker, aren't you?"

Relief made him break out in a sudden smile. "That makes two of us."

Perhaps she'd heard a question in that, for she shook her head. "Nice to meet you, but I'm just here to finish high school, and then I'm going back home to the city. So don't get used to seeing me around. Goodbye, *Jonathan.*"

Jessica turned and walked up the bank toward the road. She didn't look back once, and he found he liked that—not just because she wouldn't catch him admiring the way her skirt stretched over her rump with each upward stride, but also because it implied she knew exactly who she was and where she was going…and as a callow, uncertain youth surrounded by more of the same, he found that confidence both admirable and alluring.

Jonno retrieved his school bag from its bed of soursobs and walked up the bank to the road. Casting a glance after the retreating figure in black, he turned and headed in the opposite direction, and it was at least a minute before he realised he was still smiling.

That grin was gone by the time he reached his destination a few minutes later, pushing through the glass-panelled door that led into the front bar of the Cutters Arms. Idle musings about his exchange with Jessica were replaced with the resignation that usually preceded the start of another shift in the pub kitchen.

Mick Oliver was behind the bar, a friendly scarecrow in neat jeans and tucked-in flannel shirt, back turned to his double in the mirror behind him as he swept up a handful of change and took it to the till. Jack Nichols was the only customer at this pre-dinner hour, sipping the foam from a fresh pint; in a town with a marked taste for a cold ale, he was the pub's best customer, as if he felt compelled to live up to the reputation of his near-namesake.

"G'day, Mick. G'day, Jack."

The men tipped him nods of greeting as he made his way across the wooden floor. The old tabletop video game between the toilet doors tempted him for a moment, but *Gyruss* had been in residence for years and he'd shot all the spaceships he cared to shoot for the time being. Instead, he angled toward the end of the bar and pushed his way through the STAFF ONLY door into the pub kitchen.

Half an hour shy of dinnertime, Mary Bennington was clocked in and wiping down a counter she'd already cleaned after the previous night's shift. Mary was your archetypal country lady, friendly and dependable to a fault, and her presence at the Cutters Arms dated back to 1985, when Jonno's parents had thrown in with Mick Oliver to buy the place. She'd been an old friend of his mother's, and in that woman's absence, the source of a maternal vibe that all three men were otherwise missing in their lives.

"Hi, Mare."

She paused in her cleaning for a moment and sighed, not looking up at him, and Jonno wondered what he might have done to upset her.

"G'day, Jonno." She recommenced her work but didn't lift her eyes from the countertop. "How was your day?"

"Okay, I guess. I went out for some footy kicks with Brendan after school, and then…uh, are you all right?"

Mary tossed the rag to one side and straightened, meeting his eyes with a solemn gaze. "Nah, not really, love. Look, I've got some bad news."

"Carl," Jonno guessed. Her husband had been fighting his pervasive illness for a year now. "Is he okay?"

"He's taken a turn for the worse. He's gonna need constant care, and we just can't afford to get someone in. I'm gonna have to stay home to look after him." Mary glanced away, looking for something else she could clean, fix, make right. "So tonight's my last night here, love."

"Oh." Jonno had no idea what to say to that. Mary had been a fixture at the pub for a decade and a half; her departure was monumental. He gave her a sympathetic half-smile and hoped she understood it as well as any words he might be able to muster. And, of course, she did—women were well-versed in the inarticulation of men, and didn't get to her age without being able to read their emotions between the flat lines they spoke aloud. She returned his smile with one just as sad that told him he didn't need to fumble for words for her to understand his feelings.

"I'm sorry." That sounded lame, but Jonno was uncomfortable sharing the silence with this new bombshell. "Well, I'd better…"

"Yeah, you go get ready, sweetheart. See you in a bit."

Jonno was in a pensive mood as he trod upstairs to the second floor. Up here they kept eight rooms—four for paying guests, one each for Mick, Jonno, and Dad, and one for the pub office. That door was closed but Jonno could tell his father was inside, going over accounts or filling out order forms or whatever it was he did in there. He didn't feel like discussing Mary's impending departure with Dad until he'd processed the information himself, so he padded by the office and went to his own room.

Jonno dropped his schoolbag beside the unmade bed, a rumpled altar beneath posters of Metallica and Eminem and Korn that he'd pulled from magazines, and kicked his shoes across the room. Then he quickly stripped and dumped his clothes into the washing hamper, wrinkling his nose at the pungent scents of grass and sweat that clung to his skin from the after-school footy.

Could Jessica smell that on me? Should've sprayed some Brut on.

He strode into the ensuite bathroom and stood naked before the mirror, imagining her eyes running over this sight for the first time.

Frequent football and the constant demands of the pub had stripped him of any puppy fat, leaving his lanky body toned and capable, and puberty had bothered him with little more than the occasional rash of pimples on his forehead. Would *she* like to see him like this, in all his bare-arsed glory? The thought excited him, and his penis raised its head from its curly nest to eye itself in the mirror. Jonno opened the shower door and his mind had Jessica already in there, naked and waiting and smiling a sultry smile, her deep green eyes hotter than the water that gushed from the shower head, and from his own.

At six o'clock Jonno pushed through the kitchen door again, this time fresh and clean and ready to get started. Mary greeted him with a smile and they worked in casual silence as always, but there was an undercurrent of melancholy. He tried to avoid it by calling to mind the way Jessica's fingers had felt in his or the way her skirt stretched against her bottom when she walked, but every time he glanced up Mary was there, crumbing fillets and slicing vegetables and frying chips, and that merely strengthened the maternal connection in his mind.

Many of his fondest memories of Mum involved cooking—stumbling over the reading of recipes, passing her ingredients, shrieking with laughter when she dusted his nose with flour or chased him around the kitchen with an egg whisk. That must be why he had such a fondness and aptitude for preparing food, something that had developed along with his mind and body to the point where it seemed to bother his father, as if it signalled further womanly interests to come. Still, there was no denying that a man who could cook would never be short of job opportunities or female interest, and Jonno's talent spared Dad the chore of finding another kitchen hand, so he left his son to it.

Tonight's shift was a busy one—word had gotten around about Mary's departure, and a healthy crowd had gathered for one last counter meal by her hands. At the end of the three-hour stint, Jonno felt like he'd prepared and served a barnyard's worth of meat, but he still insisted on wiping everything down so Mary could take it easy for once. She gave him a grateful smile and got her things ready for a quiet departure out the kitchen's back door, but Jonno just shook his head and led her into the front bar. Dad and Mick were waiting with an explosion of flowers and a gift basket, and they held court for a few minutes to say some things about Mary that had her dabbing at her eyes with a handkerchief, and when she finally made her exit, the room was still echoing with heartfelt applause from the customers and friends she'd more than earned in her fifteen years at the Cutters Arms.

Jonno dreamed of her that night. He dreamed that he walked into the pub kitchen and found Mary standing at the open back door, holding a hushed conversation with someone outside, and when she saw him watching, she closed the door with an expressionless look. He hurried across the room, certain it was his mother she'd been talking to, and when he threw the door open there was a sign he'd been right—a single potted daisy sat on the threshold, nodding gently in a breeze he couldn't feel. But of Daisy Trotter herself there was no sign; she had been swallowed by the depths of the night, if she'd ever been there at all, and when he turned to question Mary, he found that she was gone, too.

At this point Jonno became vaguely aware that he was waking up, or had already done so, and yet still he stood in darkness. Ahead of him now was a vast hump of rock, gnarled and slate grey, that rose up from damp earth like a head from cold shoulders. Punched into the centre of this heap was a small cave, a hollow as deep and black as the night itself, and the longer he looked, the more certain he was that he should look away before being sucked in and swallowed whole. The cave mouth felt electric, charged with ancient secrets, a black hole at the centre of a universe that was pulled slowly and inexorably into it like bathwater into a drain, and he knew he had to look away or risk losing everything.

It wasn't until he heard movement nearby that he was finally able to tear his eyes from that bottomless pit. The sound was weighty and wet, made by something that dragged and dripped and shuffled closer by the second. It came from one side of the rock, where it slanted down to a jagged shoulder, and Jonno thought it sounded very much like the sound a drowned man would make as he staggered forward on sodden and lifeless limbs. That recalled all those nights he'd spent as a child in bed with the sheets pulled up to his nose, staring into the depths of an open closet and scaring himself giddy with thoughts of what might be staring back, and then he realised that he *was* that child, not a near-man of seventeen but a boy of seven, alone in the dark and—worse—*not* alone. Then the thing making those horrid sounds stumbled over the low crest of the rock, man-sized and man-shaped and dripping with cold water and reaching for him with crooked fingers, and just as he began to see its face he saw that its mouth was a black hole like the cave of horrors beside them, and as it opened wider he knew that what lay within was even worse.

And then he realised that the darkness was just the back of his eyelids, that he was awake and in his own bedroom, and the only movement he saw as he rolled over and fell back into dreamless sleep was the red digits of his alarm clock as they ticked over to 12:00.

* * *

The next day brought another stolid slab of school and Jonno spent the first half of it in Business Maths and Home Economics, very aware there was no alluring shadow parked in the back corner of the room. At lunchtime he headed down to the canteen to grab a pasty, but another kind of hunger awoke in him when he saw Jessica Grzelak sitting alone on a bench fixed to the side of the tuck shop. Despite the warmth, she was wearing the same all-black ensemble as yesterday. His eyes flicked of their own accord to her chest and he saw that wasn't quite true; today, the Smashing Pumpkins shirt had been replaced with a Marilyn Manson top that declared GOD IS IN THE TV.

Try not to fall on your arse this time, doofus.

"Jonathan," she said by way of greeting, without a hint of sarcasm, and he relished the way his full name sounded in her mouth. "Stared at any good creeks lately?"

"That one we saw yesterday was pretty cool. Five stars."

She didn't seem at all bothered when he took a seat beside her on the bench, though he might have expected her to be a little defensive. Few people had made the effort to approach Jessica at this early stage of the school year, perhaps leery of her appearance, and Jonno had heard a few contemptuous comments muttered in her direction: *Morticia, Draculette, cemetery girl.* She was probably assuming it was just a matter of time before she was chased with pitchforks or ducked in the school's fishpond.

"You're not on a dare or something, are you?" she asked, sounding almost disinterested.

"What?"

"Well, some of the kids here look at me like I'm going to make the crops fail or something. So, if you've come to speak to the freak on a dare, allow me to remind you what I said yesterday about making fun of Polish girls."

Jonno held up his hands. "No, no. I'm here because I want to be."

And I like your look, he almost added as she shrugged and turned back to her bucket of hot chips. *Fin de siècle* fashion had made its way even into the cloistered heart of Waterwich, and Jonno found it a refreshing change from the usual flannel shirts, jeans, and Blundstones. He made occasional trips to the city to see punky alternative bands with Brendan and Coralie, so piercings and dreadlocks and other urban trappings were not new to him. He found them interesting, exotic, and even—in certain cases—a little erotic.

"So. How was your night?"

"Blah," Jessica replied, blowing on her chips. "Watched a *Hellraiser* movie, listened to some tunes, read a book. How about you?"

"Well, I work in the pub kitchen most nights. My dad owns the place."

"Oh, okay. What's it called?"

"The Cutters Arms."

Jessica nearly choked on a chip. "What? Really?"

"Yeah, why?"

"Is it a goth club or something?"

"Huh? Oh, right. Ha. You know, I never thought of it that way before."

"Oh, come on."

"No, really! A cutter is a type of ship—this town was named after one. When I was a kid, I used to imagine a boat with arms. You know, like, to catch fish and stuff."

Now she was looking at him with one of those dark brows arched higher than usual, like *he* was the weird one, so he shrugged and went back to the previous topic.

"So anyway, last night was pretty full-on. One of the ladies who works with us had to quit to look after her husband, and none of the other cooks can do any more hours. Which means I'm going to be flat-out in the kitchen until we find someone else. Not cool."

He suspected he might be boring her, but when he glanced over, he saw that Jessica had turned on her seat to face him as if he were finally worthy of her full attention.

"So, what—you're looking to hire a new kitchen hand?"

"Yeah."

"I see." Jessica stared intently at him for a moment, and then, as if she'd made a judgement, she gave a lofty smile. "Well, today's your lucky day, Jonathan Trotter. I'll take the job."

He blinked. "Say what?"

"I've been looking for something to keep me busy in this boring little town. And I could use the cash. Boots don't just pay for themselves, you know."

"Okay…"

"And if I must, I'll bribe you with hot chips." She extended the cup toward him, then pulled it away when he reached for one, laughing at his mock scowl.

"Hmm." Jonno's mind was suddenly awash with possibilities, and he liked every one of them. "Do you have any experience in food prep?"

She nodded. "Back in town, I spent a few months working at a restaurant."

"Which one?"

"You might have heard of it. It's called McDonald's."

"Ah."

Jessica held out the cup again, and this time she let him snag a chip. Jonno regarded her thoughtfully as he chewed. The thought of Jessica standing beside him with a knife was a little scary and a lot exciting.

"Tell you what. We've got half an hour before we go back to class. You want to come over to the pub for a job interview?"

Jessica probed him with a stare as if gauging the sincerity of his statement—perhaps even his soul. Whatever she saw must have pleased her, for she smiled and said, "Sure. That'd be cool."

"Okay, then."

Jonno rose to his feet and Jessica followed suit, hefting her bag onto one shoulder. She was still smiling, and he could see himself drowning in those deep green eyes.

"Let's go see my father."

be quiet and drive (far away)

THE TENSION IN JONNY'S GUT grew greater the closer he drew to Waterwich, like his innards were wound in a windlass that cranked tighter with every kilometre travelled. He tried to ignore it and lose himself in the mechanics of driving, in the beat of the Something for Kate track that was up on his iPod's randomised playlist—but everywhere he looked, he saw things that reminded him of his destination. There to his left was the old cart wheel marking the entrance to the McCarthy farm, followed by the roadside row of discarded toilets that Mrs. McCarthy had repurposed as flowerpots; it was much longer than he remembered, two dozen pale and wide-mouthed vases with gaudy roses leaning out of each to nod their heads in the breeze, a ceramic simile. To his right, shreds of black garbage-bag plastic flapped where they'd been caught on a barbed wire fence, restless ghosts trapped in place for eternity. And here now was a road sign announcing WATERWICH 10, pointing up the fact that he was only five minutes from the home he'd hoped never to see again.

He should have been cool, what with the Clubsport's air conditioner busy at its job—he might even have expected a chill in his heart at the proximity of so many bad memories. But instead, Jonny felt flushed with a persistent warmth that might have been shame. He'd avoided Waterwich for fifteen years, refused to see his only living relative on his home turf, abandoned his best friends and everyone who'd helped him grow up. And now, today, he'd have to face them all over again.

This is a terrible idea.

It was no worse than the alternative. What was he going to do, shun his father's funeral? Gruelling as today was going to be for him, Jonny was hardly so callous as to turn his back at a time like this. Besides, Sloane would never let him get away with such a betrayal.

He turned and glanced over at the passenger seat. Sloane had one foot up on the corner of the dash, her leg bare all the way down to the hem of the summer dress rumpled around the top of her thigh, her eyes inscrutable behind red-framed sunglasses as she perused a file on her tablet. A wide-brim Panama hat was tilted back on her head, allowing her long dark hair to hang free; a few strands at the front had gone grey early, adding a distinguished look that was at odds with her youthful face. She sensed his gaze and looked up, sliding the sunglasses an inch or so down her pert nose to reveal the brown Asian eyes that were the most obvious sign of her mixed heritage.

"Watch the road, mister," she said, in a tone that made him want to forget that boring strip of bitumen altogether. "Let's get there in one piece."

Jonny gave a mordant grunt. "I suppose it'd be pretty poor manners to upstage the funeral by dying on the way there."

Sloane reached out and rested her hand on his forearm for a moment, and Jonny felt like a grumbling teenager all over again. "What are you working on there?"

"Just going over some revision notes." Sloane was an acquisitions manager for Veritable Publications, a well-regarded Adelaide small press. "You know, I can't help but feel today is like the start of a book. We're heading back to the country town where you grew up, to attend your father's funeral. If this were one of our manuscripts, your chequered past would come back to haunt you, and—I'm doing it again, aren't I? Sorry. This is hardly the time."

"Yeah, I don't exactly need any reminders."

Sloane lived with her head half in the real world and half in the land of fiction, and she was quick to relate the one to the other. If anything, this only made her more acutely aware of the machinery that ground away behind the scenes of everyday life, and Jonny tried not to wince as he recognised the truth of her remark. Waterwich *was* full of ghosts, and that was exactly why he'd shunned the place for so long.

"I know you're really stressing out about this, Jonny. But it's going to be okay, you know that. And if you need anything, I'm right here."

"I know, babe. You're a rock."

"Wow, you really know how to flatter a girl."

"A smart, sexy, independent rock."

"Ha! Better leave the wordsmithery to the professionals, chum. Speaking of which…" Sloane tapped in a few last notes, then closed the file and let the tablet fall in her lap. "How much longer 'til we get in?"

"Just a few minutes."

Jonny kept his voice steady, but his heart was racing faster than ever. The road described a sharp curve just ahead, a crash barrier following the corner where the edge of the bend sloped down to meet Cold Bath Creek. He stared at the spot, gradually becoming aware that the Clubsport was slowing as his foot eased off the accelerator, drifting to the left in preparation to park. Like his body had decided that he should stop, remember, pay tribute.

Not even there yet, and already it's too much.

This was not something he could bear to face right now, not with his soul already stretched thin upon the rack. Catching himself, Jonny wrenched his eyes back to the road and brought the car up to its former speed. But Sloane had noticed, turning her head to watch the bend blow by before fixing her partner with a curious look.

"Babe?"

Jonny gritted his teeth. "Sorry. Another…landmark, you might say."

"What, a corner? Why?"

"Before the barrier was there…if you weren't careful, you could drive right off the road and straight down into the creek."

"Ah," Sloane muttered, catching on. "So that's where…?"

"Yep."

He hoped his brusque response would discourage any further conversation on the topic, but he really should have known better. Sloane was a compassionate woman, but she had a habit of blundering straight through barriers herself.

"So, your mum drove over the edge, and all they found was the car?"

Jonny imagined the old XD station wagon dumped into the creek like a discarded toy, an empty coffin, and blinked it away. "There were a few big storms in '89. The theory was that the swollen creek took her out to sea."

She must have noticed the brittle edge to his voice. "Okay. Changing subjects, then."

"Yes, please."

"Although, you did bring it up."

"Sloane…"

"Fine. Sorry. So, about the Thing, then. I've been looking through the listings again. It would really help to know exactly what I'm working with."

And now, on top of everything, this again.

"For fuck's sake, woman. Now? Really?"

"It was the first thing that came to mind! I've been thinking about it a lot, so it's right there. But fine, no, we don't have to talk about that."

"Good. I'm about to watch my old man get put in the ground, so I hope you can appreciate that I'm not really in the mood for the Thing right now."

"I know. Sorry. Silly old Sloane, putting her foot in it again."

Her words were self-deprecating rather than sarcastic, and Jonny glanced over at the extremity in question, not willing to let a silence grow between them. "Yeah, but it's a very cute foot."

She chuffed a little laugh. "Okay. We're cool, then?"

"Of course. Always. I know I'm a bit of a hot mess right now—"

"Understandable."

"—but never forget how much I love you."

Her hand was back on his forearm now. "Duly noted, Mr. Trotter. I wouldn't be here if I didn't feel the same. And I wouldn't get all worked up about the Thing if I didn't think you were *the* guy."

"I know."

Jonny was content to leave it there for the moment. For one thing, they'd re-established equilibrium; for another, the road was beginning to bring them houses. Waterwich was opening out before them, and Jonny was coming home.

We went right past the turn-off onto Mermaid Drive, he realised as Lana Del Rey took over on the iPod. *I was too busy being shitty at my girlfriend to even notice.*

That was surely a good thing. Seeing the corner where Mum's car had run off the road had brought back enough painful memories; just thinking about what lay deep in the bush on Gavin Hunter's land was enough to turn his stomach. Dealing with the town itself was more than enough for the moment...and now they were bouncing gently in their seats as they traversed the three dips in the road that had always struck Jonny as a warning of turbulence ahead.

WELCOME TO WATERWICH—Crown Jewel of the Copper Coast, read a grand sign he didn't remember, new enough it was yet to be dulled by the sun's wilting stare. *Pop. 1,000+ Friendly Souls! Why Not "Copper Look At Us"?* He knew that if he turned to Sloane he'd see her wincing at this flagrant abuse of quotation marks, but he kept his eyes to the front as the Burr-Hill Oval slid by on his right, its yellowing grass spotted with the whites of competing cricketers. There were as many people on the field as there were watching from the boundary, and he wondered if the poor turnout was typical or affected by other, less enjoyable events being held this day.

The main street of present-day Waterwich was an odd dichotomy—everything was different, and yet everything was just the same. There was Jack Nichols's feed store, its old white face now given a vivid overhaul in navy blue and canary yellow, its name new and unfamiliar; across the road, Mino's Deli looked just the way it had fifteen years ago, its signage still promising the FISH-CHIPS-YIROS that had been a staple of his childhood diet. The old second-hand bookstore had been refitted and reopened as Crystal Empire, stocking all sorts of New Age trinkets brought in, no doubt, by some big city émigré who liked to dabble in enlightenment and babble about chakras; but Todd's Auto Repairs was right where it always had been, the garage bearing another fifteen years' wear and weather, the same old oil stains on the footpath testament to the fact that some things could never be washed away. After the modest library, the footpath still dropped away to the grassy slope that ran down to meet Cold Bath Creek, where he'd sometimes gone to be alone and stare into the rushing water; the local school had made concessions to modernity in the form of a new paint job and the angled concrete ramps of a skate park off to one side. It was foreign and familiar, alien and intact. Jonny took a deep breath that shuddered more than he would have liked.

"Seems like a nice little place," Sloane said. "Have we got time for a quick drive around, or do we need to get straight to the service?"

Jonny glanced at the dash: 3:51. "We'd better find a place for you to get changed. It starts at four."

"Did you have anywhere in mind?"

"Well, there's the pub, but that'll be closed until the wake."

He cruised down Waterwich's main drag in the direction of the pub in question, eyes flicking from side to side. Despite a recent facelift, Irene Anderton's hairdressing salon was up for sale; the local independent supermarket had become a Foodland branch; the RSL hall still sat sternly beside the ever-seedy Waterwich Hotel & Bar as if waiting to chastise its looser patrons for a lack of respect. The Cutters Arms loomed on one corner as Jonny reached the beachfront and turned right onto the Esplanade, then cut a quick left into the foreshore car park. He pulled the Clubsport up outside an ablutions block that had been brightened by a beach-themed mural, knowing Sloane would take issue with his choice but at a loss for anything else to do.

"Really? You know how I feel about getting changed in public toilets, babe. *Ick*."

He cracked his window and took a deep breath of salty sea air. "It's either this or we look for a servo with a bathroom you can use, sweetness."

"What's the diff?" Sloane sighed and slipped out of her seatbelt, heartened by the absence of any other cars nearby. "I guess I'll just have to get changed here."

Jonny nodded toward the back seat, where a fresh black dress hung from the safety handle on a coathanger. "Why didn't you just put that on this morning?"

"And drive for three hours in this heat wearing black, getting creases in the bloody thing? Not likely, babe." She doffed her hat and sunglasses, grabbed the hem of her dress. "No-one's around, right?"

The grassy strip of foreshore between the Esplanade and the beach was deserted, apart from a clutch of optimistic seagulls that hopped toward the Clubsport in hopes of a stray chip or two. The small playground that huddled between the towering pines was bare of children to give it purpose. Jonny could see a couple of people playing fetch with dogs on the sand, spotted heads bobbing in the still water and a few figures wandering along the jetty that jutted out a short way into the briny waters—but otherwise, the scene was oddly subdued for a summer day by the sea. He couldn't help but feel that his father's funeral had cast a pall over the entire town.

"The coast is clear."

Jonny watched Sloane slip out of her white summer frock and kneel on her seat in black underwear as she reached back to grab the matching dress. She remained slender as she entered her early thirties and didn't have to work too hard to stay that way—the legacy of her mother, still child-like and svelte in her mid-fifties, as opposed to her increasingly ruddy and bloated European father. He let his mind go blank for a moment and lost himself in the playful wriggle of her toes, the pronounced curve of her collarbone as it angled up to freckled shoulders, the gentle push of her compact breasts against the frilly cups of her bra.

Sloane noted his gaze and gave a wry smile. "Keep that up, and we run the risk of being *very* late to the service."

Her grin disappeared beneath the black dress as she wriggled it down over her head, and for a moment she was faceless. Jonny couldn't help but remember other bodies in black underwear, other times he'd stared, other things that had followed.

Not now.

Sloane eased the dress down over her body, adjusting as she went. She frowned at his scrutiny and so he turned to look out the window for a while as she changed her shoes, brushed her hair, applied a light lip gloss. She might have been preparing for a party, a thought that made Jonny's head ache. He'd rather have attended a dozen of her mother's Avon gatherings with their attendant wine and gossip than go through with today's ritual, but what choice did he have?

I need a drink.

There it was again, the insidious clarion call of alcohol. All week he'd been sipping at booze whenever he wasn't at work, gulping at it when Sloane wasn't around to monitor him, and for all that he knew it didn't help, in a way it did. It couldn't blank out the pain or guilt or confusion—unfortunate, especially after finding the latest black envelope slipped under his door the other morning—but it did dull them a little, blunted the edges of the blades that cut away at his soul. He hadn't brought any drink with him, though.

Not a good look, turning up pissed to a funeral. It'll have to wait until after…until the wake.

Jonny was dreading that ritual even more than the burial. At least he wouldn't be expected to say much when he stood at his father's grave, to exchange anything more than brief condolences with people who might as well have been strangers. At the wake he'd be obliged to talk, to share, to add to the din of reminiscence, when all he really wanted was for everyone to just fucking shut up and leave him to grieve in his own way.

I can't go to the wake.

But he couldn't *not* go. Blowing that off would be as bad as ditching the funeral itself. Gossip would be muttered, aspersions cast—not that it mattered much to him if he wasn't there to deal with it, but he'd been an ungrateful child long enough. Now it was time to break bread with his past, accept these burdens, make as much of a peace as he could before he fled back to the life he'd chosen over this one.

It's a shame, really, he thought, watching Sloane mist herself with perfume and give a nod of readiness. *Back in the old days, we always used to ditch out on the ceremony. Back in the old days, we always had better things to do.*

a night like this

"WE MADE IT OUT JUST in time," said Jonno as they left Jellicoe Hall. Behind them, the DJ had clumsily segued into the Baha Men's "Who Let the Dogs Out?" and was rewarded with a youthful chorus of whoops and whistles.

"But think of the others," Jessica replied, her voice dry and droll as the hall's double doors closed them off from the party. "Those poor souls. It's too late for them now."

Jonno grinned and lent her his arm so they could make their way down five shallow steps to the car park. Such chivalry was never usually necessary with Jessica, but she'd dolled herself up to the nines for tonight's Year 12 formal, and that included a rare dalliance with high heels. Once they were standing on the gravel, she leaned against him as she fetched smokes from her purse and lit them one each.

"So, are we done now?" she asked, blowing a thin grey stream into the warm summer night. "Can we go?"

"You're sure you want to leave? The other girls haven't even had a chance to drop a bucket of pig's blood on you yet."

Jessica gave a snort of amusement. "I've spent all year with these people. Any longer and I'm going to pull a Poppy and go postal. Get me out of here, *please*."

She clutched dramatically at the lapel of his jacket. He laughed, brushed her hand away, and saw two shapes slouching out of the shadows: Corey Hamble and Prickles O'Hanlon, no doubt fresh from a discreet toke around the side of the hall. They scowled at the pair, either out of habit or because they'd heard what Jessica had just said, red eyes slitted in contempt or against the brightness of the parking lot lights. They hadn't even made it back inside before Jessica spluttered with laughter.

"You know, some of the guys look *good* all dressed up—like you, babe—but those dudes look like they dug up two corpses and stole their burial suits without checking the sizes first."

"Come on, it's their big night. You'll never see them dressed like that again."

"I'll never see them again *period*, and thank fuck for that. I wonder what they'll get up to after this."

"I heard there's an afterparty at Alison Carpenter's place."

"Ah, then maybe they can lurk around until some poor bitch passes out and cop their first feel together. But what I meant was, what are they up to after this year, and you know what? I don't actually care. Are we going or what?"

Jonno checked his watch. Ten o'clock. By now, Brendan and Coralie would have swung by the bottle shop and would be waiting for them out at the 49er. "We'll go when we finish our durries."

Jessica nodded and stepped a few paces into the car park, looking up at the moon, and he watched her smoke and wander in her own thoughts for a minute. He liked seeing her in formal wear, wanted to make the most of it while it lasted. She'd certainly stunned a few of their classmates, who were used to seeing a gothed-out weirdo and not this princess from a dark fairy tale. Jessica's strapless evening dress was black, of course, her hair straightened into an immaculate fall of ebony, her eyes accentuated with kohl-dark liner—all of this in stark contrast to the cool white of her bare arms, her shoulders, and the expanse of breastbone that dropped into an eye-catching décolletage.

Oh, she was a vision tonight, but what had startled their peers most was the tattoo on her upper right arm—a skull with a cutesy hair bow and a cigarette jutting from between grinning jaws, inked in her favourite colour. Jonno had sat beside her in a Hindley Street parlour on her eighteenth birthday a couple of months back, holding her hand as the gun buzzed and pecked the design into her reddened skin; Brendan had been on the other side of the room, face tinged with a hint of green as a tribal ring was inked around his right nipple. A brilliant and permanent day, one that seemed far removed from the tame antics going on in Jellicoe Hall—and that was exactly why the four of them were blowing off the formal early to hold their own graduation party.

They tossed their butts into a nearby empty flowerbed and Jonno again lent an arm as they made their way across the car park to his XF panel van. When the back doors were open, Jessica sat carefully on the tailgate and removed her heels, tossing them into one corner with a grateful sigh. She plucked the dress up to her knees and crawled into the back of the van, and Jonno closed the doors as he followed her in.

They'd each brought a change of clothes, and Jonno was keen to get out of his borrowed tuxedo. It had been gathering dust in Mick's closet for five years since he'd worn it to his sister's wedding, and it made the differences in their builds painfully obvious—the sleeves were a little long, the crotch too tight, and seams would dig into his skin at the least provocation. But as much as he wanted out of the suit, he only managed to pry off his leather shoes before pausing to watch Jessica disrobing beside him.

She unzipped the dress and peeled it gently off, folding it like a delicate tapestry and putting it to one side. The moonlight beaming in through the small side windows made her skin glow, made shadows of her black underwear, cast her in monochrome—a chiaroscuro angel. Jonno felt the familiar excitement lifting him as she knelt there, unselfconscious and unaware of his scrutiny, and reached back to unclip her strapless bra. It dropped on top of the formal dress as she reached into her bag and grabbed a more comfortable one.

That second bra fell from her hand as he pounced on her with a growl and swept her to the carpeted floor of the panel van. She let out a startled yelp that became a laugh, meeting his questing mouth with kisses of her own that grew longer and deeper as she recognised his desire. Jonno ran his left hand down to clutch at one generous breast, fingers rolling a nipple that quickly stiffened beneath his touch. The cut of his suit's crotch became even more uncomfortable as her thigh brushed against the pressure there, and she made a contented sound as she slung her arms around his neck.

Her skin was cool, but Jonno found heat when his hand continued down to the front of her panties, stroking labia that swelled and parted at his touch. Jessica gave a moan of approval into his mouth before reluctantly breaking off the kiss.

"Babe, we don't have time for this now. We've got to meet the others."

"They won't be going anywhere," he pointed out.

"Besides, we're in a public car park…"

"Yeah?"

"People could come out at any time…"

"Yeah?"

"They'll see the van rocking and know *exactly* what we're doing…"

"Yeah?"

"They might even peep in the windows and watch us."

"So?"

Jessica giggled and placed her hands on his shoulders. "I've taught you well. But seriously, J, we really should get going."

"We really should get *coming*," he disagreed, locating her clitoris with his thumb.

"Oh, babe…we really fucking will. But right now, I need you to hop up and get changed." She laughed at his playful scowl as he begrudgingly sat up and let her rise. "Don't worry. There'll be plenty of time for this later."

He felt a smile stretching his face and knew that now was the right moment.

"Actually, you're right. We'll have all the time in the world."

Jessica was reaching again for her bra, but something in his voice caused to her to look askance at him. "Oh?"

"Yeah. I made up my mind." Jonno felt his heart tingle and swell as if it were even more potent a sexual organ than the one that was tenting his rented trousers. "When you go back to the city, I'm coming with you."

Now it was Jessica's turn to shriek and throw him to the floor, kissing him like she hadn't seen him in a year. He positioned his crotch against the heat of her own as his hands rose up to cup her breasts, thumbs circling their firm peaks. They lay nose to nose for a few seconds, lost in the depths of each other's eyes.

"That makes me so happy, J. I'm so, so stoked." She sat up and gently detached his hands from her breasts. "But I'm still not going to fuck you."

He made a sound of exaggerated frustration, and she laughed. "Not right now, anyway. But later, when we're alone again…oh, *baby*. And maybe we'll even try that thing we talked about. Right now, though…"

Jonno sighed, admitting defeat. "You're terrible, woman."

"I'm the best, J. And you know it."

"This is true," he allowed. "Go on, then. Get dressed. But I'm holding you to what you said about later."

"Good," she said, slipping into her comfy bra. "I like it when you hold me."

She held his eyes until a Nine Inch Nails shirt dropped over her head. Jonno took this as his cue and began struggling out of Mick's tux. Hopefully, he'd never have to wear one of these bloody things again.

But what if I get married one day?

To her…?

That was getting ahead of himself somewhat, but who was to say it was altogether out of the question? Things had been going so well for the last nine months, and now they would be moving in together. Maybe it was all just a matter of time.

Despite his father's proclaimed aversion to weirdos, he'd quickly been won over when Jonno had brought Jessica in for an impromptu job interview; by the end of that first meeting Dad had offered her the position, and they shook on it with a smile. So then Jonno started spending a few hours with her in the kitchen most nights, and from there it had seemed natural to hang out when they weren't at school or at work. The process had been so organic, so right, and when they'd ended up sitting by the creek where they'd had their first conversation...well, where else would they share their first kiss? Heavy petting in public places had soon been replaced by heated sessions under the blankets in Jessica's caravan, a flat-tired old thing parked out the back of her aunt's house. And when Jonno had bought the XF cheap from one of Dad's mates, life had become a non-stop rolling party for two.

Except for Brendan and Coralie.

Of course his best friends were not excluded from this newfound happiness, but he had been a little worried when first telling them about his fresh romance. After all, they'd known him since the age of seven, and they'd never liked any of the other girls he'd taken a shine to—as if they knew Jonno better than *he* did, knew when he was fooling himself. But by the end of their first double date Coralie was hugging Jessica like a sister, and Brendan was giving him a discreet nod of approval; by the end of the second, they were all referring to themselves as the Fantastic Four and arguing over who was who. You'd have thought Jessica had been one of them all along.

"Seriously, hon, I'm so happy right now." Jessica finished wriggling into black tights and smoothed her skirt down over them, her eyes seeming to gleam in the moon's shine. "Going to New Orleans is going to be *insane*, but I can't wait 'til we get to town and find a place together. I have such sights to show you! It'll be *awesome*, baby. Me and you. Me and you."

Jonno liked the sound of that, and he paused the lacing of his Converse sneakers to lean forward and kiss her eager lips. "I know. I can't wait."

"I love you, J."

"I love you, too." He sat back, basking in unadulterated happiness. "Tell you what—I'm *so* glad I met you, Grzelak."

"Bless you."

"No, seriously. I don't know what the hell I'd have done without you." He shook his head, shuddered at the very thought. "If I hadn't met you, I probably would have just stayed here forever. Stayed here until I got old and died. Another Trotter, dead and buried in Waterwich."

forgive our fathers

JONNY HAD NEVER FELT SO present and yet strangely disconnected from reality as he did at his father's burial.

Everything around him loomed large in his senses with lysergic clarity, from the shuffling and sniffling and throat-clearing of the black-clad townspeople around him to the birds obliviously singing their signature songs in the trees that fringed the cemetery, and yet he was trying so hard to disappear into his own mental shadow. He could feel the eyes of his erstwhile friends and neighbours running over him like ants, taking in all the changes he'd made to himself over the years, and had never felt so *urban*. Every hushed word that passed between the funeral's attendees was about him, whether it was or not, and each syllable was loaded with inaudible judgements. Coming back here made him uncomfortably aware of the person he used to be, and that young man was a poor fit inside the skin he'd come to wear. Even now, he thought he might have just cut and run if Sloane hadn't been at his side, clutching his hand in hers. She was his anchor, keeping him weighed down in the present as if to prevent him fleeing his past all over again.

The disconnect might also have been a safety mechanism. Jonny thought that if he actually listened to what the local priest was saying, he might either burst out in ugly laughter or just sock the man in the mouth. What the fuck did this guy know, anyway? By his own admission, he'd had little more than a passing acquaintance with Alan Trotter. Would he have spoken so kindly today if he'd heard the jokes Jonny's father had used to make about the clergy? Probably so; no doubt these people jumped at any opportunity to turn the other cheek and be the better man, to have the last word. Jonny tried to ignore the piety in the priest's speech and was glad when the man finally shut up and stood aside to watch the coffin's slow descent into the earth. The unoiled screech of the lowering mechanism grated on his ears like a blade against bone, but it was a welcome relief after the platitudes of a stranger.

Jonny shuffled on the spot, keen to leave. Sloane must have mistaken his unease for another emotion, for she squeezed his hand tighter and leaned against him in silent support. So braced, he looked on as Mick Oliver stepped forward and stooped to scoop up a handful of dirt.

His father's best friend watched the soil trickle through his long fingers, then stepped in slow motion to the hole in the earth and let the dirt fall on the coffin below. Mick stared down for a few long, painful seconds, and Jonny came outside himself enough to recognise the depth of despair in the man. He'd been Alan Trotter's best mate and business partner for thirty years, single all that time, and he'd been the one to find the old man by the kitchen's open back door, felled by his first and last heart attack. Jonny couldn't even imagine how a bloke might cope with such a brutal sight, and he realised the desolation Mick must be feeling today left his own selfish concerns in the dust.

Then Mick stepped aside, and Jonny saw that eyes were turning to him next. Sloane noticed too and gave his fingers a subtle squeeze before letting them slip out of her grip. Steeling himself as if about to step onto a stage and sing for millions, Jonny took a breath and walked toward the hole that had swallowed his father. The priest tipped him a sympathetic nod, and he hadn't the heart to blank the man at such a time, so he returned the gesture before stopping at a pile of fresh earth and squatting to cup some in his hand.

Dad would have cracked some joke about being so full of shit that he'd make good fertiliser, Jonny thought as he ground some grains between his fingers, and a sudden pang of anguish stabbed at his heart. His head hung low for a moment, but then he remembered he had an audience. Standing, he stepped over to the grave and watched as the soil fell in a gentle rain upon the box that held his father's remains. He was glad nobody was expecting a speech right now. He couldn't have forced a single word out through the knot of muscle that was blocking his throat.

I'm sorry, Dad. I'm sorry for what I did—sorry for what you *did. But I missed you so much sometimes. I hope you knew the truth that we country men could never say to each other: I loved you. Still do. Always will.*

Goodbye, old man.

Jonny turned away, blinded by sudden tears, and might not have found his way back to his place at the front of the crowd if Sloane hadn't been there to guide him. She folded him into her arms, accepting him, offering any solace she could give. Overwhelmed by her kindness as much as his loss, Jonny let out a single sharp sob into the soft fall of her hair.

Her soothing hand paused on his back for a moment, and he realised this display was unprecedented for her—in the year they'd spent together, she'd seen every emotion in his array other than this. If he'd had his way, she wouldn't have seen it even today. Jonny knew that Alan Trotter wouldn't have wanted waterworks at his funeral, especially not from the men, and to shed a tear seemed almost an insult to his memory. Sloane wouldn't have understood that, would have asked why—and what could he have said in reply?

Boys don't cry.

But those three words turned his thoughts in another direction, one he wanted very much to avoid right now, so he focused on regaining his composure. With a deep, shaky breath, he pulled back from Sloane's embrace and tried to throw the sadness off, wiped its evidence from his eyes. Hers were full of sympathy and support as she watched him try to be the man his father would have wanted him to be on this day.

Clearing his throat and swallowing his tears, Jonny half-turned and stared out across the cemetery. Rows of teeth jutted from the earth, grey and slate and marble white, souvenirs of the sorrows of a thousand days like this; one section was dominated by weeping angels and pre-mortem portraits, monuments to the extravagant grief of Waterwich's small Greek community. Every now and again, a small grove of trees broke the miserable monotony of graves, and in the nearest of these, he saw the ghost.

She stood in the shade of a cedar tree, a vision in white—her long dress, her gloves, the hat atop her head and the veil that hung from it to hide her face. For a moment Jonny thought she'd come dressed as a bride, either in total error or as a deliberate statement. She was tall, but crooked over by age or infirmity or some horrid circumstance of her death. She might have been young beneath all that white finery, but Jonny just *knew* that she was not—as he now knew that she was no ghost, for she stood solid in the daylight. And what spirit would need a caretaker like the slender young rust-haired man who waited at her elbow, elegantly conveyed in a suit of butler-black? No, she was alive and real, and though Jonny had never seen the like of her before, a chill penetrated the heat of the summer afternoon.

The strange pair was watching the funeral, of course, but he couldn't shake the impression that they had eyes for him alone.

"Who's that?" Sloane whispered. "You know her?"

Jonny gave a dismissive shrug, but he didn't look away. He was waiting for those odd spectators to show their hand, to admit some sign of their interest in this matter—but before they could, he felt Sloane shift beside him and give his fingers another quick squeeze, this one an alert.

Turning back to her, Jonny saw that the funeral party was breaking up. Mourners were drifting away from the graveside, and through them came Mick Oliver.

He was as thin as ever, like he'd perfected his diet decades before, but Jonny was shocked to see the lines the last fifteen years had etched on the man's face. Mick was one of those men who'd looked middle-aged even as a schoolboy—but something, whether the passing of time or recent bereavement, had aged him considerably. Seeing him again was another strong reminder of how much time had passed while Jonny sought to find himself, and what he'd left behind to do so.

"Jonno," Mick said in greeting, his voice low and full of shared suffering. A large hand swung up and Jonny clasped it with a firmness born of sincerity. He'd always appreciated this man's kindness, his honesty, his unspoken support.

"Mick. I'm sorry, mate." Jonny heard himself say that and wondered at the weakness of those words. "Shit, sorry just doesn't cut it. I wish I—"

"Don't worry about it." Mick cut him off with a shake of his head and the ghost of a smile. "Not today. I'm just glad to have you back here. It's heaps good to see you, mate."

"You too, Mick."

The man held onto his hand a little longer, indulging in the moment while he could, and little wonder—after Daisy Trotter had disappeared, Mick Oliver had become a kind of back-up parent for young Jonathan. He'd never married or had children of his own, and only now did Jonny realise just how much filial affection had been transferred on to his younger self. It was an odd feeling, and it only deepened his shame at having fled Waterwich without a backwards glance. Shit, would it have killed him to come back here once in a while and spend a little time with the old man and his best mate?

You know where to find me.

Well, there was that.

"And this lucky lady must be Sloane," Mick said, turning his heavy gaze away from Jonny. She took his hand, and those slight fingers disappeared entirely inside the man's grip.

"Pleased to meet you, Mick."

"I don't know about lucky," Jonny said, and Sloane let out a delicate snort of amusement. "I think she lost a bet or something. I'm the lucky one."

"He's right. Not about the bet, though. I had to take him on for community service."

Mick managed a smile. "I like you already, Sloane. I hope I'll get to know you a little better before you go…?"

"We're not running off just yet," she assured him.

"Okay, then." Mick let go her hand, straightened a little. "Well, I better get back to the pub before this mob gets restless. Nothing helps with grief like an open bar."

"We'll see you there," Sloane promised, and the two of them watched Mick slope away toward the car park, pausing here and there to receive a handshake and solemn nod from a friend. Then she turned to Jonny and folded her arms, resolute.

"Don't say it."

"Wasn't going to."

"Good. I know this is hard for you, but we can't skip the wake."

"I know, Sloane."

"It's just, the way you were talking before—"

"All right," he cut in, hating the petulance in his voice. "Okay? Yes, we're going to the wake. I was only saying that, back in the day, me and my friends would have blown it off because that's how we used to roll."

"He's right, you know," someone said nearby, and Jonny felt the strangest jolt of recognition. It was partly love, partly dread, like seeing an ex-girlfriend in the street a moment before they see you and remembering the best and worst days of your life at the very same time. He braced himself for both extremes and turned around.

Like the rest of Waterwich, Brendan Swain had barely changed in fifteen years, and he had also changed completely. He'd always been on the beefy side, and nothing had changed there—an observation made easier by the fact that he'd crammed himself into a suit clearly bought a few years and more than a few pounds back. As a teenager, he'd let any hair on his head or body grow indiscriminately, but now he was more selective: the locks that had reached down past his ears back in the day were kept neat and close to the scalp, but the goatee he'd affected ever since he could grow one was in place, more neatly groomed than Jonny remembered. Brendan's face was still youthful atop this bigger, older body, a pair of stylish spectacles the only true concession to age, and overall Jonny thought the last fifteen years had been kind. He felt a rush of affection and was immensely relieved when his extended hand was taken and shaken with what felt like the same.

"B-Dog," he said by way of greeting.

"J-Man," Brendan shot back. "So. You finally made it back, eh?"

There was no trace of recrimination in his voice, but Jonny felt pricked by guilt regardless. "Yeah. Took my time, I know. But…well, you know."

"I do." And he did, better than most. "But never mind, you're here now. And you're coming to the pub. That'll do for starters."

"Been a long time since we bent an elbow together," Jonny noted, realising all over again just how much he'd missed that.

"No shit." To Sloane, Brendan said, "He hasn't turned into a two-pot screamer, has he?"

She smiled. "He can hold his own."

"Yeah, he always did like that." Brendan grinned at her little laugh, then nodded at the pair of them. "Well, let's save the catch-up for the wake so we've got something to talk about. See you there directly, eh?"

"No worries," Jonny said, and watched Brendan head off after the rest of the mourners. He walked with purpose, a man who held himself tall and never let doubts cripple him. Jonny had always been a little envious of his unpretentious poise, his simple power.

"Nice guy," Sloane said as he slid his hand back into hers.

"Oh, yeah."

Jonny gave her fingers a little squeeze as they walked away from the grave, trying not to feel that he was turning his back on his father all over again.

"Was he a good friend?"

"He really was." Jonny smiled a little at last, picking over a few select memories as he and Sloane followed the path through the cemetery back to where they'd left the Clubsport. "In fact, for ten years or so, Brendan Swain was my best mate."

anthem for the year 2000

JONNO PULLED OUT OF THE Jellicoe Hall car park and headed south down the main drag as Jessica fumbled with his cassettes until she found one she liked and slotted it into the tape deck. Inside a minute they were rolling out past the city limits sign to the strains of Nirvana's live album, the streets of Waterwich falling behind them; and not long after, as "Drain You" squalled into life, Jonno was slowing the XF and indicating to make a right turn off the main road. A street sign pointed two fingers off in this direction, one marked with the dirt road's name, the other with its destination.

Mermaid Drive cut west between the borders of the McCarthy and Hunter properties and ran straight through for three kilometres or so until it reached the coast, where it opened out into a local fishing nook known as Tiny Point. The popularity of this haven amongst the men and boys of Waterwich was why the narrow dirt road was well-worn by the tires of passing cars, but there was another place of interest out this way, one less widely known but more infamous, and that was where Jonno and Jessica were headed tonight.

The panel van bumped and rocked on the dirt track, a thousand branches looming in the headlights as the bush reached for them. Ranks of trees loomed over the property fences on either side of Mermaid Drive, their gnarled hands held high, and at certain points the branches had grown long enough to create a natural canopy over the road. Jonno sometimes got the impression that the trees were blocking out the moon's pale eye so they could feed on trespassers without being witnessed—and this impression, of course, had been planted in his mind by Jessica, who could never come down this track without smiling up at those frozen fiends as if welcoming friends.

Nothing is too creepy for that girl.

One could tell that her tastes ran to the darker end of the spectrum just by looking at her, but Jonno thought people would be surprised to find out just how morbid Jessica Grzelak could be. Even after nine months together, he had barely begun to plumb the depths of the black river she called a soul. Things that would freak out a normal person often gave her a delicious little shudder that made him think of the way she came when they went at it slow and deep, and it worried him that he might never understand why.

Case in point: a few weeks ago in class, Mr. Ferrano had asked his students to share what they most wanted to be. Some kids still harboured dreams of becoming rock stars or touring car champions or professional footballers, while others had more modest ambitions and simply wanted to be happy or fruitful or sexually active…but when the question had reached Jessica, she'd given a dark little smile and said, "A ghost."

Down by the creek after school, Jonno had brought that up. "Why'd you choose *ghost*," he asked, "instead of, say, *vampire*? At least then you'd still have a body. And you'd get to rock a cape."

"Because vampires are just like us," she'd said, staring at the running water as if unable to cross it. "We can understand them. Their needs are our needs with a new lick of paint—hunger, desire, the lust for life and flesh and feeling. But a ghost…I mean, can you even begin to *imagine* what the existence of a ghost must be like?"

"No."

"Me either. And that's why, J."

I'm in love with a girl who understands vampires and whose ultimate ambition is to be a ghost. Can't say I ever saw that coming.

About halfway along Mermaid Drive, the fence on the right-hand side gaped where an open gate had swung wide and stayed that way. Even the initiated might have missed it entirely if not for the red reflectors someone had affixed to the trunks on either side that flashed back at headlights like the eyes of some unseen beast. Jonno slowed the XF to a crawl, tapping on the steering wheel as the beat of "Aneurysm" kicked in, and hauled to the right. This end of Gavin Hunter's land had been sectioned off from the rest in order that it might act as a kind of unofficial nature reserve—from here it was all untamed bush until it reached the wide band of rock that separated the trees from the coast, and it was common knowledge in the area that Hunter allowed anyone to wander in and do what they would so long as they didn't burn the place down.

This second dirt track did not warrant a name and was only wide enough to allow one car at a time. After a hundred metres or so, it opened out into a clearing the width of two tennis courts. Brendan's prized Holden, an LX Torana SL/R 5000 he'd been nursing into rude health since his sixteenth birthday, was dozing just to the left of the entry and Jonno parked the panel van alongside. He twitched off the ignition, and Kurt Cobain's voice was silenced all over again.

"About time!" Jessica crowed, piling out of the panel van and stretching her back. "Fuck, I need a drink."

"Drink, I need a fuck."

She laughed and took his hand. They walked across the dirt floor of the clearing to the far side, where the old school bus waited for them.

Jonno had no idea who had left it here or why, but the wreck of the bus made for an incongruous and somewhat creepy sight. It sat on four flat tires, its once-bright yellow hide faded to a weather-beaten jaundice by the passing of many seasons, its rows of windows smashed in by careless youth. Visitors had made weapons or souvenirs of its windscreen wipers, and some industrious vandals had brought out spray paint cans to decorate its sides with tags and WAS EREs and crude depictions of anatomically absurd genitals. Black lettering beneath its broken eyes read 1349 SCHOOL BUS 1349, hence its nickname—*see you at the 49er* was a phrase recognised by any young person in Waterwich who'd passed through puberty, and many of them had gone there at least once to get drunk or high or laid. One other message was stencilled above the shattered windscreens: CAUTION, it stated, as if boiling twelve years of education down to a single imperative. Or perhaps it was a warning to those who might make unwise decisions on board.

The first time Jessica had seen it, she'd shuddered and smiled and said it made her think of the train carriage in *Twin Peaks*. Jonno didn't get the reference, but he understood her feeling—cloaked by night's shadow, the 49er looked like a place where dark deeds were done. Of *course* she loved it.

As they approached the bus, a pale figure appeared in its open doorway. Under other circumstances Jonno might have been startled by the sight, but tonight they were expected.

"About fuckin' time!" Brendan declared, stepping down to the ground and spreading his arms wide, a beer in each hand. "You guys took forever. You stop off for a root along the way, or is it just because you drive a Ford?"

He handed Jonno a beer and then stepped in to embrace him with a hearty slap on the back. Jonno glanced away as his mate turned to welcome Jessica with a tight hug. Then another figure skipped out of the bus, this one short, dark, and lithe, and stole her out of his arms.

"You looked so gorgeous tonight!" Coralie cried, squeezing her best girlfriend. She'd also changed out of her prom dress, but her hair remained up in a formal do, a black curl dangling down either cheek like Hasidic sidelocks. "You were *stunning*, Jess. I bet the guys were all kicking themselves that they missed out on you."

"They should have said something. I could have done the kicking for them."

Coralie let her go and stepped over to Jonno, arms wide. He held his old friend close for a moment, all too aware of the beautiful brown body beneath her casual clothes and trying not to let his recent discomfort show. Oblivious by deed or design, she kissed his cheek with booze-wetted lips.

"And you looked *very* handsome, Mr. Trotter."

He shrugged off the compliment. "Walking in there with you two tonight was like *Beauty and the Beast* squared."

"Aw, come on," Brendan protested. "The girls didn't look *that* bad."

Coralie turned and poked him in the stomach. "Hey!"

"It's what horses eat. Come aboard, you guys. We got some drinks that would like to meet you."

Brendan stepped up into the 49er and led them down the aisle toward the back, where they always sat. The seats there had not yet cracked in the sun to release bulges of foam, nor had they cultivated sprays of mould, though their metal tubing had grown spotty with rust and coarse to the touch.

As they passed a middle window, Jessica reached one hand up to a gentle shimmer of spider-silk and cooed to whatever lurked at its heart. This was just the kind of place she liked to seek out—dim and busted and dusty, full of cobwebs and countless tiny creatures. Jonno could imagine her moving in here to join them with her cigarettes and her books, lying on the back seat in a sleeping bag and smiling up at the moon, just waiting to pupate and transform into something strange and new.

Though the summer night air found free admittance through the broken windows and ran warm, soft hands over Jonno's skin, he couldn't resist a shudder at that thought.

Brendan and Coralie dropped onto the back bench where a picnic rug was draped over the torn vinyl, sliding to the left-hand side opposite an esky of drinks. Jessica took the next seat back, curling her legs up, and Jonno knelt on it beside her. They all lit smokes and looked at each other with satisfied grins as Coralie passed around beers.

"So here we are," Brendan announced, raising his drink. "The graduating class of Waterwich High…or the cool ones, at least. Cheers!"

"*Na zdrowie*," Jess said, and they all tapped their bottles together.

"How was the formal going when you guys left?" Coralie asked.

"Huh. Like a dream," Jessica sighed. "One of those dreams where you're surrounded by morons. Did you know the theme song they chose for our formal was "It's My Life"? Bon fucking *Jovi*, man. As if it wasn't bad enough having to put up with Killing Heidi and "Freestyler" and motherfucking *Wheatus*."

"Oh, dear lord. Well, we're much better off here."

"At least they *had* music. Even if it was shit."

"Hang on, give me a minute." Brendan slid across the seat and reached over the esky, producing a portable tape deck. "Ta da!"

"O me of little faith," Jessica said.

Brendan grinned and pressed PLAY on one of the punky mixtapes he put together for driving around or hanging out—Testeagles, Silverchair, Regurgitator, Bodyjar. Jonno grinned at Jessica as Frenzal Rhomb kicked off the first side with "Let's Drink A Beer", savouring the way she rolled her eyes.

"*Now* it's a party," Brendan stated. "Fuck the formal, *this* is where it's at."

"Oh, it wasn't all that bad," Coralie argued. "It was cool to see everyone dressed up for a change."

"Not everyone! Corey and Prickles looked like a couple of shaved apes. And did you see what Mandy was wearing?"

"Mandrill!" Jessica crowed. "What was she *thinking*?"

"She must have bought that dress ages ago," Coralie mused. "She looked like ten pounds of pork in a nine-pound bag."

"No shit!" Brendan shook his head in amazement. "Every time she turned around, I thought those massive titties were gonna pop out of her dress and clock some poor bastard in the head."

Jessica laughed. "The people around her weren't dancing, they were just trying to keep from being pulled into orbit around her boobs."

"You're not supposed to notice things like that when I'm all dressed up," Coralie told her boyfriend. "Well, not ever, really, but especially not then."

"I couldn't help it! They were like…oh, what were they like—"

"The elephants in the room?" Jessica suggested.

Brendan clicked his fingers. "*Led Zeppelin I* and *II*!"

They all convulsed with laughter. Coralie's amusement was brief and her smile had an edge to it. Brendan was possibly the last one to notice, but when he did, he placed one hand on hers.

"Ah, come on, Coz. You know I got no interest in Mandrill or her bits."

"Ha! In Year 9, they were all you ever used to talk about."

"Well, yeah. But these days, I only take *brown* sugar."

As irreverent as he could be toward his girlfriend's colour, Brendan took a dim view of anyone else whom he felt had no right to do so. He and Jonno had been regular and welcome visitors to Coralie's house for most of their lives and the Aboriginal side of her family had accepted them just as warmly as the white, so they tended to take racist jokes personally. They had jumped into a few schoolyard tussles over the years because of casual bigotry, but Brendan's recent and deeper love for Coralie had made him merciless. Even the hard nuts around town who didn't give two fucks for anyone's feelings knew to keep certain words out of their mouths when Brendan was in earshot.

"I seem to recall you quite *liking* white sugar," Coralie pointed out, a teasing lilt to her voice now. "What about Rebecca Liddard?"

"Ah, geez," Brendan groaned, squirming at the sound of that name in Coralie's mouth—much as he must have squirmed when Rebecca Liddard had had something else in hers. "Why do you wanna bring that wench up?"

"I'm just saying—I know all your little secrets, boyfriend."

"What, *all* of 'em? Even what I used to do with that Elle McPherson calendar in my dad's shed?"

"No!" Coralie shrieked. "Not all of them, apparently! And now I don't want to."

"You really don't."

Jonno turned to look at Jessica, found her regarding him with a thoughtful stare. "What?"

She waved at Brendan. "Well, after that little revelation, I was wondering what *you* used to jack off to when you were younger."

"Ah," he said, thrown, as Coralie and Brendan dissolved into a fit of hilarity. "Well, that's for me to know and you to find out."

"Duh, that's why I'm asking. Well? Come on, just give me one example."

Jonno wanted to demur further—indeed, he would never even have considered answering such a question around anyone else. But these were his closest friends and they'd been through a lot, especially since Jessica had made it her duty to broaden everyone's horizons. He saw the dare in her eyes and knew he couldn't back down.

"Oh, man. Fine. There was this crappy sci-fi video we hired a few years ago—*Slave Girls from Beyond Infinity*."

"I remember that!" Brendan crowed.

"I dubbed off a copy because it had some nice topless scenes in it. And, er...we'll leave it at that."

"And to think you prepare food for people with those hands," Jessica cooed with a grin, tapping her beer against his.

"So, then—who'd *you* used to jill off to, sweetie?"

Her smile grew wider, and she didn't hesitate to answer. "When I was twelve, I used to read the naughty bits from *Lolita* and imagine it was my English teacher who was writing it—writing about *me*. I got off so hard I could barely look him in the eye at school. I was such a dirty little bitch back then."

"And so much has changed," Brendan said, sarcasm rank on his breath. "Jesus, Jess. Trust *you* to get off on being statutorily raped."

Jessica blew him a raspberry. "*Statutorily* is not a word, smartarse."

"Whatever," Coralie cut in, "and furthermore, let's change the subject now, because I am *not* telling you guys *any* of that stuff."

They finished their beers and tossed them under the seat to be collected later. Brendan and Jonno fetched fresh ones whilst the girls poured themselves a Beam and Coke. Jessica produced a joint and passed it around, and soon Jonno sat slightly outside of himself, feeling like he was watching someone else's POV on a television.

"Well, the first year of the millennium's almost over," Brendan declared. "So much for a brave new world and all that shit."

"Actually," Jessica began, and Jonno grinned, knowing what was coming, "*this* year is the last year of the millennium. I mean, we didn't start counting from 0 AD, did we? We started at 1. So the 1980s actually ended in 1990, and the '90s will end in three weeks, along with the second millennium. Though technically, for us humans, this is actually something like the *thirty*-second millennium."

Brendan shook his head and grinned. "You don't half talk some shit when you're stoned, Jess."

Coralie sipped at her Beam. "Well, new millennium or not, I wonder what the new year's going to be like."

"Just the same as this year, babe. Shit don't change but the date, yo!"

Jessica wrinkled her nose at Brendan's forced accent and *faux*-gangsta pose. "Can you not?"

"Hey, I'm pretty fly for a white guy."

"What you are is wrong—it's all change next year. We've finished school for good, and I'll be going back to the city…*and*—big news, dun dun-dun *dah*—guess who's decided to come with me?"

Jonno smiled and nodded on cue, though he wouldn't have chosen this way to let his oldest friends in on the news.

"Aw, that's great, you guys." Coralie's voice bore a genuine that's-so-cute whine, but Jonno found himself wondering if there wasn't an undertone of sadness to it; after all, now she was looking at losing two of her best friends instead of one. "You're so good together, it's going to be wicked."

"I know! I can't wait for us to get a place, and as soon as we do, the two of you are coming up for our housewarming, or flatwarming, or whatever."

"Of course! We wouldn't miss that for anything."

"Any excuse to get pissed," Brendan agreed, looking a little solemn himself. "Especially with you freaks. And you'll always be welcome back here, too. No way are we breaking up the Fantastic Four."

Jonno heard the sincerity in his best mate's voice and shared it…but there was no getting around the fact that the Fantastic Four would soon be splitting into two Twos, and after that, nothing would be the same. He harboured a vague hope that Brendan and Coralie would acquire a taste for city life and decide to move close by, but in his heart he knew it would never happen. Brendan was a country boy through and through, and Coralie could never bear such distance between her and her family. No, they'd be staying in Waterwich, keeping the home fires burning, and it wouldn't be long before they had their own place here—and then it was only a matter of time before Jonno and Jessica got that phone call to say they were starting a family, that Coralie was going to be a—

Mum.

Jonno took a mental step back out of the conversation as the others carried on, his stoned brain hanging on the echo of that word and what it meant to him.

One cool night a few months back, lying in the back of the XF with Jessica's sweaty skin bare against his and the raw scent of fuck mingling with the smoke of their shared cigarette, Jonno had told his lover why he sometimes stood and stared into Cold Bath Creek—why he sometimes did the same at the edge of the sea. He told her he was imagining a pale figure tumbling along below the surface, limp limbs akimbo as she washed from the site of her accident to some far-off destination; he told her that when he stood on the beach, he imagined something sodden and lifeless washing up on the shore, coming home at last. He told her that sometimes that figure remained motionless and sometimes it lifted dripping arms and held them out to him, that sometimes he saw himself walking over and settling into that wet embrace for the first time in eleven years—that sometimes he wished she would take him back into the water with her, down into the unseen deeps where she now made her home.

He'd stared at the ceiling of the panel van as he spoke, and only when he'd finished did he turn to look at Jessica. Her eyes were as deep and wide as the sea of which he'd spoken, her lips parted, captured and enraptured by his tale. He was convinced that if they hadn't just finished, Jessica would have jumped and ravished him then and there. Maybe she'd discovered unsuspected depths in him, been surprised by this uncharacteristic spurt of articulation, or maybe he'd just hit one of her erotic triggers with all that talk of death and undeath. His lover had some pretty dark kinks in her hose, that was for sure.

And I wouldn't have it any other way.

Jessica was laughing along with Brendan and Coralie, enjoying their horseplay. He reached up and gently ran his knuckles down her jaw. Pleased, she nuzzled into his fingers like a cat keen for pats, gave them playful kisses.

What a woman. *His* woman—and in six weeks or so, his housemate and partner. Who knew where all that might end? He'd already rolled the name *Jessica Trotter* around in his mouth to get a feel for it, and the enormity of those five syllables made his head and heart spin. He wasn't anywhere near ready for that, of course, and Jessica herself might disdain even the concept of marriage—he hadn't the guts to ask her opinion on it, not this year and maybe not the next. But it didn't really matter in the end, did it? It was just a piece of paper. They didn't need the pomp and the ceremony, they just needed what they already had: each other.

I love you, Jessica, he thought, and she glanced at him as if somehow able to hear. He cast his thoughts into the dark pools of her eyes and hoped they were echoed somewhere in the depths beyond. *I love you and I need you and I'm never going to leave you. Like you said earlier: me and you. Me and you.*

Forever.

the funeral party

JONNY HAD BECOME WELL-ACQUAINTED with a number of drinking holes during his first decade in the city, and returning to them now in older and saner times had taken on the feel of a nostalgia tour—he'd thrown up vodka and potato chips in this corner, swapped drunken gropes with a stranger on this dancefloor, made one-night friends over shots at that table. Those pubs had been a home away from home at times, but the Cutters Arms had been his *actual* home between the ages of three and eighteen. There were more ghosts in these rooms than the rest of the town combined—some pleasant, some less so—and if they didn't include the very worst Waterwich had to offer, they nevertheless hung heavy on Jonny as he pushed open the bar door and led Sloane inside.

I can do this.

The front bar was full of people from his past, and he didn't really want to see any of them with the exception of Brendan and Mick, but he knew he'd have to talk to them and share real condolences in trite terms and explain what he'd been up to over and over again as if it were an apology they couldn't quite believe. Two things made this knowledge bearable: Sloane at his side, and free drinks at the bar.

Jonny could feel eyes gravitating to him as he walked in, so he turned his own to the room. The *Gyruss* machine between the toilet doors had been replaced by a digital jukebox; the old TV corner had been upgraded into a shiny Sportsbet console, a new thirty-six inch flat-screen installed on the wall at the end of the bar; and at some point, the rag-tag selection of stools and seats had been replaced with a matching set which had itself done enough time to qualify for retirement. But the floorboards groaned and creaked beneath his feet the way they'd always done, the old tin signs Alan Trotter had collected as a young man still hung in their traditional spots above the spirits rack, and the air was thick with that distinctive pub-perfume that never failed to give Jonny the craving for a pint.

"Let's get a drink," he said to Sloane, less a suggestion than a plea. Somewhere in the back of his mind, an internal boombox started spinning "Let's Drink a Beer", a song he hadn't heard in almost exactly fifteen years. As a sign of respect, perhaps, no music was playing in the pub today, not even Dad's beloved Johnny Cash. The TV drew wandering eyes with its parade of light entertainment images, but it too was muted. Conversations in the bar had begun that way, but Jonny knew intoxication would push the volume slider up as the afternoon dimmed into evening.

"You know what, that's actually a great idea," Sloane admitted. "After you."

Jonny nodded at faces he recognised on the way to the bar, hoping to avoid conversation until he could recall the names that went with them. A few came straight away: Danny and Teddy Smith, Coralie's older brothers, were pumping coins into the pool table, and Gary George from the service station was grumbling to his wife as he wrestled his too-tight tie, and—shit, that had to be Corey Hamble over in the corner, widened and weathered but otherwise barely changed. The bloke next to him was thus easily recognisable as Prickles O'Hanlon, now shaved bald and carrying a drooping beer belly. Corey caught Jonny looking, and though he was laughing at something Prickles was reading off his phone, his eyes were flat and hostile.

Some things never change. Finally, some of that resentment I was so looking forward to.

Jonny pushed through to the bar and rested both hands on it, relishing the cool sponge of the Hahn Super Dry mat beneath his fingers. He'd half-expected Mick to put the needs of others before himself even today, but the pints were being pulled by a pair of young people he didn't recognise. He ordered a Coopers Pale for himself and one for Sloane, and while he waited, he found his eyes roving up to the mirror above the till.

There he stood, Jonathan Trotter at thirty-three, a stranger in this familiar scene. Once that bloke had looked much like the people around him, would have blended in as if rendered by the same brushstroke. Now his hair was side-swept in a metropolitan fashion, his jawline shadowed by a neat beard that he would have scoffed at ten years ago, and he couldn't have felt more urban if he tried. Even the stylish cut of his black suit looked like an alternative statement in here, one only reinforced by the presence of his elegant biracial girlfriend. He looked like he should be running a pop-up coffee bar in the city centre, the kind of place that kept battered literary paperbacks on hessian-sacked shelves near a turntable spinning indie LPs. He looked like the kind of guy who used to get beaten up in bars like this.

Don't get to thinking like that. You look for a fight, you'll find one. And right here and now, that's the last thing you need.

The girl returned with their beers and they took grateful draughts of the deep amber. Sloane licked away a foam moustache and sent him a smile, ignorant of the thoughts behind his fond look.

This is alien territory for her, and yet here she is at my side, without question, without complaint. She's a saint, this one. I can't lose her.

Better work out what I'm going to do about the Thing, then.

Jonny reached over and gave her earlobe a gentle tug, an endearment that had become a running joke between them, and Sloane's smile widened.

"What's that for?"

"Thank you, that's all. For everything, ever."

Her smile remained fixed, but her eyes deepened, and he knew she was thinking more about the future than the past. But whatever she might have said then was forestalled by the arrival of Mick Oliver at their elbows.

"Here we are again, then," he said, with a tone of forced jollity. Maybe he was trying to draw attention away from the gentle trembling of his drinking hand. "Cheers, Jonno. Cheers, Sloane."

He tapped his pint against theirs and took a sip, glancing around the room. He appeared a little agitated, his eyes and hands always in motion. Jonny got the impression that if Mick stopped moving, stopped *doing*, the full implication of today's events would catch him up and knock him flat.

"Packed house today. Lot of folks miss the old man."

"And none more than us," Jonny said, but it sounded hollow, so he continued. "Although I know I haven't exactly been, you know—"

"Knock it off," Mick advised, his voice low and soft. "Alan always understood, you know. He could hardly blame you for running off after what happened. And he still got to speak to you on the phone, make the odd trip into town to see you. Trust me, mate, he didn't take any ill will with him into the…"

Mick paused, faced with a choice of words he couldn't bear to use: *ground, grave, afterlife*. Jonny saw the pain in his eyes and froze, unable to break through the sudden awkwardness. It was Sloane who reached out and touched the man's arm.

"I'm sure you're right. You were his best friend, no-one knew him better than you. Jonny knows you're right, too, but he'll come to terms with that in his own time."

Mick nodded at the wisdom of her words, while Jonny felt a brief flash of irritation at her for speaking on his behalf. He glanced away at the front window to hide any sign of it, and as if cued by some unseen director, two people moved out of the way to give him a clear view of the park bench across the street.

The ghost in white sat there in the open sun, her face shaded by the veil, the besuited young aide at her side.

Who IS that…?

No clues were forthcoming. But again, Jonny couldn't help but feel their attention was focused on a specific person—that they were watching *him*.

They weren't the only ones. Sloane had noticed his distraction and followed his gaze to find its cause.

"So, who's old Miss Havisham out there?" she asked. Mick frowned, not understanding until he half-turned and glanced outside himself.

"Ah. That's our local eccentric, I guess you'd say. We don't see her out and about too often." Mick took a fortifying swig of beer and gave Jonny a loaded look. "We call her the White Widow."

"So, who is she? Why doesn't she come inside?"

"She generally doesn't talk to anyone except her butler, or whatever he is," Mick said, giving the job title a touch of derision. "Usually she stays at home and does whatever crazy old sheilas do. She's kind of a local legend around town, among the kids, anyway. They dare each other to run up and knock on her door after sundown. A rite of passage."

Not the only one around these parts, Jonny thought, and then: *shut up*.

"Did she get left at the altar or something?" Sloane asked, visibly intrigued by the narrative possibilities this sad spectre offered the day's play.

"Nah, not quite. She was married once, but her husband died in a car crash. She wore all black after that—a bit weird, but a decent sort, really. Then there was another…incident, and she became a recluse. Never been quite right in the head since. Now she wears white, and if there's a good reason, she ain't sharing it with us."

Jonny experienced a sudden chill, as if one of the bar staff had leaned over and dropped an ice cube down the back of his shirt. Mick was already watching him to gauge his response, and that told him his sudden suspicion was on the money.

"*Fuck*. So that's…"

Mick nodded. "Kassia Rzepka."

Another ghost that had been lurking here all these years, awaiting his return—this one alive, but somewhat less than whole. Jonny shuddered, and it did not go unnoticed by Sloane.

"Someone you know, babe?"

"Sort of. I knew her niece. Who's the guy with her?"

"That's Colin Perkins. Or at least, it used to be." Mick shrugged at the ways of the world. "Local kid, five or six years younger than you, always a bit of an odd one. Runs all her errands, drives her around in the car occasionally, and you don't wanna know what else people think they get up to."

Sloane pulled a face. "Eww. Just gossip, surely."

"Probably, love, but who knows? Rumour goes that Colin was one of them kids who dared each other to go up to Kassia's house. Apparently, a few of 'em actually broke in looking for a hidden fortune, but they found the Widow instead—and when the others ran, Colin stayed. Now he's her personal assistant, butler, whatever you wanna call it—*she* calls him Mr. Dogsbody. Never was close to his family, now he doesn't see 'em at all, or anyone else. I don't think she even pays him. Like I said, he was always a bit odd."

Jonny tried not to look, fighting the feeling that the strange couple outside knew exactly what was being said, and failed. But now a woman had stepped into his line of sight, blocking his view of the bench outside with a figure that had gone well beyond generous into downright charitable, and he was strangely unsurprised to see that it was Mandy Hill. No, a modest wedding band was disappearing into one swollen finger, so Mandrill had managed to land herself a husband along the way. *Led Zeppelin I* and *II* must have done the trick, though these days they resembled a pair of *Hindenburg*s. He felt a sudden and savage urge to laugh, one that passed when Mandy saw him looking and flung him a polite twitch of the lips. She was on her mobile, talking to a child judging by the inflection of her voice, and Jonny's mockery subsided. She was alive and sane and happy and doing just what life expected of her, of anyone—what the fuck was so funny about that?

"So how did you and Alan meet, anyway?" Sloane asked Mick, and Jonny turned back to the conversation—in surprise, if nothing else. It wasn't like her to drop the discussion of what sounded like a pair of very colourful characters. She must have found another narrative knot to unpick.

Mick gave a short bark of something that was trying to be laughter and rapped the bar with his knuckles. "We can thank *this* old place for that. The Cutters went up for sale back in '85, and both of us wanted her! Turned out to be too expensive for either of us on our own, so I suggested we join forces. I don't think Daisy was too chuffed, but it turned out okay, didn't it?"

Jonny felt a strange spiritual tic at the sound of his mother's name in another's mouth. He didn't think he'd reacted, but Sloane shot him a glance.

"Jonno was only three at the time, and his mum didn't think a pub was the best place to raise a kid—see, we had to live on-site as well, having sold our houses just to buy this joint. But you took to it right away, didn't you, mate? You used to love exploring this old place, roaming around the hallways all day with your Transformers and whatnot."

Sloane smiled, and Jonny had one of those flashes that convinced him of their bond's strength: she was imagining him as Danny in that movie *The Shining,* riding a tricycle around the upstairs corridors, maybe meeting strange twin girls or watching a lift disgorge a torrent of blood. He also knew that if he mentioned this, she'd feel obliged to note that she preferred the book. If that wasn't true love, the kind of soul-synch that brought two closer to one, then what was?

"You must have come to know her very well," Sloane said, and the warmth in Jonny's heart flash-froze. He knew exactly where she'd be going with this. "It must have been a huge shock when the accident happened."

Mick glanced at Jonny for a moment, ascertaining how much he'd told her. "Yeah. Poor Alan, he was devastated. We mourned, then we moved on, and we never talked about it much after that. Better to leave tragedies in the past where they belong, I reckon."

That was a less than subtle admonishment to drop the subject, and neither of Mick's listeners missed it. He downed the rest of his beer, sadly eyeing the empty pint like it was an hourglass.

"Well, you're gonna have to excuse me for a minute. I got a lot of these to get through today, if you don't mind."

"No worries, mate," Jonny assured him. "We've got plenty of time to talk."

Mick gave him a distracted smile and a pat on the arm, then walked back to the bar. Sloane watched him raise his empty glass to summon one of the staff, her eyes soft.

"Poor guy. He and your dad must have been quite close."

"Mick's never really had anyone else. A sister he hardly sees, that's about it. Never married, never had kids—I can't even remember him ever having a girlfriend. What you might call a confirmed bachelor."

"And your dad never married again, did he?"

"Nah. Too busy, I suppose. That, and too scared of losing her as well." A grunt of dark amusement escaped Jonny's lips before he paraphrased a quote she was sure to recognise. "To lose one wife may be regarded as a misfortune; to lose two looks like carelessness."

Sloane's eyebrows shot up. "Really? *Now* you start quoting literature?"

"It was just something that—" *Something that Jessica used to riff on.* "—someone used to say when I was younger. Never mind. No, Dad never married again, or even got involved with anyone else after Mum. Unless there was someone he never talked about."

Maybe Mary…?

Strange how that idea had never occurred to him before. Mary had played a maternal role in the lives of the men who lived at the Cutters Arms; was it so strange to imagine that role might have extended to warming Dad's bed, especially since her husband was so ill? Jonny found the idea of her cheating on Carl somewhat outlandish, but people were always surprising you. He turned to mention this theory to Sloane, but she was fixing him with a look he knew all too well. The look that told him she was waiting patiently for his brain to catch up to his mouth.

"What?"

She eyed him a moment longer, then shook her head in a way that left him feeling too thick for words. "Never mind. Oh, I think someone's trying to get your attention."

Jonny followed the direction of her nod and found a couple of older men waiting to shake his hand and offer their condolences. One was Jack Nichols, whom Jonny was both surprised and pleased to see considering his advanced age and fondness for the amber, and the other was Mino from the eponymous Deli, whose aftershave and beer breath couldn't completely cover his traditional scent of FISH-CHIPS-YIROS. They'd always been good blokes, and Jonny was glad to see that hadn't changed; neither of them seemed to bear him any ill will, and he began to wonder why he'd been expecting a hostile reception in Waterwich at all. That thought led him to glance toward the window, but now someone else was standing in front of it, and if the living ghost of Kassia Rzepka still sat outside staring in, he was at least free of her veiled gaze for the moment.

Jonny clasped a few more mournful hands after Jack and Mino moved on, and each seemed too hot and clammy for comfort. The whole room was beginning to feel that way, as more people filed in and filled the air with their noise and body heat—Dad and Mick had never gotten around to installing ducted air conditioning, so the job was left to the four old ceiling fans that chopped at the heavy air as fast as they could. Jonny ordered a second beer that seemed to evaporate in the summer air, and by the time he obtained a third, Sloane was following him for another.

Mandrill didn't make her way over to say hi, but her husband did. Jonny was startled to realise that stout, outgoing Mandy Hill had married thin, reclusive Michael Gregson, with whom he'd been good friends in Year 6. He couldn't even remember one occasion when those two had interacted in high school, but here they were—parents to three kids under ten, running a modestly successful IT business that covered the nearest five towns. Jonny shared a few reminiscences with Michael about childhood sleepovers and that time Brendan had egged Mrs. Gregson's old white Nissan instead of the principal's old white Nissan, swilling beer between the laughs before Michael made his farewells and left to attend his wife.

It's not been so bad, after all. What was I so worried about? Fifteen years is a lot of water under the bridge.

That thought conjured images he didn't want, so Jonny, already tipsy, fetched himself a fourth pint. Sloane arched an eyebrow at him but understood. He thanked the bartender, turned around, and found Mary Bennington standing at his elbow.

"Mare!" he exclaimed, delighted, wrapping an arm around her shoulders. "Hey! Is it just me, or have you gotten younger?"

He was exaggerating, of course, but Jonny was relieved to see that Mary was largely unchanged and still rather robust for a woman approaching sixty. The grey had annexed more of her hair and the careworn creases in her face had deepened over time, but it might have been only five years since he'd last seen her. Mary rolled her eyes at his irreverence but let him squeeze her for a moment before stepping back. Of course, this was hardly the time for frivolity.

"Hello, Jonathan."

The long years spent looking after an ailing husband must been hard on her. Mary had always been quick with a laugh, but now she appeared quiet, restrained—brittle, even. Sloane seemed to notice something, too, and edged closer.

"Oh, hey—Mary, this is my partner, Sloane."

"Hello, dear," Mary said in her general direction. "So, Jonathan. This is what it takes to bring you back to Waterwich."

"Yeah." Jonny dropped his smile a notch, let out a sigh that relieved some of the weight he'd been buckling under this past week. "I know I took my time, but...I guess I just wasn't ready."

"Wasn't *ready*." Mary threw up a vacant smile. "Reckon I shouldn't be surprised, really. You see, Sloane, Jonathan always was an ungrateful little shit."

The air froze in Jonny's lungs.

"I'm surprised you even remember who I am." Mary nailed him with a glare, really *looking* at him for the first time since she'd approached, and he quailed before it. "I mean, I only watched you grow up—*helped* you grow up, after what happened to your poor mother. You know what he used to call me as a kid, Sloane? *Aunty Mary*. And now it's been fifteen years, and guess what? Not a single bloody word to me. No *how have you been, Mare*, no *miss you, Mare*—nothing. And as for your father…how *dare* you run off and turn your back on him after everything he did for you?"

Jonny panted out a single breath, totally lost for words. He wished Sloane would jump in and help, but she seemed just as stunned. And what could he say in his defence? All he had to offer was that he'd ended some of his phone conversations with Dad by adding *say hi to Mare for me*. He couldn't even recall what Carl had been suffering from, or when he'd finally died. Fucking hell. Why had he never thought…?

"I, I'm *sorry*—"

"Of course you are, anyone can see that—a sorry excuse for a son. I just wanted to let you know that the Jonno Trotter I knew, the boy I cared for…he disappeared fifteen years ago, and don't even get me started on *that* night. As far as I'm concerned, you and your mongrel can bugger off back to the city and stay there. Goodbye."

Mary turned on her heel and stalked away, head up and spine straight. Jonny watched her go, paralysed, barely noticing as the people around him glanced over and then went back to pretending they hadn't heard anything. He turned to Sloane, who was staring after Mary with her mouth hanging open.

"I'm so sorry about that, babe."

His partner blinked and closed her mouth. "I don't believe it."

"That was so out of line. I never would've expected that kind of talk from her."

Sloane turned to him now, and her pointed gaze pinned him to the spot. "You never even spoke to her in all that time? *Jesus*, Jonny! Is this what you're like when you move on? Is that what'll happen to *us* if we end it—you'll just turn your back and forget I exist?"

Jonny reeled under this new blow. "What? No! *Sloane*. Never going to happen. I'm not going to lose you, too."

"You just might, if you're not careful." She placed her half-empty glass on the bar, avoiding his eyes now. "You need to think about things. You need to think about *the* Thing. Because, babe…I can do this on my own if I have to."

She puffed out a tense breath, shook her head, and moved her arm away when he made to touch her. "I'm sorry—this isn't the time, I know.

But I need an answer soon, Jonathan. And I need to know who you *are*. Because I get the feeling there's a lot you're not telling me."

Jonny swallowed a knot of desperation, gripping his glass tight. "Sloane—"

"I need to go to the Ladies. Where is it?"

He pointed it out. "Over there. Hey—"

"When I get back, we'll be cool, okay? I'm not going to make this day any harder for you. I love you. Just keep that in mind, all right?"

He nodded, not trusting his tongue with words, and Sloane slipped him a quick smile before stepping through the small crowd. Jonny took a deep breath—hoping that most of that conversation had gone ignored by the people around them, knowing it hadn't—and finished his beer.

This is going to make it a lot harder to avoid getting pissed today.

And that association sparked an awareness that he, too, needed to visit the toilet. Leaving the empty pint on the bar, Jonny made his way through fellow mourners with a series of polite nods until he'd reached the other end of the room. The pool table here was now manned by three rough-edged blokes who stood guard with cues and watched a fourth aim down his own stick like a surveyor. Corey and Prickles scowled as their opponent sank the black, turning their displeasure in Jonny's direction like it had been his fault all along. He ignored them and saw Sloane disappearing into the Ladies toilets as he approached the Gents.

Mino tipped him a parting nod as he washed his hands, and then Jonny was alone in the restroom as he stood at the trough and unzipped. Relief came, but it was of the physical kind only—Sloane's words rang in his mind like the echo of a gunshot. *I can do this alone if I have to.* Christ, did she really think that was what he wanted? His thoughts swirled, tipsy, and he knew he'd be back here at the trough every half-hour now that he'd broken the seal. As his flow slackened, he heard the toilet door open again and tried to pay it no heed as he finished his business.

"Mate, you remind me of someone," said a voice behind him, and Jonny would have recognised it anywhere, even after all this time. "Only I don't reckon I know any hipster faggots."

Jonny let out a breath that was almost a sigh. This, he could handle.

"G'day, Corey. Funny how you wait until I've got my dick in my hand before you talk to me."

"You still think you're so smart," Corey Hamble sneered.

"Yeah, a fuckin' smartarse," came the inevitable echo—Prickles O'Hanlon, the perennial dumb sidekick. That guy had never been too bright; wherever he'd written his nickname back in the day, whether on a school desk or the fading skin of the 49er, Jonny had amused himself by adding a second S.

"All these years and you still think calling someone smart is an insult," Jonny said, zipping up and flushing before bothering to face his old classmates. Corey and Prickles were standing a few feet inside the bathroom door, penning him in and bristling with drunken hostility.

"You cunt," said Corey. "You always had it good and you never deserved it. You thought you were better than us, and what did you do? Huh? You fuckin' wanker."

"What you did," Prickles added.

What happened wasn't my fault, he almost said, whether he truly believed it or not. But they'd had so long to make up their minds, and men like them never changed their position on anything, especially not when it gave them the chance to look down on someone. So fuck it—he'd talk to them in a language they *could* understand, and it had been a long time coming. Jonny remembered all too well the resentful looks these guys had given him back in school when he'd been the one to hook up with Jessica, the hateful shit they'd said about her and especially Coralie, words like *zombie slut* and *coon cunt* and fuck, he was so ready for this.

"I used to be so patient with you guys," he said, stepping to one side to wash his hands. He showed them his back, oddly calm now that he was prepared to explode. "Because I didn't give a flying fuck what you thought. While you were talking shit, I was getting laid—and I still am. What about you, Prickles? Popped your cherry yet?"

"Fuck you!"

"Yeah, your pick-up line needs some work, mate." Jonny turned to face them, wiping his hands on a paper towel. "Now, I just put my old man in the ground today, so I'm thinking you picked a bad time for this shit."

"Yeah, 'cause you cared so much about your dad that you ran away like a pussy and never came back. He was a good bloke, our Alan. You?" Corey snorted, spat on the floor. "You're just a soft cock who's about to get what's coming to him."

"Faggot," Prickles chucked in.

Jonny felt his face twisting into something that might have been a sneer or a smile or both at once. He crumpled up the used paper towel and threw it down at their feet like a gauntlet.

"Come on, then," he said, low and dangerous, and barely recognised his own voice.

Then the toilet door swung open, forcing both of his antagonists to step quickly aside, and there stood Brendan Swain. His eyes snapped from Prickles to Jonny to Corey, reading the situation in a heartbeat.

"You two," he said, nodding back toward the bar. "Fuck off."

Corey scowled. "Hey, we were just telling this prick—"

"Now." Brendan's voice was quiet, almost friendly, but his gaze was flat and pitiless. "Think you've had enough. Reckon it's time you went home."

Corey spluttered. "I came here to pay me respects to Alan!"

"Yep, and that's appreciated, but now it's time for you to fuck off."

"*You* fuck off," said Prickles, taking a quick step back as Brendan swivelled his head to stare at him.

"Really, Prickles? You wanna go there?"

"Hey, hey," said Corey, finally deciding to try diplomacy. "Come on, mate."

Brendan nailed him with a look. "You got five seconds to get gone or else you'll be shitting your own teeth for a week. *Mate.*"

Prickles looked to Corey to make the call. Corey shook his head in disgust and turned away from Jonny with one last look: *we ain't done, cockhead.* Brendan stood aside and let the two of them slope out of the toilet, and when the door fell shut again, he looked at his old friend with no more warmth than he'd offered them.

"You all right?"

"Yeah." Jonny let his fists fall loose, trembling with unspent aggression. "I might look like a *hipster faggot*, but I haven't gone soft."

Brendan snorted and stepped up to the trough. "They can't talk. I reckon those idiots have had about one grope of a titty between 'em. Seeing you rock up with another hot missus must've made 'em mad enough to shit."

"Thanks," said Jonny, trying to shake off the adrenaline as Brendan unleashed a torrent of processed beer. "I'll be sure to tell Sloane you approve."

"Ha! Just don't say it around *my* missus, or I'll be in the shit."

Jonny leaned against the basin, folding his arms, biting his lip. "So. How is she?"

Brendan shrugged, staring at the ceiling. "She's good. We all are."

"How many again?"

"Three."

"*Dude.*"

"I know, right? But they're the best." Brendan shook and zipped up. "Anyway. We haven't had that beer yet. You still up for it?"

"Fuckin' oath," Jonny replied, wondering how many years it had been since such a phrase had passed his lips.

Brendan grinned and made a cursory attempt at washing his hands. "Come on. My shout."

They took up a place by the end of the bar and got comfortable on stools; Corey and Prickles seemed to have heeded Brendan's warning and made themselves scarce. Sloane wandered over, dangling a familiar plastic tag from her hand.

"Mick just gave me the key for a room upstairs. He doesn't seem to think we're going to be in a fit state to drive home tonight."

"Okay." Jonny didn't especially relish the idea of spending the night in Waterwich, but he found himself unable to resist a tickle of warmth when he imagined sleeping under the roof of his old home. "Let's see how we go."

Brendan requested three pints from the young bartender. Sloane rolled her eyes and tucked the room key into her handbag.

"So, how are you finding Waterwich?" Brendan asked her.

"Oh, it's delightful. I just had a woman ask me, in the bathroom, where I'm from. I say, 'Adelaide,' so she asks where my parents are from. I say, 'Adelaide.' She looks confused, and I know what she's getting at, so I tell her my mum's parents came from China. And she says, 'I bet you can't wait to go back there.'"

"Wow," said Jonny. Brendan winced.

"Yeah. I'm guessing they don't see many *mongrels* around these parts, right?"

Jonny and Brendan exchanged a glance.

"My wife's Aboriginal on her dad's side," Brendan said, "and it's a big family. And we've had three kids of our own. So you'd think they'd be used to it by now."

Jonny dropped his eyes to his old friend's hand, and there was the ring. A wave of melancholy rolled over him as he pictured the wedding he'd missed. He should have been at Brendan's side, the very best of men. Instead, he'd had to hear about it from Dad.

"Congrats, by the way. You're a lucky, lucky man."

"Cheers."

"Can't say the same for her, though."

Brendan laughed. "That's 'cause she's not a man! I think we'd have noticed that, eh?"

Jonny slurped beer and tried to smile. "Is she here today?"

"Nah, she's looking after the kids."

"How old are they?" Sloane asked.

"Mae's nine, Tara's six, and Jesse's fourteen."

"Jesse?" Jonny repeated, seeing the answer in Brendan's eyes.

"Yeah. We reckon he was conceived on the night of our Year 12 formal."

"Ah." Jonny remembered the two of them fooling around in the grass of the meadow and tried not to remember what had happened after he'd walked away. "At least something good came of that night, then."

"Yeah, he is a good kid. Can't be arsed doing anything we want him to now he's a teenager, but he's got a real knack for footy. Chip off the old block. Even better than you and me, J-Dog."

"You, I can kind of see it," Sloane said, "but if you tell me Jonny was a football hero, I may never recover."

Brendan scoffed at the idea. "We played footy for a few years—Waterwich Warriors under-eighteens, premiers in '98—but we were hardly golden boys. We weren't, like, *jocks*. We went to punk gigs in the city, got tattoos, smoked weed out on the 49er. We were the *cool* kids."

"I wouldn't know about that kind of stuff. While my friends were out bumping Nelly and learning how to give blow jobs, I was at home reading Jane Austen and playing chess with my mum."

"Well, you got there in the end," Jonny quipped.

"Ha ha. I'll get *you* in the end."

"Don't forget to lube up first!" Brendan said, and they all laughed. Sloane tapped her pint against his. Then Jonny remembered where he was, and the smile decayed on his lips. Much as a wake was for celebration of the life that had passed, he could imagine the people of Waterwich seeing him laugh and thinking Dad's death had barely touched him—just another shallow city prick paying lip service to custom. He cast a discreet glance around, but no-one seemed to be watching and judging, so he turned back to the conversation.

"Most of the people I've met here are pretty cool," Sloane was telling Brendan. "But you can keep Condescending Racist Toilet Lady—hey, that sounds like a weird anime character, doesn't it?—and that Mary woman was a bit, um, harsh. Oh, and then there's old what's-her-name. Oh, yeah—the White Widow."

Brendan glanced at Jonny much the way Mick had not so long ago. "You saw her, then. You know who she is?"

Jonny nodded. "Sounds like she's a few sheep short in the top paddock these days."

"Hear that, Sloane? It's like the guy never left. Yeah, old Kassie's gone a bit…odd. Harmless enough, but Colin freaks me out a bit. What's he get from spending all his time with a crazy old sheila? I don't even wanna *think* about *that* shit."

Sloane might have let her imagination go there, for she shuddered and declared her intention to inspect the finger food that had been laid out. Jonny watched her slipping through the crowd until he lost sight of her, that uncharacteristic black dress blending in with dozens of other outfits in the shade of mourning. Brendan regarded his beer with a heavy look that became more weighted by the second, and when he spoke again, his voice was low.

"You're not going out there, are you?"

Jonny took a long breath—he'd been wondering if the two of them would dare to broach this subject. He supposed he should have expected it from Brendan, whose lack of pretension had always made him frank and direct. Jonny shook his head, never more certain of an answer.

"Mate, that's the last thing I want to do."

"Good." Brendan supped his beer, keeping his eyes forward. "It's boarded up, anyway. Not long after you left. We couldn't have it happening again."

Jonny felt the memories pressing up against the walls of his mind, but he'd had years of practice ignoring them. The beer helped.

"The past is past. We all got regrets about it. But it looks like you're on to a good thing there, dude. Best to focus on that."

"I know," Jonny agreed, thinking about the decision he still had to address. "She's great. But it's so hard to avoid the past today, man. It's like everything's been waiting fifteen years to catch up with me, and now it won't let me go without a fight."

"So fight it," Brendan advised. "Kick its arse. Trust me, the past is a piece of piss. It's the future that scares me."

Jonny lifted his beer, and they toasted each other with a clink of glass. "Cheers, B-Dog. Fuck, it's good to see you. I was so worried about facing you again, man. I mean, we didn't exactly part on the best of terms."

"I know, brother." Brendan shook his head in disgust, even as Jonny thrilled inside to hear that endearment on his lips once again. "Sorry about that. I was a dickhead. I didn't know any better. Oh well. Older and wiser, yeah?"

"That's the idea." Jonny rested one hand on his mate's broad shoulder. "I missed you, you great lump. What have you been up to, anyway?"

"Well, when Coz told me she was pregnant, I knew I had to get my shit together—there was no way our families were gonna let me be a deadbeat dad on the dole at nineteen, and fair enough, too. I'd never really wanted to be a sparky like the old man, but it came easy, so…"

Brendan shrugged, and Jonny could imagine him in the black Swain Electrical uniform his dad had worn for so long; he'd be much more at home in that rig than the too-tight suit he was rocking today. He had always been happier in daggy old track pants and a pair of thongs than anything with the slightest hint of class—unlike Sloane, who now returned munching on a stick of dip-coated celery.

"Well, the good news is, there's lots of food. The bad news is, it's like someone killed a zoo over there."

"Sloane's a vegetarian," Jonny explained.

"Oh, that's all right, I don't care where she's from," Brendan said, and she grinned. "So, what do you do with yourself these days, Jonno?"

"I've been working in restaurants ever since I left here. Now I'm kitchen manager at a place called the Hamburger Hilton."

He refrained from adding that he might not be for much longer. The owners were good friends of his and he'd been working with them for years, but the Hilton wasn't making enough to stay afloat—the recent spike in pop-up bars and cafés had torn a big hole in their hull. They'd already stripped the staff down to essentials, and Jonny often found himself wondering how much longer they could afford to keep him on.

"Oh, hello, it's Gordon bloody Ramsay! So, when are we gonna see you on *My Kitchen Rules*, then?" Brendan chortled at his friend's mortified expression. "Just kidding. You always were the best bloke to have around the morning after a party."

Jonny thought of all the times he'd whipped up bacon and coffee and French toast for his hungover friends, the work at hand helping him to forget his own wretched state. The act of creation was a way to take control of his environment, to make something positive from the raw materials he had been given. Even washing dishes afterward was a task he could find some small pleasure in; if his troubles didn't exactly sluice down the drain with all the grime and mess, it was a reminder that perhaps someday they could be washed away, that even the dirtiest of souls could come clean in the end.

"I'd kill for one of your veggie burgers right now," Sloane confessed. He imagined slapping one together, field mushrooms and chargrilled eggplant and leaf salad and creamy blue cheese sauce, and his stomach just about barked at him. "Babe, we have to get something to eat. Especially if we're going to keep drinking."

Jonny wasn't about to ask Mick if he could whip up a couple of cheese toasties on today of all days. "Yeah, you're right. We should go for a walk and suss something out."

"There's a neat little pizza place just up the road," Brendan suggested. "Dino's. So yeah, now we got a Mino's *and* a Dino's. I keep wondering when someone's gonna open a Gino's. We get pizzas from there a fair bit."

"Okay, cool. I should probably walk off some of this booze, anyways."

They chatted a while longer, occasionally folding passers-by into the conversation. Jonny felt stronger with Brendan at his side, less inclined to worry about the judgements of others, but no further attacks on his actions or person seemed forthcoming. The faces he saw were all friendly—Coralie's brothers came over as if Brendan's presence had marked him as safe, unchanged, and seeing Danny and Teddy's familiar grins made him miss their sister all the more. Eventually, Sloane returned from the Ladies again and sent him an impatient look, so Jonny finished his pint and placed the glass on the bar.

"Looks like it's time for dinner, but I need another piss first. Let's hope this one's a bit less eventful."

"I'm going to have a smoke out front while I wait for you," Sloane declared. She rarely smoked nowadays unless she was drinking or especially tense. "See you in a tick."

She disappeared outside while Jonny relieved himself, and this time the worst thing he had to deal with was an unseen flatulent presence in the stalls. He returned to Brendan and slapped him on the back, feeling a warm rush of affection for the man who'd once been the closest thing he'd ever have to a brother.

"You're coming back, right?" Brendan asked. "We still got a lot of catching up to do."

"Yeah, mate. I think we're going to be glad Mick gave us that room key. See you in a bit, B-Dog."

"I'll be here, J-Man."

Jonny made his way across the Cutters Arms to the door, doing the polite nod routine again; he was almost pathetically grateful that Mary, Corey, and Prickles were nowhere to be seen. As he pushed outside into the sunlight and the oppressive heat, he checked his phone and saw that more time had passed than he'd expected—it was almost six o'clock already. He glanced up as he shoved the mobile back into his pocket, looking for Sloane. She wasn't sitting at one of the outside tables, flicking ash into a black plastic tray; she wasn't on the footpath in either direction, impatiently tapping her little foot. She was standing on the other side of the road, a cigarette smouldering in her right hand as she talked to the White Widow.

Fuck.

Jonny's skin crawled at the sight of Sloane with that veiled ghost, two parts of his life that should never touch. What might Kassia be saying to her right now? The possibilities jerked his feet off the footpath and onto the road. He had to wait as a ute cruised slowly by, and then he was across and standing on the traffic island. But by now the White Widow had said whatever it was she had to say, and her Dogsbody was leading her away. The pale wraith seemed to have a limp, depending on her carer for support; they looked like a bizarre, inverted wedding-day family, the young son leading his ailing mother up the aisle to give her away. By the time he crossed the other lane and reached Sloane, they were metres off and paid him no mind at all. A hint of sandalwood lingered in the air, the ghost of a ghost.

"You all right?" he asked.

Sloane turned, regarded him with a knitted brow, then seemed to remember she had a cigarette burning between her fingers. She took a last drag, butted it out, and tossed it into a nearby bin, all without saying a word. Jonny's bad feeling intensified.

"Let's go eat," she said.

"What did *she* have to say?" he asked. "The White Widow?"

Sloane shrugged the question off as they walked in the direction of Dino's Pizza. "You feel like going halves in a veggie? I'm not as hungry as I thought."

Jonny said nothing, walked, waited. Half a minute passed before Sloane came to a halt on the footpath outside a closed newsagent, and he turned to face her.

"Okay," she said, her deep brown eyes meeting his, and folded her arms. "So then, Jonathan. Tell me about her."

"Her?" Jonny echoed, trying to put off the inevitable.

"The White Widow told me to ask you about her niece." Sloane stared at him, keeping a close eye on his reaction. Whatever she saw on his face, it only strengthened her resolve.

"She told me to ask you about Jessica."

i put a spell on you

"I THINK THEY LIKE ME," Jessica said, standing on the sidewalk outside the Cutters Arms as she and Jonno watched the taillights of Brendan's Torana recede down the Waterwich main drag.

"Of course they do." Though Brendan and Coralie had been introduced to Jessica at school, tonight had been the first time they'd really all hung out, and Jonno had been pleased to see them taking to her as quickly as his father had. "You're a likeable sort, Jess."

He cringed a little at that, thinking it was too on the nose, but she just smiled and turned to look at the pub. It loomed over them in impassive silence, its doors locked and windows on both floors dark; the Cutters Arms closed at midnight on a Saturday, and that had been two hours ago.

"Well, here we are," she offered. "Back at work."

"Yeah, but it's also my home. I'd invite you in, but I'm sure you already see enough of the place."

That was another line that came perilously close to revealing the depth of his interest in her, but again, she didn't bite or even seem to notice. "This is true. The kitchens, anyway. You know, where a mere woman belongs."

Jonno snorted in amusement and matched her dry tone. "You're lucky we let you do that much. Really, you should be off in a room somewhere, having babies."

She nodded, a lopsided smile emerging as she latched on to the concept. "Yeah, me and all the other women—battery bitches. I can totally see that. Sheds full of pregnant women squeezed into tiny cages, pumped full of steroids, forced to feed and breed and never even able to stretch their legs. Fuck free range, just stick 'em in cages and keep 'em in their place. Pay your money and you can impregnate 'em right through the bars."

Jonno shook his head in wonder, though he was getting used to her flights of fancy and the dark paths they took. "Christ. You're a weirdo, Grzelak."

"Problem?"

"No. Look, I'm not really tired yet. You want to go for a walk or something?"

"Sure."

They picked a direction at random and began wandering down the footpath, away from the flat expanse of sea that glimmered under the touch of the moonlight. Waterwich was almost dead silent around them, with only the occasional drone of a passing car to suggest the town supported life.

"Everyone's gone to bed," Jessica mused, a hint of condescension to her voice. "So they can get up early in the morning for church, I suppose."

"We could go, too. I hear red wine is on the house."

"Ha! No, thank you. I'm fairly sure that if I ever cross the threshold of a church, something's going to catch on fire."

"Oh, you're so *evil.* When are you going to stop messing around and sacrifice me to the Devil?"

"Let's not rush things, Jonathan. I'm a good little bad girl. I don't kill boys on the first date."

So she thought of this as a date, too. Jonno was pleased to know she had no problem with that formality. He hadn't pitched tonight as such, just as a chance for the two of them to hang out with Brendan and Coralie, who were well beyond courting and deep into a relationship. They'd ended up driving to nearby Killian in the Torana and catching a screening of *The Blair Witch Project* at the local cinema—a "new release" film Jessica recommended with some amusement, having already seen it in Adelaide three months ago. Then they'd kicked their heels around Killian for a bit, chatting and drinking Cokes and getting to know each other, before driving back to Waterwich and doing the same down at the foreshore car park. It hadn't exactly felt like a date, but if Jessica thought it one, that meant she was aware of its possibilities.

She'd started at the pub that Monday, and the next two days at school and in the kitchen had gone well enough that he'd nerved himself up to ask if she wanted to hang out after work on Wednesday night. She did, and on the Thursday and Friday nights, too. It seemed effortless, and Jonno, who had little experience with this process, felt increasingly certain that their rapport was building to something more than just friends and workmates.

"Oh, hey! We should go down here." Jessica paused at the side of the road near the library and pointed to where the ground sloped down to a thick ribbon of running water. "Remember your five-star creek?"

Jonno shrugged in acquiescence. This was where they'd first met, and that seemed to lend tonight's visit some weight. Of course he was in.

They picked their way down the slope until it became the bank of Cold Bath Creek, and Jessica led the way to an outcropping that would let them dangle their feet over the water. They sat and watched it babble by, then turned to look at each other. An invisible chorus of frogs soundtracked the scene with a pulsing batrachian ballad.

Think of something to say. Witty and charming would be good.

Jonno came up dry. It didn't help that Jessica's eyes were able to dash all thought from his mind with a moment's contact.

"So," he said as a preamble, and left it hanging.

"You smoke weed?" Jessica asked, casual as you like.

"Er, sometimes, yeah. Why?"

She shook her head as if dealing with a slow child, then opened her cigarette packet and produced a slim joint. "Here's why. You want to smoke this with me?"

"Yeah, sure."

Jessica sparked it up, hit it and passed it over. Jonno paused for a moment, worrying that the weed would make him paranoid and ineffectual, then threw caution to the wind and took a drag.

"So, how long have Brendan and Coralie been together?"

Jonno managed to let out the smoke without coughing and passed the joint back. "About six months now. But it'd been on the cards for a while before that."

"Is it weird? I mean, the three of you have been best friends since you were kids. Does it feel strange that two of you are together now?"

Jonno gave this some thought. "It was a little weird at first, but not much has changed, really. It kind of seems right that one of us ended up with Coralie, partly 'cause we both had little crushes on her at times when we were growing up, and partly 'cause her going out with some other bloke would seem…strange. Like he didn't know her well enough to deserve her. She's been like a sister to us, so we've always been real protective of her."

"Mmm, incest."

"Okay, not a sister, more like a…cousin?"

Jessica laughed. "Oh, that's all right, then."

"Look, you know what I mean." It occurred to Jonno that he was stoned, every puff was going to take him higher, and already he was losing his grip on coherence. "She's so cool. I love Coralie. I mean, I'm not *in* love with her. She's just awesome. Nicest person you'll ever meet."

Jessica watched the joint burn, thoughtful. "So you've never hooked up with her?"

"Nah."

"But you wanted to."

Jonno knew this was perhaps dangerous territory, but Jessica seemed to encourage honesty in others by virtue of her own, so he went with it.

"Now and then, you know…like when we went through puberty and stuff. New things to get used to—suddenly one of your best mates has got boobs and long legs and you feel funny when she smiles at you. There were a couple of awkward moments, but we all came through okay. I got over it, but I think Brendan's been in love with her ever since then."

"They're really cool. I hope it works out." Jessica passed the joint over, and her cool fingers brushed against his. "And what about you, Jonathan? You in love with anyone?"

He tried to laugh and shrug it off, suspecting that may have made him look twice as guilty. "No, I wouldn't say that."

"What *would* you say, then?"

Jonno hit the joint to give himself time to think. The answer rode out of him on a grey plume of sweet-smelling smoke. "I'd say there's not been anyone around I found interesting enough to even ask out."

"But you asked *me* out."

He nodded. "Well, you *are* interesting."

Jonno passed back the joint, and this time he was sure the touch of her fingers on his was intentional. "Thank you. A girl tries."

"But you don't, that's the thing. You're just *you.* You know exactly who you are, and you don't give a fuck what anyone else thinks about you."

Jonno couldn't quite believe he'd been that honest. He watched as Jessica responded with a little smile that looked almost sad.

"Yeah, I do," she said, her voice low, and then she hit the joint and blew a soft cloud of dope smoke straight at his face.

There. Even a clumsy, stoned dickhead knows that's a sign.

She was watching him with those sultry, almost sleepy eyes, and her gaze was intense. Jonno got the sudden impression that she was as nervous as him, and almost laughed until he realised how she might take such a response. She'd put herself out there, and from knowing her a week, he could already see that was rare. This moment was pivotal, and he couldn't, *mustn't* fuck it up.

Jonno lifted his hand and slowly slipped it into hers, half-expecting at each moment that she would pull away and ask what the hell he thought he was doing. Instead, her cold fingers closed gently on his. When he looked up, she was glancing away with a wide grin, pulling on the joint and trying to look casual and failing.

They said nothing for the next minute or so, the physical contact being all the communication they needed for the moment. Jonno's mind was awhirl with a thousand thoughts, with dreams and doubts both. This was rarely trod territory for him, but how often had *she* done this? His history with women amounted to a few drunken pashes at parties and that night last year he'd fingered Alison Carpenter out on the 49er; Jessica was a seen-it-all city girl, and there was no way she'd gotten this far without taking at least one lover. Maybe more. Maybe he wasn't even her first guy in Waterwich.

Oh, stop it, you whacked idiot.

As if underlining this thought, Jessica butted the roach out on the grass of the bank and popped the stub into her cigarette packet.

"Would you like one?"

"Sure."

Jonno didn't smoke cigarettes that often, but both Brendan and Coralie had picked up the habit in the last couple of years and he'd often shared theirs. And in this moment, he would gladly have accepted a punch in the face if it came from Jessica.

She lit them a pair of cigarettes and they stared into the water for a moment. She didn't look up when she began to speak.

"You haven't asked me what I'm doing in Waterwich. I guess you're just being polite, but it's the first thing I'd want to know if I was in your shoes. I mean, it's obvious I'd rather be back in town, but here I am, spending a whole school year out in the sticks."

The question had indeed occurred to him, but she was right—he'd been waiting until she felt comfortable enough to tell him.

"Thing is…I got into a bit of a weird place last year. I'd always been into going out and running amuck, but me and my best mate Anjelica, we started getting into it hardcore. We were hanging out every night, crashing parties, looking for new experiences. My folks didn't mind so much at first, because my grades were good and they figured I was smart enough to not do anything too stupid.

"What they didn't know is that I didn't feel comfortable at home anymore. It wasn't because of them—as far as parents go, I think I got a pretty good deal. It was because…well, you'll probably think I'm a freak, but…I became convinced that our house was haunted."

Jonno blinked, said nothing.

"That's mental, right? I mean, it wasn't like there were any stories about previous occupants dying in horrible ways or anything, but I just started to feel like…like something was *watching* me. I never actually saw anything, it was just a feeling, you know? And it wasn't all the time, either, but it could happen anywhere—I'd be in the kitchen, or in the shower, or in my room doing homework, and I'd just *know* that someone was close by. It got so I didn't even want to sleep because I couldn't stand to think that something was in my room, watching me while I was helpless.

"I spent as little time as I could at home—as little time as I could sleeping, too. Me and Jeli would stay out late and I'd crash at her place, or we'd just get on some gear and stay awake all night. I thought maybe we could party away the darkness, you know? Ignore it until it went away. But it didn't. And when I came home high on speed or whatever, it was *worse*. Because it just made me more aware of the weirdness, more paranoid about what might happen, and I couldn't even sleep to block it all out. Shit was fucked.

"Eventually my grades started to suffer, because I wasn't bothering to do much schoolwork. I just didn't care. I had more important things to worry about—where we could score some drugs, what hot guys we might meet, what club we might be able to sneak into. My parents got worried, started trying to pull me back in line. But by that stage, the last thing I wanted was my folks coming down on me. I wasn't a kid anymore, you know?

"The last straw was when it touched me. I'd been partying all night, and I convinced some random dude to drive me home because I'd had a fight with Jeli and I didn't want to stay at her place. I crashed on my bed, still off my tits on meth, trying to make sense of everything, the chaos my life had become—and *then*…

"I felt something cold—like, *deathly* cold, like *fingers*—take my hand.

"I jumped up, and of course nothing was there, but fuck that—I *felt* it. My hand had gone numb. I started freaking out, screaming and trashing my room and shit, and my parents came storming in. *Man*, they were pissed off, and they didn't want to hear any bullshit about ghosts—they'd had a gutful.

"So, the next day, we made a deal. If I came out here and spent a year living with Aunty Kassie, if I buckled down and got good grades and stopped getting into trouble and doing drugs and all that shit, they'd not only chuck in the money for uni, they'd send me on a trip anywhere in the world I wanted to go. They made it pretty clear that saying *no* wasn't an option. So…here I am."

Jessica turned to look at him now, gauging his response. He had no idea what to think, but whatever she saw in his eyes seemed to be the thing she was after.

"This is me, Jonathan. I'm a weirdo and I have a strange sense of humour and I do silly things sometimes and I thought I was touched by a ghost. I just figured you should know what you're letting yourself in for."

Jonno smiled and squeezed her hand. The whole ghost thing was bizarre, and the drug angle was a little worrying considering she'd just gotten them stoned, but he'd actually been more concerned about those references to hot guys. He knew it was dumb, but he would rather imagine a ghost laying hands on her than another dude.

"Okay," he said.

Jessica smiled a smile then, and it was unlike any he'd seen her wear before. Bare of her usual snark, there was something childlike in it, joyous even. It struck him that what he was seeing was unfiltered happiness.

"Cool," she said, her eyes burning holes in his mind. "Now, just fucking kiss me already, will you?"

Her lips were as cool as her fingers, and the tip of her nose was chilly against his cheek, but her mouth was warm and welcoming. Jonno pushed aside what she'd told him and focused on the business at hand, giddy with delight and triumph. He'd spent a sizable portion of the last week wondering what her kiss would feel and taste like, and now that it was here, he wanted to stay inside it and be happy and warm for as long as they could keep the rest of the world out.

When their lips finally parted, Jonno kept his face close to hers and murmured, "No going back now," and Jessica laughed, a bright and delighted sound at odds with the dark face she presented to the world, and he knew that laugh would echo through his mind and through his dreams for the rest of his life.

about a girl

"YOU WENT OUT WITH A goth?" Sloane asked, casting him an amused look. Jonny thought she might have been exaggerating it to show she was at ease talking about his past partners. "I guess that explains why you keep buying me black underwear."

Once she'd voiced her question about Jessica, Jonny had led her back to the foreshore and into the still-deserted playground—pizza would have to wait, because there was no way Sloane was going to let this go until she was satisfied. They'd walked across a carpet of woodchips, past an ageing fort that poked out a slippery dip like a dull steel tongue, and sat on some swings at the back that gave a clear view of the sea spread out before them. Jonny remembered playing here as a kid and was frustrated to find that his rear end now barely fit into the seat. Sloane drifted back and forth beside him, one foot tucked under her, smoking another cigarette already—a sure sign of tension.

"So, you and this Jessica were best friends with Brendan and his girlfriend?"

"Coralie, yeah. The three of us had been mates for ten years before Jess came along. We just totally clicked from the get-go. It never seemed weird to us that Coralie was a girl, or that she was brown. She was a real tomboy, and a lot of fun to have around, and her family was dead-set lovely. We just were what we were, you know?"

Jonny grinned to himself, a hundred sun-bright memories crowding the front of his mind and begging to be shared.

"Man, we used to do everything together. The shit we got up to…You see how Brendan's got that goatee? He's had that forever. He grew it in to cover a scar on his chin that he got when he was nine. We were racing our BMXs down a dirt track, and Coralie ran him off the road into an old fence, and this big rusty nail took a chunk out of him. He got up yelling, wondering why we were staring at him in horror, and all the while blood's pissing out of his face…Coralie felt so bad that she was physically sick. Like, she actually threw up right there in the dirt. She cared about us so much that she probably still hasn't forgiven herself for hurting him."

"Two guys and a girl grow up together—it's a classic. So, did this turn into a love triangle?" Sloane asked, with a little grin to show that she was joking, but not entirely.

"You've got to stop thinking of life in terms of tropes, babe. Nah, it wasn't like that. I remember Coralie referring to us as her boyfriends once, but that was long before we cared about such things. Shit got a bit awkward when we hit puberty, but not so much that it affected our friendship."

Unbidden, Jonny's mind flashed back to a dream he'd had at thirteen. He'd been playing football with Coralie on the school oval, and whenever someone kicked a goal the other had to remove an item of clothing. They'd both ended up naked before Coralie had run off with the ball, and he'd chased her down until they'd tumbled onto the grass together, laughing as they fought over the Sherrin. The way her body had looked, the raw sensual power of her imagined nudity, and the way it had felt wriggling and writhing beneath his—

My first wet dream. But I never even told Jess about that.

"That was about the time Brendan fell in love with her. He wouldn't admit it for ages, but we could all tell what was going on. Coralie just tried to ignore it at first, I think. But his feelings didn't go away, though he cared too much to act on them in case it all went wrong. I guess that, over time, she came to realise she felt the same way. They've been together ever since."

"How sweet," Sloane said. "So that was that? You and Coralie never hooked up?"

The way her body had looked, the way it had felt wriggling and writhing beneath his—

"No."

"How did Jessica come into all this?"

"I met her when she moved to Waterwich to finish school. She'd been having problems in Adelaide, so her parents sent her here to live with her weird aunt. I got her a job at the pub, and we hit it off. And then there were four."

"Hmm." Sloane flicked the cherry of her cigarette into the woodchips below, stamped out the glow with her sandal, fiddled with the butt like a magician about to make it disappear. "So, what am I missing here? Why would that White Widow woman tell me to ask you about Jessica?"

"Because she's Kassia. She's the weird aunt."

"Ah, right. But that still doesn't explain it." Sloane gripped the chains of her swing and made her seat sway from side to side. "Was Jessica at the funeral, or the wake?"

"No."

"So where is she now?"

"I have no idea."

Sloane didn't speak for a while, didn't look at him. Jonny got the distinct impression she wasn't satisfied with his answers. And fair enough, too—there was a lot he wasn't saying. Some of it he didn't know how to put into words; some of it he just wanted to keep locked in a dark mental basement where it couldn't get to anyone.

"What I find strange," Sloane said eventually, "is that you've never mentioned any of these people to me before."

"Why should that be strange? The past is the past. When I'm with you, I'm more concerned about the present."

"You *should* be thinking about the future." She shook her head, deciding not to direct their conversation back that way. "Thing is, I've told you about my childhood. You've heard all about Tam and Min, and my obsession with the Spice Girls, and the shitty novel I wrote in high school. I didn't even realise until today that you'd never told me *anything* about how you grew up. Why?"

Jonny frowned, fumbled for an answer. "What? I must have said *something*."

"Oh, you've told me about this place, the pub, your parents, and you've told me things that have happened since you moved to the city—ex-girlfriends, old jobs, all that stuff—but until today, I had never heard you mention Brendan or Coralie, and certainly not Jessica. Not even once."

Jonny hadn't noticed that. He was so used to eliding elements of his past that he didn't even realise he was doing it anymore. What justification could he give?

"When I left this place…it was under a bit of a cloud, okay? I had a falling out with my dad, and my best friends, too. There was nothing left for me here, Sloane—so I ran away. And it was too painful to look back. That's why it was so hard for me to come here today. Not only because my relationship with my father never really recovered, but because this town is just chock-full of bad memories. Good ones, too, but…so much I just don't want to think about."

Not that he could avoid doing so for long. The stiff edges of the envelopes in his jacket pocket ensured that.

"I'm not the person I was back then. I left Jonno Trotter behind when I moved to Adelaide, and I wanted to leave his past behind, too. Start over."

Sloane planted her foot in the woodchips and pushed her swing over enough that she could rest one hand on his arm. "What could be so bad that you'd turn your back on everything like that? I don't mean to pry, my love—I'm just saying, whatever happened, you can tell me. If you need to. I'm here for you."

He stroked her fingers, gentle, loving. "I know, sugar. I couldn't have done this without you. You're the best. But…I don't know. Coming here again has opened up a whole can of worms, and I don't know how to deal with it. I kind of just want to go back home and forget all about it again."

"But you can't outrun the past. Whenever you look around, there it is, right behind you. You need to come to terms with it, Jonny."

He nodded. *But that means telling her everything,* an internal voice protested. *And some of it, even* you're *not sure really happened.*

"Let's go get that pizza," he said. "We'll take it down to the creek. And I'll…I'll tell you things. I'll tell you everything."

You can't do that! Because then you'll have to admit that you've been lying to her. How do you think she'll like that? How do you think that breach of trust is going to help, what with things already up in the air and Things to think about? Better to keep her in the dark.

What, like Jessica?

He winced at the thought. Sloane must have misread his expression, for she slipped out of her swing and stood between his knees, one palm on his cheek. She gave his earlobe a little tug and kissed him, slow and soft.

"Thank you. Now, come on. I'm starving."

She kept his hand in hers as they crossed the little playground, tossing her cigarette butt in the nearest bin, and they walked back past the Cutters Arms on the opposite side of the road. Jonny spotted Corey and Prickles drinking in a parked car, smoking hands hanging out of the windows, and averted his gaze in case they spotted him and remembered they had unfinished business. He figured he could handle himself in a scrap if it came to that, but it would still be two on one, and the last thing he wanted was to cop a drubbing in front of his woman.

The walk took a couple of minutes and they said nothing along the way, allowing the silence to speak for them. This lack of conversation was not uncomfortable, but Jonny could almost feel desperate thoughts percolating madly inside his skull and knew Sloane's head would be just as busy. When an A-frame sign appeared on the footpath to direct them into

Dino's Pizzeria, he was glad of the context it provided for less weighty interaction.

Jonny remembered when this place had been a tackle store. His old man had never been much for fishing, so he'd only been in once or twice when Brendan had been stocking up for a quick trip out to Tiny Point. Now the shop was painted a passionate shade of red and heavily redolent of cooking pepperoni, a scent that never failed to get his stomach juices flowing.

Sloane scanned the menu board above the counter for a moment. "We'll grab a veggie and go halves, yeah?"

"Sure."

She stepped up to the counter and recited her order to an ageing Italian man with shiny hair and shiny teeth. Trying not to think about the conversation they'd just had—and the one he'd promised to have—Jonny glanced around the room.

The shop floor was tiled, two plastic tables sitting by the front window with their attendant chairs, an aluminium bench fixed to the far wall. A teenaged boy sat slumped on the end nearest the window, staring at his phone like he wished it would whisk him away from this mundane reality and show him something truly worth seeing. Presumably this was at least partly due to the noise made by the two little girls sitting beside him, swinging their legs under the bench and singing a mangled melody he vaguely recognised as a Taylor Swift song; judging by the shade of skin they all shared, these were his sisters, and currently the bane of his sullen, self-centred existence.

You were a teenager not so long ago. When did you get so grumpy, gramps?

Ah, but he'd grown up, much like the woman who sat on the other side of the girls and dabbed at the cheek of the youngest with a Wet Wipe. She was probably about his age, had kept herself reasonably trim despite the three pregnancies she'd gone through. Jonny was just about to pull out his own mobile, maybe not so far removed from the teenager after all, when the woman brushed aside a dangling lock of black hair and he saw her face.

That face—it was careworn around the edges, no longer that of a girl but still one of the most beautiful he'd ever seen. Her beauty was humble, everyday, and all the more poignant for it. Her skin was a shade darker than that of her children, and now he realised their little faces all resembled hers enough that he should have noticed immediately.

When she tucked the Wet Wipe in her purse and turned to look his way, he froze. And then so did she, her eyes widening in shock as they took in the man before them and realised who that man had once used to be.

Jonny took a long, slow breath, pushed headfirst into a busy intersection of memories.

Coralie.

she's lost control

GASPING, JONNO LEANED HARD ON his hands where they plunged into the beanbag on either side of her head. His face hung down so that he was looking at the flushed plum of his glans where it rested on her wiry-haired pelvis, the glistening frills of her pussy beneath, the pearly spatter of his come as it puddled and spread across her stomach. His head and heart were pounding, and he couldn't help feeling he'd come so hard he'd lost part of himself with it.

That was…

He closed his eyes and groped for a firm feeling, but his head was reeling for a number of reasons. Jonathan Trotter was a cocktail of chemicals tonight, and not all of them had been naturally produced. He was rushing like an athlete who'd just pushed themselves to the limit, and for a moment he imagined a roaring crowd in the stands, a commentator running up to stick a microphone in his face and ask how he felt about his performance.

Opening his eyes, he saw her belly rising and falling in a rapid rhythm and watched as the movement caused his semen to bead and streak down toward her sides. A bauble of sweat, his or hers, hung from one dark nipple. As his gaze reached her face, he found her staring back at him, a distant quality to her rich brown eyes. Jonno's thoughts were starting to return to something approximating order, and he realised that this moment carried with it a weight, a sense of profundity. Also, sadness.

Jonno leaned in and kissed Coralie one last time, trying to transmit everything he felt about her with that one action. Her lips were slow and soft against his, and he got the impression that she knew. How could she not, after all these years? Their bond was deep, none deeper now, and in many ways, they were one. Or maybe that was just the E.

The glow began to fade. Jonno found his bliss tainted by ambivalence, then guilt.

That was…amazing.

And terrible.

Because it wasn't Jess.

As much as he loved Coralie, as close as they'd been, the sight and feel of her beneath him was starting to jar his senses. Even as he drank in every detail of the body he'd imagined many times over the years, drank it deep so as never to forget, he was cursing himself for ever letting this happen. This…this was *wrong*. Coralie was gorgeous, but she was his *friend*, not his lover. What the hell had he done?

No going back now.

His own words to Jessica after their first kiss. Remembering the happiness in her eyes, in her laugh, Jonno turned his head to the left, and he saw her.

Jessica sat astride Brendan on the lounge, naked and shaking and so beautiful, one hand clutching at the backrest as she caught her breath, the other letting go of his cock to give his cheek an affectionate stroke. She glanced over and saw Jonno watching, stared back with inscrutable emeralds for a few seconds, her expression not changing—he might have been an insignificant stranger, or a literal fly on the wall. Then she winked, and everything was fine.

Jonno pushed himself back, rolling off Coralie and onto the rumpus room carpet. She sat up slowly, still looking dazed, and tried to stop his come from escaping onto the beanbag. Jessica stood on unsteady legs, her belly shiny where Brendan had exploded up from her furious fist, then tore some tissues from a nearby box before tossing it to Coralie.

"Okay, that happened," she said, wiping clots of pearl from her skin. "And we did it out of love, and just this once. No regrets, no recriminations, right? Now, who wants a bong?"

She threw her tissues in the little plastic bin on the coffee table, then picked up Brendan's ceramic smoking implement and a wooden bowl. She sat cross-legged on the carpet beside Jonno, her knee resting casually against his thigh. Her skin was as hot as his, her splayed sex as flushed and fragrant, and she chopped up a fresh bud as if distracting herself from thought. When she noticed his eyes on her and leaned over to kiss him, he felt no slackening of the love she held for him, no impurity in the promises her lips always made. They'd pushed the limits tonight, but their bond remained intact.

Just don't think about it.

"Love you," she whispered, and he said it back as he ducked his head to her upper arm and kissed the grinning mouth of her skull tattoo.

She smiled and turned back to the bowl before her, packed a cone of finely chopped mull. Jonno couldn't imagine there was much point to smoking weed right now; the Ecstasy Jessica had scored for tonight, two tablets they'd broken into halves and shared a couple of hours back, seemed to be soaking up as much booze and pot as Jonno could throw at it. Coralie sat on the couch beside Brendan now, their hands linked, and both accepted the bong from Jessica. When they had all partaken, they lit smokes and sat in what seemed to Jonno an uncomfortable silence.

They were in new territory now. This was monumental.

Or maybe just mental.

Of course, this had been Jessica's idea. She'd been working on it for a while, Jonno now saw, gently nudging them all into position. To be fair, no-one had protested too much tonight, but that might have been the influence of the E. The pills had loosened them up, brought their affection buzzing to the surface, and in that headspace, it had seemed perfectly sensible that they exorcise their mutual attractions out in the open, where everyone was involved and permissive.

Going to take me a while to get used to the idea, though.

Jonno looked around the rumpus room at the back of the Swain house, vibrantly aware that it had witnessed many of their exploits over the years. That PC in the corner had once been a Commodore 64, around which he and Brendan and Coralie had sat to take turns on creaky joysticks, and they'd shared that couch dozens of times to watch cartoons and movies, first on VHS and then DVD. The three of them had spent so many hours in this room, engaged in more innocent pursuits—how could any of them have foreseen what would one night come to pass here?

I hope Brendan does a good job of cleaning up and airing out before his folks get back from Alice Springs.

Jonno imagined Mrs. Swain sitting on the couch and watching one of her programmes on the TV, her fingernail picking idly at a pearly scab on the cushion, and stifled a horrified laugh.

Jessica stubbed out her cigarette in the empty tuna tin they'd been using as an ashtray and rose to her feet.

"Guess we don't really need to talk about it, do we? It's done, and done in love, and we're all cool. Now, I could really do with a shower. Coz, you want to join me?"

"Yeah, I'm a bit…icky." Coralie gave Brendan a parting kiss and stood. Jonno ran his eyes up her body one more time, from the tips of her toes to the unfurled fleshy rose between her thighs, across the sticky plain of her belly to the wonderfully soft jut of her breasts, and then his gaze met hers. She threw him a conspiratorial little smile that was half-pleased and half-embarrassed as she stepped by him.

"See you in a minute, boys." Jessica took Coralie by the hand, tousled Jonno's hair with her free fingers, tipped him a wink. Then the girls turned and walked out of the rumpus room, completely bare and beautiful, and the boys watched them until they were out of sight.

Jonno turned back and finally met Brendan's eyes. "Well."

"Yeah."

"So…we *are* still cool, right?"

"Yeah, man, of course." They finished their smokes at the same time and Brendan rose from the couch. Not wanting a drooping dick in his eyeline, Jonno stood as well. "You're my best mate. Nothing's gonna change that shit."

Jonno felt a surge of relief, intermingled with a rush of affection. The E was definitely in play—thinking about Brendan had never given him the warm and fuzzies before.

"Awesome. You're my bro. I couldn't stand to have something come between us."

Brendan snorted, finding some amusing innuendo in that. "Nah, man. Not us. We're the fuckin' Fantastic Four!"

"Yeah…but, it's just—well, the Thing never banged Reed Richards, you know?"

"Ha! That kind of works, though, hey—I'm the Thing, obviously, and Jess is Mr. Fantastic—you did say she was flexible—and Cozza has to be Susan Storm, so I guess that makes you the Human Torch, dude."

Jonno twisted his face into something between a grin and a grimace. "In a weird way, I do kind of feel like I just shagged my sister."

Brendan stepped close and smiled, dropping one hand onto Jonno's shoulder. There was more weight in the grip than the grin. "Yeah, but it'll never happen again, mate. Now we got something to laugh about when we're too old and worn out to get it up anymore, but it's done. No more funny stuff, eh?"

"You say that, but our dicks are almost touching right now."

"They're like an inch apart. Your tiny tacker would never reach that far. Now: there are two naked hotties in my shower, and I reckon we should go and supervise to make sure they're not getting up to any mischief."

Jonno liked the visual that conjured up. "You're right. We wouldn't want that."

"Yeah, we would."

They laughed, stark naked and staring into each other's eyes and more comfortable with that in this narcotic moment than they would ever have guessed. Brendan threw one sweaty arm around Jonno's shoulders.

"Fuck, you're a good bloke. Tell you what, before we go, we gotta have a shot. A toast, mate. To you and me."

"Cool."

Brendan located the Beam bottle while Jonno fought off the urge to light another cigarette. When two shot glasses were brimming with liquor, the boys raised them.

"To us, motherfucker."

"*Na zdrowie*," Jonno agreed, and they downed the shots. "Now, didn't we have something important to do?"

Brendan led the way down the corridor of his house toward the bathroom, though Jonno had used it countless times and could have found it with his eyes closed. The door was open and the sound of running water echoed down the hall. Beneath it, a giggle from Jessica.

"Maybe they're getting kinky," Brendan muttered with raised eyebrows. "Maybe the night's not quite over y—"

He came to an abrupt halt just inside the bathroom, and Jonno stepped around him to avoid a collision. He bumped into his best mate anyway, because he wasn't watching where he was going either.

Coralie was standing in the shower with the curtain pulled aside, facing them with her spine arched and her head thrown back. Jessica stood behind her, kissing her neck as the showerhead gushed onto their faces, one hand grabbing Coralie's breast and teasing the nipple as the other worked away at her best friend's clitoris.

"Bloody hell!" Brendan breathed.

As those fingers circled and dabbed on the tip of Coralie's cunt, she began moaning and clutching at her friend's hair, staring at their spectators in helpless rapture. Jessica looked up from Coralie's neck and grinned at the boys like a vampire interrupted in its feeding.

"Brutal," Jonno whispered.

He watched that passionate clinch intently and took in every minute detail—every drop of water that raced down the slopes of Coralie's breasts the way his own ejaculate had just minutes before, every purse of Jessica's lips as she laid kiss after sensuous kiss on that soft throat, each gentle thrust as she ground her needy crotch into Coralie's arse. He'd exploded less than ten minutes ago, but his eager and ecstatic teenage body served him well; already he was thickening, rising, ready for more. Beside him, Brendan grabbed at his own fresh erection.

Soon Coralie let loose a string of hitching breaths and slumped in Jessica's embrace with a moan of completion. By now, both boys were matching the girls' rhythm with their own hands and eager to play a part.

Jessica kissed Coralie's mouth, lingering, then withdrew her arms and left her to find her own feet.

"Brendan, you get in here and look after your woman."

She was staring intensely at Jonno as she spoke, and the desire in her eyes gave his cock a core of unbending steel. Jessica stepped onto the bathmat with care, but as soon as she was out, she came at her boyfriend like a ravenous tiger. She slammed into him, wet arms wrapping hard around him, fingers curling to claws in his hair, his dick pushed up almost vertical against her stomach. Jonno gave as good as he got, kissing her hard with teeth and tongue, but he knew what she really needed.

He pushed her back until her buttocks hit the bathroom basin and then kept pushing until her arse popped up onto it and her head bounced against the mirror, her legs locking around him, and he followed his own momentum right up and into her body. She sucked in a deep, low breath like a death rattle and worked with his strokes, pumping back hard like she wanted to see blood out of this. She pulled his head close and kissed him, letting him put his tongue in so he was penetrating her at both ends, then sucking at it and spitting it back into his mouth with a gasp of pure animal joy.

Jonno fucked his girlfriend like it was the last time he ever would, losing himself in her fleshy depths. *This* was what he wanted, needed; *this* was what felt right, like home, like heaven. This wasn't just Ecstasy, it was *ecstasy*, truth, love, infinity. Every thrust, every beat became a single syllable, a percussive cry that lent a lyric to this sweetest of songs: *Jess, Jess, Jess, Jess, Jess.*

Their position was precarious, but their fucking was frantic and fast reached its climax. Jonno came inside her this time, like he'd agreed he wouldn't with Coralie, like they both wanted and needed, and promised to himself that he'd never do this with another woman. They kissed long and true like silver-screen lovers as Brendan and Coralie gasped together in the shower, and he knew that this was a promise that would always be kept.

* * *

After the debauchery died down, when everyone was dry and dressed and mellowing out as the E wore off, Jonno went out onto the porch for a cigarette. The night air was getting warmer as summer approached and he opened himself to it, let it flow through him as if it might carry away his confusion.

Having sex with Coralie had been good in some ways—it was something he'd had occasional guilty thoughts about even before puberty, and he'd felt so close to her heart when inside her—but it still felt like a betrayal, even if both Jessica and Brendan had encouraged him in it. And that was even worse, that someone else had been inside his girl where only he belonged, that he'd even watched it happen. How often was that vision going to come back to him? Would he imagine Brendan's dick inside her when it was his own, and lose his connection to the moment? Would he remember his mate's come shining on her skin when they were having an argument about some petty bullshit, ratcheting his rage higher still? They'd all gone into this with the best of intentions, but there were so many ways it could go wrong, that this sweet could turn sour. This love-in had brought them closer together, but if they weren't careful, it could end up tearing them apart.

Why did she have to push us into this?

Why did Jessica do anything? Because she wanted to. Because it was there to be done. Because she refused to accept any kind of boundary or limitation, made that a point of pride, and never stopped to wonder if that pride might be setting her up for a fall.

Jonno smoked and stared out into the black and realised he had one of Jessica's favourite songs looping in his head—"Love Will Tear Us Apart", how very apt. The tune might even have summoned her, for he heard the sliding door open behind him and knew it was her even before those familiar arms snaked around his waist.

"Hey, lover. Did you enjoy tonight?"

I'll let you know when it doesn't destroy us all.

"Yeah," he said, because that was easiest.

"You're welcome," she sighed, slipping between his body and the porch railing, pinching the cigarette from his fingers to steal the last few drags. He held her there and pressed his lips to the back of her head, perhaps to keep them still and silent.

The breeze blew soft and warm. The leaves of the trees in Brendan's yard shushed like a brushed cymbal.

"The year's nearly over," Jessica murmured. "The formal's coming up, and then it's only three weeks until 2001. I wonder how much of an odyssey next year's going to be…?"

That might have been a subtle prod, asking him to make up his mind about their future. She was moving back to the city next year, and she wanted him to come with her. His mind was spinning too much for him to consider something so big right now, so Jonno said nothing.

"Still, there's time left. Time for treats. And I've got another one lined up for us soon, babe. Nothing like tonight, though. Something…different. Just for us, the pure and true."

Jessica flicked the cigarette away, and the glow of its fading life disappeared into the night. Then she turned and breathed warm, smoky words into his ear, and he told himself it was the ticklish sensation rather than their meaning that made him shiver.

"We're going to the Chapel."

after all these years

"JONNO," CORALIE SAID, AS IF he'd knocked on her front door at the worst possible time. He didn't know what to say, so he just smiled and nodded, waiting for his old friend to set the tone of this unexpected encounter. Her girls eyed him curiously for a moment, and even the teenager glanced up from his phone to see what might bore him next.

"Hi. I figured you'd be back in town for the—today, but I wasn't sure I'd…wow." Coralie rose to her feet and took a step toward him. "Look at you!"

"All grown up," he quipped, for lack of anything better.

"You look good," Coralie said, and enough time had passed that he couldn't tell if she was being sincere or just polite. "And here's me, all bummed up to the nines."

She gestured at her outfit, a plain yellow T-shirt and a pair of old black track pants with pearly paint spatters down one leg. Sloane had paid for the pizza and now roamed back to Jonny's side, clicking her fingers.

"Hang on, I've got this. You're Coralie, aren't you? Jonny was just telling me about you."

"Good things, I hope!"

"Oh, yes. I'm Sloane."

"Pleased to meet you."

"And who are these little darlings?"

"Ah, these are my pride and joy, the light of my life, the pains in my bum." The girls laughed at this while the boy shook his head in embarrassment. "That's Tara, Mae, and Jesse."

Sloane smiled at the girls and took a seat on the bench beside them, ready to make friends. Jonny could tell she was giving him space to talk to Coralie, and felt another surge of desperate affection for her.

"Did you see Brendan at the, the thing?" Coralie asked. "Sorry, I'm not used to—I'm so sorry about Alan."

"It's fine, you can say it. Yeah, I spoke to him at the funeral, and we had a drink together at the wake."

Her eyes lit up. "Good! You know, he'd never say, but he was really looking forward to having a catch-up with you. So much to say…so much has happened. I told him, if it went well, to invite you back to the house for a drink so I could say hi."

Jonny smiled, feeling a sad tug on his heartstrings. "Cool. Well, here we are."

"Yeah."

Silence for a moment, but only between them. The kitchen clattered and sizzled, a TV quietly muttered the news from one corner, and the girls explained to Sloane how much they loved pizza and wished they could have it every night. Then Jonny shook his head and chuckled.

"Man, who would've thought we'd ever have a conversation this awkward?"

Coralie laughed too, the same laugh he remembered from a thousand childhood memories. "I know, right? It's just weird. I mean…what, fifteen years?"

"Yeah. Last time I saw you we'd just finished school, and now you're a wife with three kids."

"Oh, doesn't time fly? So, what do you do with yourself these days?"

Jonny filled her in on Sloane and the Hamburger Hilton, feeling he was on safe conversational ground and also that it should never have been so hard to talk openly with Coralie. It got to the point where he had to address the situation.

"I've got to say, I'm so relieved that you guys have been cool. I didn't know what to expect. I mean…the way we left it…"

Coralie winced. "I know. I'm so sorry about that. We never should have…it was just such a terrible time."

"It's okay. I never blamed you guys. We were all messed up back then."

She shook her head. "No. We should have been there for you. God, it was bad enough for us, but you…you were really hurting. And after all those years, we didn't even stand by you."

Coralie put a hand to her mouth, and Jonny realised she was close to tears.

"Hey, don't. We're all good, really."

Dropping her hand, Coralie stared at him. "I missed you," she said. "I've missed both of you so much."

He still knew how to read her. He opened his arms, and Coralie embraced him with a ferocity born of absence. Looking over her shoulder, Jonny saw Jesse watching them with a frown—some stranger, hugging his mum! Sloane didn't look, but she noticed, though her patter with the girls didn't miss a beat. It wasn't like she had any reason to feel jealous, unless she suspected that Jonny hadn't been entirely truthful about his past with this woman. That gave him a stab of guilt, especially with Coralie in his arms again, warm and just as comfortable a fit as she always had been. He broke off the embrace and stepped back, his eyes falling on the spatters of white that adorned Coralie's pant leg and making an unwanted association.

It was just once, between the four of us—our own little Thing. But maybe it hadn't been so little after all, and maybe that memory had been at the front of Brendan's mind that last night. Maybe that had made it easier for him to say what he'd said, do what he'd done. In her attempt to bring the Fantastic Four even closer together, maybe Jessica had only driven a wedge between them all.

Coralie sniffed and regained her composure. "I really needed that. You know, there were a few times I saw you pop up on Facebook, and I thought, *should I?* I just wasn't sure how you felt about us. The last thing I wanted after growing up together, being so close, was for it to come down to you ignoring a friend request. For all I knew, you...you hated us."

"No. No. Never. Come on, Coralie. You guys were the closest thing I ever had to a brother and sister. I never hated you. Myself, yeah. I mean, you might say it wasn't my fault, but if not, then whose?"

"You weren't to blame, Jonno."

"Coming back here, I figured everyone else would think so. For all I knew, you guys did too. But it's actually been okay. Mostly."

"What happened?"

"Well...Mary tore strips off me, but I guess that's fair enough. Corey Hamble and Prickles O'Hanlon tried to start a fight with me in the pisser, but Brendan sent them packing. And Sloane had a run-in with Kassia."

"Oh, no. Those guys always were dicks. So, Sloane met the White Widow? What did she have to say?"

"All I know so far is she got her to ask me about Jessica."

Coralie shot a quick look over her shoulder, to where Sloane and the girls were forming a loose triangle on the floor to play some little game. "Have you told her what happened?"

"I'm right in the middle of it, actually. I was scared to bring it up before—never told any of my other girlfriends about Jess, or Mum, or anything. I just wanted to bury it all. But she's amazing, this one. She deserves to know."

"She seems lovely. The kids like her, and they're great judges of character. What does she do?"

"She's an acquisitions manager for a small publisher in town. Proper book nut, that one. She picked up a manuscript last year that's gone on to win awards, biggest seller they've ever had."

Jonny cut himself off there. No need to go on. No need to mention the news Sloane had dropped on him only the day before Mick had called to tell him about Dad. He glanced over at his partner, who was grinning widely as her palms slapped against little hands in some playground pat-a-cake game he dimly remembered from school.

"That's great. Remember when I thought I could be a writer, when we were, like, twelve? I was going to be the next R.L. Stine, for all of a week, anyway! I started writing a—hey, girls! Come on, not that."

Jonny realised he knew the simple melody Coralie's daughters were singing. More than that, he knew the words, though he'd missed the verse. Now Mae and Tara were singing *"Bang! Bang! Bang! Bang!"* as they punctuated each word with a clap, coming to a halt as they turned to stare quizzically at their mother.

"Why not?" Mae asked.

"Just don't, please. Where did you learn that, anyway?"

"At school."

"Of course you did. Just—pick another one, okay?"

Coralie turned back to Jonny, apologetic, as if the girls had been singing a dirty limerick or something. He smiled to show he didn't mind, though the song threatened to dig up memories he'd kept buried for so long.

Billy and Poppy, oranges and apples—

"Sorry about that. God, I haven't heard that in years."

Jonny had a feeling he might have heard it in his dreams, though he couldn't remember any specific instance. It just felt true, like when he bumped into someone he knew in the street and was suddenly certain he'd encountered them the night before in the nonsensical patchwork of visions and memories that danced across his unconscious. And furthermore, he was convinced the voice singing that simple, chilling melody had belonged to Jessica.

The pizza man called out a finished order, and Coralie's head twitched toward him. "That's our dinner. I'd better…"

"Yeah."

Coralie grabbed his hand like an impulsive schoolgirl. "Look, like I said before—you two should come out to the house when the wake wraps up. We'd love to have you."

Jonny had a brief, painful vision: fucking this adult Coralie in a beanbag, spurting on her belly as Sloane rode Brendan's cock on the couch beside them.

"That'd be great," he admitted, pushing his wretched imagination to one side. "I don't actually know what we're doing yet, how things are going to play out, but Mick's given us a room key so we can stay the night."

"Then you should definitely come out while you're here." Coralie dropped his hand, sniffed in his direction, gave a wry smile. "But don't drive. You smell like you've had a few, and I know hubby dearest will be knocking them back tonight."

"Yeah, some things never change, eh?"

"Right! But some things do. And we forgave you a long time ago, Jonno. I hope you can say the same for us. Because we'd love to stay in touch."

"I'd like that, too."

"Great." Coralie turned and beckoned her brood to her. "Come on, gang. Tea's ready. Let's get you home and fed."

The girls milled around her as she walked up to the counter and took possession of two pizza boxes. Jesse slouched in their general direction, a hint of interest in his dark eyes as his stomach began to speak louder than his boredom.

"It's so good to see you again," Coralie said as she led her tribe to the door. "And it was lovely to meet you, Sloane. Say goodbye, girls."

Mae and Tara chorused a farewell to their new playmate and Jesse tipped the two of them a slight nod. Then the Swains had left the building, and a relative quiet fell over the pizzeria.

"Someone's made some new friends," Jonny ventured as Sloane returned to his side.

"Oh, aren't they just adorable? They're such little sweethearts."

"Getting broody?"

"So, that was Coralie," she said, ignoring the question. "She seems really cool."

"She really is. She's still the same old Cozza." Jonny let out a breath that took a good amount of tension with it. "I was so worried that she and Brendan would, I don't know, blank me or something. I was scared they'd hate me. And now they've invited us out to their house."

"The way we're going, neither of us will be able to get there. But I like those two. And I'm happy that you guys seem to have mended fences."

They sat at one of the tables for a few minutes and browsed their phones in comfortable silence. Jonny logged into Facebook to send Coralie a friend request. When their pizza was ready, he carried it out the door in Sloane's wake.

"So where are we eating, then?"

"We'll go to the creek. It's not far."

Jonny led her down the main street to the library, laughing when she faked a junkie's cravings at the sight of the place.

"Sorry, babe, but it's closed. Anyway, we're going down here."

He led Sloane off the footpath and onto the slope that led down to Cold Bath Creek, and they picked their way past explosions of soursobs to settle at the edge of the bank. As she adjusted her dress so she could sit with her legs beneath her, Jonny glanced over to his left. The tree was still there, poking its thick branch out over the shallow water, but no-one was perched on it today.

Ever wonder where it all goes?

He hadn't back then. But in the ensuing years, that question had come to carry several meanings, the worst of which he could barely bring himself to face.

Where did you *go in the end, Jessica Grzelak?*

He turned back to his partner and pizza, trying not to look in the water—trying not to imagine a pale figure tumbling along in the gentle current, and the face it might wear.

Did you get what you wanted? Did you become a ghost?

A fear of such things had fuelled Jessica's breakdown and sent her out here in the first place. When had she changed her stance, come to embrace the notion—and why?

The food was good after those generous pints, and Jonny started to feel a little better about things. With pizza in his belly and his oldest friends ready to pick up where they'd left off so long ago, he was back on an even keel. Until Sloane dropped her half-eaten slice back in the grease-stained box and spoke for the first time in several minutes.

"There was something else the White Widow said to me."

Jonny paused, then continued to chew slowly so as not to choke on it. "Oh? What was that, then?"

"It's funny, but it's something that came up in the song the girls were singing. Another thing Kassia told me to ask you about."

Jonny knew exactly what she was going to say. And he knew that this time, he was going to have to tell her everything—the story behind Mum's disappearance, what had happened the night of the Year 12 formal, and everything that had come after.

It's okay. I'm ready for this now. It's time.

"Tell me about the Chapel," Sloane said.

my own summer (shove it)

"SO, YOU GUYS HAVE HEARD of the Chapel, right?"

Jessica was leaning forward on the back of the bus seat, her Beam and Coke almost tipping out of its glass, a glint in her eye. The post-formal celebrations were proceeding apace.

"Yeah, of course." Brendan lit a smoke, blowing a plume of grey out through the nearest broken window. "It's one a them urban myths."

"*Rural* myths," Coralie suggested. "It's a story the local kids have been passing on for years. Why's that?"

"I'm curious," Jessica admitted. "I heard a few things, so I've been looking into it. My special little project."

"And?" Jonno prompted.

She shook her head. "I want to hear what *you* guys know."

"Well, apparently there's this cave," Brendan said, and Jonno shivered. "Out in the bush 'round here somewhere."

Coralie took up the story. "Supposedly it looks normal if you go in, but if two people enter it and they're in love, they find something else. Another place. They call it the Chapel."

"The story goes that you can only leave if your love is pure and true. Kind of a test, I guess. To see if you're meant to be together."

"There was this rhyme about it. Some game we used to play as little girls, you know, sitting in circles and clapping and stuff."

"Really?" Jessica licked her lips, intrigued. "So how did the rhyme go, Coz? Do you remember?"

"Geez, that was *ages* ago. Let me think." Coralie tucked her glass between slender thighs and raised her hands, clapping a couple of times like a drummer testing their kick pedal. "*Billy and Poppy, sitting in a tree*—no, that's not it—oh, *man*—"

"That rings a loud frickin' bell," Brendan stated, and Jonno agreed. He could remember Coralie sitting on the school oval with her friends from primary school, Georgina and Cathy and that girl who used to catch spiders and keep them in her lunchbox, clapping and chanting like miniature acolytes enacting some playful ritual.

"Billy and Poppy, did you say?" Jessica sat up a little straighter, looking excited now. "Go on."

"Um…I'm trying! *Billy and Poppy…*"

Brendan clicked his fingers, a hard sound like snapping bone. "Oh! *Went to the Chapel.*"

"Yeah, that's it! Okay, shush now—um…okay. I think I got it." Coralie began to clap and sing a simple playground melody. "*Billy and Poppy went to the Chapel. Billy and Poppy, oranges and apples. Mummy and Daddy said, "No way!" So Billy and Poppy blew them away. Bang! Bang! Bang! Bang!*"

"Wow." Jessica wore a wide grin. "Have you guys heard about Billy and Poppy, then?"

Brendan frowned and nodded. "Everyone around here has. They're like the local Romeo and Juliet or something."

"More like the local Charles Starkweather and Caril Fugate."

"Who?"

"Never mind. But they were real, all right. Billy Ross and Poppy Diamantopoulos."

"Say *that* five times fast."

"So who were they, then?" Coralie asked, twisting one of her fresh curls around dark fingers. "I mean, I've heard some things, but, you know…small town stories, you never know whether you should believe them or not. Like the one about the Chapel."

"Or the one about Knackers O'Brien rooting his dog," Brendan offered.

Jessica pulled a face and waved this away. "Babe, did you ever notice that framed newspaper page my *ciocia* has in the lounge?"

Jonno didn't spend much time in Kassia's house, usually just popping in from the caravan to use the toilet or sometimes watching a movie with Jessica on the ancient VCR, and only vaguely recalled the page in question. He gave an apologetic shrug.

"Typical! Completely oblivious."

"Usually I'm distracted by something else," he pointed out, one hand on her thigh. She grinned to show her appreciation and stroked his fingers before carrying on.

"Okay, so it's 1964, and Billy and Poppy have fallen madly in love. He's eighteen, a high school dropout; she's going on fifteen, the daughter of immigrants with a successful fruit and veg business. They figure they're meant to be together forever and decide that they'll get married when she turns sixteen…but not everyone's keen on the idea. Poppy's family is real traditional, and they insist that she'll get hitched to some good little Greek boy, not some Aussie white trash with no prospects. They try to break the pair up, but of course, that doesn't work. Eventually it gets so bad that they lock her inside the house and won't let her out at all, won't even let her use the phone. They reckon Billy will just give up and go away eventually."

"Obviously, he didn't," Coralie murmured.

Jessica grinned, in her element. "Nope. The night of the school summer dance, Billy rocks up in his car—he'd promised to take Poppy, even though he'd dropped out at fourteen, and she's been looking forward to it for months. She's all done up for it and ready to go, even though she's not allowed out of the house. Her father and brother go charging out to send Billy away, shouting, throwing rocks, threatening to thrash him within an inch of his life. So, what does Billy do? He pulls out a rifle and shoots them dead, right there in the front yard."

"Ouch," Brendan, sucking on his teeth. "That's a tad extreme."

"Then he goes inside, lets Poppy out, and goes after her mother and little sister. Not with the rifle, though. They were stabbed to death with his dad's World War II bayonet. And apparently, Poppy was the one who finished them off."

"Jesus…!"

"Yeah, I know. That's so hot, right? I bet they fucked right there on the floor, in all that blood."

Coralie made a retching sound. "Eww, Jess!"

This is the girl you love, Jonno thought, shaking his head with a little smile. *Joking about being turned on by slaughter, and probably not entirely kidding.*

"After that, they go to the summer dance like nothing happened. Everyone knows Poppy's family has been trying to keep them apart, so they're surprised, but no-one could have guessed what they'd just done. They stay long enough to have their picture taken and share a slow dance, then they hop in the car and hit the road. They must have known they wouldn't get far, but they just fuckin' light out and make a run for the sun anyway. They rob a service station for petrol and money, kill the clerk, hide out at a farm for a night, kill the family who lived there. They decide to switch cars, so they bump off an old lady and swipe her wheels.

"After two days on the run, the cops lay an ambush for our dashing young couple, and there's a shootout. Poppy's killed outright, but Billy survives his injuries long enough to go to trial. He was one of the last people hanged in Australia before we ditched the death penalty."

Jessica paused to wet her whistle with Beam.

"And no-one lived happily ever after. The end."

"Bloody hell," Brendan exclaimed. "What a couple of psychos."

"*Natural Born Killers*, retro Aussie style." Jessica settled back against the side of the bus, looking contemplative. "It's fucked up, I know. But…I think it's kind of romantic."

"Oh, totally." Brendan flicked his cigarette out into the night and turned to Coralie. "Babe, if you really loved me, you'd let me take you on a psychotic killing spree."

"Wouldn't you, though? I mean, if you guys were in their position and that was the only way you could ever see Coralie again? Wouldn't you trade the rest of your life for a few intense hours? Wouldn't you kill for the woman you loved?"

Brendan's answer was immediate. "No."

Jonno blinked in surprise. Brendan was willing to fight any number of men at any time over the use of a single derogatory word toward Coralie; his devotion to her was absolute.

"I mean, if I *had* to—like, to protect her or something, then yeah, of course I would. But murder? No way. 'Cause the Coralie I love, the last thing she'd want is for anyone to get hurt—especially her family. So, no."

Coralie beamed and kissed him. "Good answer. As much as I love you, Mr. Swain, I don't know if I could be with you if you had blood on your hands."

"Awww," Jonno cried. "You're such a big softie, mate."

Brendan laughed. "Shut up or I'll smash you, cunt."

"There's more to my story," Jessica said, dropping her patient smile, and everyone piped down to listen. "Before he was hanged, Billy explained why they did it. He said he and Poppy were destined to be together, and they couldn't let anything keep them apart. They were meant to be, and he knew that beyond the shadow of a doubt…because, he said, they'd been *tested*. And their love was pure and true. Sound familiar?"

"Ah." Jonno clicked his fingers. "You think they went to the Chapel?"

"Well, it's right there in the rhyme, isn't it? Yeah, I think they did. I think they found it, went in, and were tested. And I think they passed."

Jonno wasn't sure how to respond to that, so he just said, "Interesting."

"I thought so, yeah. And the thing is, they can't have been the only ones. Rumours of the Chapel have been going around for decades, right up to this day…so how many other people do you think have found it? How many were tested? And how many passed?"

Jessica let them ruminate on that for a moment while she lit a cigarette.

"I've been looking into this for weeks now. And it's funny, but out of all the people I've spoken to around here, not a single one seems to know where the Chapel is supposed to be…or if they do, they're not willing to talk about it. But I did find someone who was. Babe, do you remember those extreme sports guys who stayed at the hotel earlier this year?"

"Yeah." Jonno remembered them, all right: a pair of taut and toned cover boys, all easy-going charm and wide white grins through macho stubble. Summer Bay surfer stereotypes—the kind of guys who could catch a girl's attention just by strutting into the room, could get her knickers wet with a long look and a knowing smile, and never mind that they were like Easter eggs, brightly coloured and tasty but hollow inside. "Wankers."

"Well, when I took their meals out to them, we got chatting. They told me their thing at the moment was cave diving. They said they'd heard about a massive underground cave system in these parts, and they'd been told about a place nearby where they might find a way in. They were heaps keen to go down. They even invited me along."

I'll bet they did. Jonno knew his dislike of the divers was irrational, rooted in envy and insecurity, but he didn't care. Those guys—strangers, virile and vile—had asked his girl to go along and be alone with them, and Jessica hadn't even mentioned that to him until now. What else was she keeping from him? Maybe she'd actually gone with them, given Jonno some line about homework or needing time alone as she sometimes did, and who knew where that might have led? He imagined the bastards tag-teaming her in their room at the pub, high-fiving each other like smug pricks as Jessica pushed those boundaries she hated so much and Jonno slumbered on unawares just up the hall—

For fuck's sake! Jess wouldn't do that, you idiot. She's curious and rash but you KNOW she's loyal and faithful to a fault.

Except when it came to his best friends, of course.

"Anyway, I bumped into them again before they left and asked how it went. They said it took them a while, but they eventually found the cave. There was a shaft at the end of it that angled down into water, so they went in. But it was narrow, and after a while there was no room to turn around, so they gave up. They reckon it probably just kept going down and out until it met up with the sea. Poor guys, they were really disappointed. No underwater caverns—and by the sounds of it, no Chapel, either."

Jonno tried to imagine being trapped in a tiny tunnel hundreds of feet below the ground, caught tight in a claustrophobic nook with no way out and no air left to breathe, then remembered he was stoned and tried not to.

"I know what you're going to say," Coralie declared. "They didn't find it because they weren't lovers."

"You read my mind," Jessica said with a smile.

"I don't know if I'd want to do that. Your head must be a pretty freaky place to live."

Jessica laughed. "You have no idea. But anyway, all this is going somewhere, so I'll get to the point. Those dudes told me the location of the cave. And since I got interested in this whole Chapel thing and started poking around, I've found that there's only one known cave in this area. And that's the one."

She watched them with amused eyes, dragging on her cigarette, waiting as ever for them to catch up to her.

Jonno said it first. "You think you've found the Chapel."

"I do. What's more, it's not far from here. Not very far at all." Jessica pointed out through the hole where the 49er's back window used to be. "Maybe ten minutes' walk that way."

Uh oh.

"Why am I getting a sinking feeling in my guts, babe?"

"Because you know you'll come if I ask you to. And you know I'll ask."

"You want us to go tramping through the bush in the dark, looking for a spooky mystical cave?" Brendan sighed. "That is *so* you, Jess."

"We're not doing that," Coralie said, her voice flat and abrupt, arms folded across her chest. "Don't even go there, Jess. No."

Jonno was startled by Coralie's sudden and adamant stand, and judging by the short silence, so were the others. Jessica leaned her elbows on the back of her seat and fixed her friend with a penetrating gaze.

"Interesting. What are you not telling us, Coz?"

Coralie sighed, and Jonno knew full well what that sigh meant. If she told Jessica her reasons for refusing to go look for the Chapel, it would only make her all the more determined to do just that.

"Well?"

"Fine." Coralie took a deep draught from her Beam and Coke. "The Chapel might be a myth, but it's older than you think. It's *really* old. Like, Dreamtime old, according to Granny Mae."

Jonno had fond recollections of Granny Mae: a dark face almost always split open by a broad yellow grin, a plump body that looked too heavy for her skinny little legs, a raucous and infectious laugh. All the kids in town loved her because she treated them like they were her own grandchildren, black and white alike, and she always had butterscotch lollies in the pocket of her apron. He'd surprised himself by bursting into tears when told that she'd passed away. Coralie had been distraught for weeks.

"When I was a little girl, Granny Mae overheard me singing that rhyme with my friends and came over to tell us a story. We always loved her stories, so we stopped and listened.

"Long before the whitefella came, this land was home to the Narungga, my dad's mob. They lived well around here for many, many generations. But there were some places they knew not to go—bad places. And one of them was a cave."

Jessica flinched as her cigarette burned down, so entranced she hadn't even noticed. She pitched it out the window and stared at Coralie with wide, hungry eyes.

"Granny Mae said that her people—*our* people—went nowhere near that cave, even if it meant missing out on good hunting, and they never drew water in that area." Coralie told them the name the Narungga had given the place. "That means *ceremony house*."

Jessica took in a sudden quick breath that sounded almost sexual to Jonno's trained ears.

"So please, Jessica...I don't know how much truth there is to any of it, but I really don't think we should go looking. And I know you're probably keener than ever now, but I'll say it anyway. Let's not, okay?"

Coralie reached out and touched her friend's hand with a blatant appeal in her eyes, but even she must have known it was doomed to fail. Jessica gave her a look that said *I really am listening, I really do care*...and then it was replaced by the expression that they were all expecting. It was the look wolves wore when they caught the scent of blood, the aspect of men who've found a map with a big X drawn on it. It was the look she'd had on a few weeks ago when convincing them to take Ecstasy and swap sex partners in Brendan's rumpus room.

"But *think* about it, guys—what if this is for real? What if there *is* a Chapel in that cave? There's nothing for *us* to be afraid of. Brendan, Coralie—you guys are so made for each other it's unbelievable. You're the kind of people who know each other all your lives and go on living until you're, like, a hundred, and the whole time you're together and madly in love. And J—now that I know you're coming back to the city with me, I know for *sure* that what we have is real, that you love me as much as I love you. We're going the distance, baby. What I'm saying is...what we have, between each other and the group, is *love*...and it's pure, and it's true."

Jessica slipped her feet to the bus floor and stood, holding out her hands.

"So. Who wants to go and prove it?"

Brendan saw the look on Coralie's face and decided to mind her mood. "Ah, man…I think we're better off here. We got beer, we got weed. We'll just get lost out there."

"No, we won't." Jessica squeezed past Jonno into the aisle and pointed out the empty back window into the dark. "Look."

Jonno rose after her as Brendan and Coralie turned on their seat, and all three of them followed her finger. They saw nothing out of the ordinary.

"At what, exactly?" Coralie wanted to know.

"The trees. Shut up for a moment, all of you, and just *look*."

The silence lasted maybe five seconds. Then Coralie let out a gasp of surprise, and that was the moment Jonno saw it, too.

"Huh," Brendan grunted, trying to sound unimpressed. "I never noticed that before."

The 49er was backed up to the trees, and Jonno had always assumed this edge of the clearing was as unremarkable as the others. How strange that he and his friends had sat on the back seat of the bus so many times, but none of them had seen that the trees just a few feet away thinned out in a ragged line, forming a narrow path through the bush that became clearer the longer one looked at it.

It was there all this time, just waiting to be seen.

Coralie shivered and shook her head once more, but Jonno knew this was a foregone conclusion. He remembered what Jessica had whispered to him that night at Brendan's, out on the patio as his cigarette disappeared into the dark: *we're going to the Chapel.* She'd been planning this just as she'd been planning the partner swap, letting the idea build up steam until it would not be stopped by anything so flimsy as disagreement. Jessica knew what she wanted and her stride did not falter on the way to it, nor slow for anyone else. Her confidence was one of the things he'd first been attracted to, but he sometimes felt powerless against the way it pulled him in and along like a strong current pulled driftwood, or a body.

"Drink up," Jessica said. "Tonight won't last forever."

* * *

"You're unbelievable, Jess," Brendan huffed five minutes later, as they tramped through the night-shrouded bush. "We're supposed to be having a party, and somehow you've talked us into going on a hike."

"It's not going to kill you," she replied, and Jonno saw a sly smile appear on the pale half-moon that was all he could see of her face. "Anyway, you wouldn't miss a couple of pounds."

"What? Are you saying I'm fat?" Brendan turned to Coralie, indignant. "Is she saying I'm fat?"

"No, dear." Coralie slapped his belly, which did describe a slight outward curve. "And you're not. There's just more of you for me to love."

"You get plenty of me as it is." In case his girlfriend didn't pick up on the innuendo, Brendan patted her on the behind.

At least Coralie seems to have calmed down a bit, Jonno thought. When making her stand on the bus, Jonno thought she might have point-blank refused to go along with Jessica's sightseeing plans—but, as usual, Jess had won them all over with the promise of just going for a look, nothing crazy, another little adventure for the Fantastic Four. Whatever reservations the group might have had regarding the trip had been buried under their usual carefree bonhomie, as if they might lessen any gravity in this situation by ignoring it.

Five minutes into the journey and the four of them were still traversing the path they'd seen from the back window of the 49er, with no clear end in sight. The trail was less distinct than the rough roads that also cut through the Hunter land, but once it was spotted there was no unseeing it. The trees didn't step aside to allow the track room, but it wound and ducked around them whilst maintaining enough clarity that it could be followed by moonlight. An invisible choir of crickets chirped their songs of lust all around, an aspect Jonno found fitting considering their destination.

By now, he was used to Jessica's strange fixations. Usually they took on more harmless forms: there was that afternoon when they'd ditched school and gone back to her caravan because she just *had* to hear a certain song to get it out of her head, or the time he'd driven to the next town over because their service station was the only place that stocked Fry's Turkish Delight and Jessica just *had* to have some, and never mind that it was almost midnight. Those he could understand, but he thought he might never get a grip on the part of her that produced deeper obsessions such as this one. So there was a cave, and there were myths about it—why did they have to go see it *now*? Couldn't they come back tomorrow, with their celebrations behind them and the benefit of daylight to boot?

Of course not. That's not the way Jessica's mind works. It's spooky, so it has to be done at night.

"You know, I'd feel better if we weren't stumbling around in the dark," Coralie said, as if she'd been reading Jonno's thoughts. "Didn't happen to bring a torch, did you?"

"Of course I did," said Jessica.

"What?" Coralie slammed to a halt, meaning Brendan did too. "Then why aren't we using it?"

Jessica turned to face her, Jonno's fingers in one hand and her canvas satchel in the other; she'd fetched it from the XF before beginning this walk, so Jonno assumed the torch was inside. "Because we don't need it yet. The torch is for if we find the cave."

"This just gets better and better," Coralie sighed.

"How did those divers hear about the cave, anyway?" Brendan asked. "This place is the arse end of nowhere, so how did they even know it was here?"

Jessica shrugged and turned back to the path. "Someone must have told them. No idea who. And it's not like I can just call them and ask."

Jonno would not have been the least bit surprised to discover that the men *had* left her their number, but that quiet rumbling of jealousy quit when he tried to imagine her using it.

Think of something else.

His mind went back to Brendan's question, which had been more pertinent than Jonno had initially realised. Even if those scruffy studs had heard tell of the Chapel—and they hadn't seemed aware of that aspect, just the cave itself—how could their source have known where to find it? It was stashed out in the middle of the bush, and the path to it was obscured by the 49er.

Is that why the bus is there? To hide the path?

Jonno shivered a little at the thought, despite the warmth of the summer air. If someone had gone to all that trouble to block off the path, they must have thought—or *known*—it was dangerous. Perhaps that was why they'd used the bus in the first place, for its fading signage: CAUTION. But who had left it there? He remembered asking Gavin Hunter at the pub one night, and the bloke had simply shrugged. *Too much hassle to have it towed away, so I just left it there.* Hunter himself had given no sign he was aware of the cave, despite it being a local legend that happened to be located on his property.

If it exists at all.

There was little point in mentioning any of this to Jessica; it would only brighten the gleam in her eyes. She'd once quipped that she'd had her caution surgically removed as a child.

"Hey, look!"

Jonno snapped out of his thoughts and saw that Jessica had lifted the hand holding her satchel to point straight ahead. He followed her finger and spotted the bush opening up some twenty metres away to reveal a clearing.

"Is that it?" he asked.

"Are we there yet?" Brendan added in a childish whine.

"I don't know," Jessica replied, distracted, picking up the pace. "Let's go see."

Shortly the four of them stepped out of the bush and into a small meadow about fifty metres across. Thick grass carpeted the ground beneath their sneakers, and bunches of soursobs sprouted here and there about the clearing. There was no sign of any cave.

"Nice place for a camp," Brendan noted.

Or a picnic, Jonno thought.

"It's not here," Jessica muttered, her fingers slipping out of Jonno's grasp as she stomped further into the clearing. "Obviously, we haven't gone far enough yet."

Coralie begged to differ. "Come on, Jess. We gave it a bash, but we can't go wandering through the bush all night. We'll get lost, and then what will we do?"

Brendan agreed. "We should probably head back, eh? I could do with another beer or six under me belt."

Jessica was shaking her head. "There must be another path."

"What did those dudes tell you?"

"They just said they followed the trail behind the bus until it ended."

Brendan gestured around. "Looks like it's ended to me."

She shook her head, adamant. "No."

"Where now, then?"

"I don't know, all right?"

Jessica was frustrated, perhaps on the verge of giving up the search. Jonno quite liked that idea, but his girl was unhappy, and it was his job to fix that. He turned to cast his eyes around the edge of clearing as she had already done, and immediately spotted what she hadn't.

"There," he said, pointing off to the right where two trees stood slightly further apart than the rest—how had she not seen that? It was obvious. "You see it? Maybe that's where we need to go."

Jessica stared that way for a moment and a smile spread across her face. "Nice one, babe. I knew I kept you around for a reason."

She stepped closer and patted his chest, closing her eyes and tilting her mouth up when he leaned in for a kiss.

"Nearly there, guys. Don't worry, we'll be back at the 49er for drinks in no time. Shall we?"

Coralie sighed, and Brendan said, "Well, we've come this far, I suppose."

They cut across the meadow toward the natural gateway, and the closer they came, the more it resembled just that. The two main trees stood on either side like stoic security guards, and between them was another path like the one they'd just left. Jessica took Jonno's hand again, and her chilly fingers sent a shiver up his spine.

Cold hands, hot heart, she'd once said. This had been in the back of his panel van in the middle of winter, Jessica straddling him naked as if unable to feel the ice in the air. Jonno had imagined for a moment that she was changing into a ghost from the outside in, that the heat within her was merely the heat she stole from him, and then that bizarre idea was smothered by her all-consuming passion.

Why was he thinking of this? Jonno had the disconcerting notion that his mind was flitting about almost at random, as if to avoid something.

A splintering *crack* came from behind him, and he turned in time to see that Coralie had stepped on a discarded branch unable to bear her weight. She cried out and toppled, bringing Brendan down with her, and the two of them collapsed into the grass at the edge of the meadow.

"You guys okay?" Jessica asked.

"I'm fine," Coralie replied, with an embarrassed laugh. She'd landed on her back with her legs splayed out, and Brendan had tumbled atop her like an eager lover. "Oh, get off, you great lump."

"As you wish," Brendan murmured, and began pumping his crotch against hers. Coralie squawked in amused outrage, then lifted her own legs to clamp him in place.

"Gotcha!"

"You have."

Jessica sighed as the two of them shared a long, deep kiss. "Okay, guys, come on. We've got all night for hanky-panky."

"Yeah," Jonno agreed, recalling that his own ardour in the XF had been postponed. "If I'm not getting any until later, why should you?"

"There's no rush," Brendan declared between kisses. "Your spooky cave ain't going anywhere."

Jessica tapped her foot as the couple in the grass carried on, their hands moving further afield in what looked suspiciously like foreplay. Would they go ahead and fuck right there, in front of their friends? Jonno would not have been surprised. After that night four weeks ago, they had nothing to hide from each other.

"Fine." Jessica yanked Jonno's arm and led him away from their friends, into the trees. "You two can catch us up."

"They'll only be a minute," he replied, making sure they could hear him. "This is Brendan we're talking about here."

"Oi!"

His cry of protest faded as Jonno and Jessica walked between the two sentinels and into the bush once more. They had no real fear of losing their friends, as the path this time was only fifty metres long, and it soon opened out into another small clearing...but this one was far from empty.

The dirt gave way to rock here, and it rose in a large hump directly before them like a head from slate shoulders, as if a featureless giant were forcing its way out of the earth. No, not entirely featureless—a mouth gaped in the rock, two metres high and blacker than anything Jonno had ever seen. That frozen scream seemed to loom closer with every moment he stared at it, a dizzying dolly zoom that caused his gut to twinge in dismay.

Oh God.

The ground sloped down as if pulled by the immense weight of the rock and the path they'd followed ran straight into the cave mouth, conveying the unwary to their fate. Some intrepid visitor before them had apparently heard the same tales as Jessica, for they'd daubed a sigil in white paint above that gaping maw: a crooked Christian cross inside a crude love heart. The pale graffiti had faded like the elements were trying to erase its blasphemy.

"We found it," Jessica whispered, but Jonno barely heard her over the accelerated pounding of his heart. He could hear his breath shaking, could feel the hairs all over his body standing on end. The sight of the cave stunned him like the gaze of a gorgon, and he thought he might never be able to tear his eyes away. That black hole seemed to promise depths and darkness such as he could never truly comprehend.

"J? Hey, you okay?"

Jessica's hand grabbed at his elbow, and he managed to rip his head to one side and look at her. She flinched as if meeting the eyes of a madman.

"Babe? What is it?"

He let out a sound that was somewhere between a laugh and a sob. "I dreamed this place…or thought I did."

"*What?*"

"But it's real. It's real! It wasn't a dream." Jonno lifted his hands to his head and squeezed, trying to rid himself of this *déjà vu*. "Oh, man. It wasn't a dream. It was a *memory*."

Jessica dropped her satchel, stepped before him and placed her hands on his chest. "Jonathan. Are you saying you've been here before?"

He nodded, close to tears. "Yeah. But it wasn't…there was something else. Coming toward me. Over there."

He pointed to the right side of the cave, where the rock sloped down and flattened to a near-level outcrop. There was a hint of a path there that would lead the curious around the cave itself and further into the maze of stone that separated the bush from the sea.

"It came over that. Wet. Dripping. *Moaning*. I was just a little kid, I…I thought it was going to *eat* me—but…it wasn't a monster. Oh, Jess…it wasn't a monster at all."

His lover placed one cold hand on his cheek, snapping his attention back to her. Her eyes were worried, loving—and needful. Hungry, almost.

"Honey…*what was it?*"

Jonno swallowed hard and let himself remember what he had clearly tried so hard to forget for so many years.

where boys fear to tread

THEY ATE ROAST BEEF SANDWICHES for dinner, and when they were done Mum frisbeed the paper plates across the meadow and laughed as Jonathan chased them like an eager puppy. Dad sat and watched with an indulgent smile, perhaps tolerating this foolishness because they weren't at home. They had chocolate mousse for afters, and the summer sun was sitting low in the western sky by the time they were done.

The picnic had been Mum's idea, of course—Jonathan couldn't imagine Dad coming up with such a footloose notion, though he had agreed it might be fun to eat Sunday dinner outdoors for once. Mum said she knew a place, and though they'd had to search for the trail and then tramp through the bush, the little meadow was a fine destination. Mum had dressed up like it was a special occasion, wearing her white frock with the coloured dots on it that always reminded Jonathan of a Twister mat, even doing her hair nice and putting on some make-up. Dad looked pretty much the way he always did, slouching impatiently around in his jeans and polo shirt as if there were matters awaiting his attention; Jonathan guessed that was true, though he had little idea what running the pub entailed other than pouring beers.

After dinner, Dad pulled a West End Draught from a little esky and poured Mum a glass of wine. Jonathan figured they'd probably just sit around and talk boring adult talk, so he took off across the grass to make the most of his evening. After agreeing not to leave the meadow or his parents' sight, Jonathan ceased to exist. Now it was Optimus Prime racing around in circles, shooting laser blasts up into the sky as Decepticons chased him across the field. After twenty minutes of battle he made a triumphant swing past the blanket where his parents sat, intent on picking up some refreshing Energon in the form of sparkling apple juice. Mum and Dad barely noticed, intent as they were on their conversation. As usual, Mum was doing most of the talking while Dad grunted and occasionally muttered rejoinders. Jonathan took pride in knowing that they had been able to have their little picnic without being bombed into oblivion by evil robots.

When he tired of being a heroic truck, he fetched his football from the bag they'd brought and pretended to be Stephen Kernahan for a while. Play had to be contained in the middle of the meadow though, as the light was dimming fast and his parents didn't want him going off into the bush. He kicked several difficult and crowd-pleasing goals, including an incredible punt after the siren to end play. With sweat pasting his clothes to him like fresh glue, he walked off the field to a rapturous response.

As he approached the blanket, he saw that Mum hadn't stopped at one glass of wine. Her hands were more animated than usual, and he could make out her raised voice as he drew closer. Dad had one hand on her knee to placate her, but his quiet grumblings didn't seem to be having the desired effect.

"Bottom line, Alan, is this," he heard Mum saying as he slumped closer with the football tucked under one arm. "You made vows to me, and I need to know you still mean them. I need to know that everything is going to work out."

Dad muttered something that the direction of the breeze kept from Jonathan. Judging by the tension in his turned back, it was probably less soothing than curt.

"Then prove it," Mum said, so abruptly that it sounded like an angry insult. Then she noticed Jonathan closing in and took a sip of her wine, and by the time he reached them she was wearing a smile again. It was one of her pretend ones, even he could see that, but he felt safe so long as she made the effort.

"How was your play, darling?"

"Good, Mum. Can I have some more apple juice?"

Jonathan sat on the blanket beside them, and Mum absently stroked his arm for a minute as she finished her wine and kept an expectant gaze on Dad. When Jonathan finished his juice, he lay on his back and watched the last of the sunlight fade and fall over the horizon. Daylight saving was a mixed blessing as far as he was concerned—he liked having more time outside in the sun, but no sooner had dusk fallen than it was bedtime, and that didn't seem fair. He had an extension tonight, but the routine still held sway; by eight-thirty, he was ready to doze off.

He realised he already had when Dad's arms scooped him up off the blanket. "Come on, little man," said that familiar voice, and he felt it resonating in Dad's chest as much as heard it. He turned inward to the comfort of a parent's embrace and was only dimly aware of the trip back to the car.

He came partly awake as Dad lowered him onto the back seat and tucked the picnic blanket over his weary body. "You go back to sleep, Jonno. Me and your Mum'll be back soon. Just stay here and you'll be right."

Jonathan snuggled into the leather of the bench seat as the door closed, vaguely wondering why they were leaving him behind. He could hear Dad murmuring about some time when someone could babysit; he couldn't make out what Mum was saying, but she had her worked-up voice on again. He was imagining what she might be upset about when he dropped off the ledge of consciousness into the deep.

He wasn't sure how much time had passed when he woke. The interior of the car was completely dark, and when he listened for anything that might have woken him, such as the approach of his parents, he heard nothing but crickets and the wind. He needed to do a wee, so he sat up on the back seat and rubbed his eyes. All the doors were locked, but the knobs were easy to reach. Jonathan hopped out, hurried to the nearest tree, and pulled down his pants.

Going out in the open was still new to him, and he couldn't shake the feeling that something was watching even as he shook himself and pulled his pants back up. There was still no sign of Mum or Dad, and only the interior light of the car offered him any comfort in this dark wilderness. What if something had happened to them? Jonathan had no idea where they were, or how long it would take him to walk back to Waterwich, or even which way the town lay.

This wasn't good. He'd been planning to give a morning talk tomorrow at school about the picnic he'd had with his family, and he didn't want to have to tell the class that he'd lost his parents. But if Mum and Dad were gone, how was he going to get to school to *give* his morning talk? How was he going to get home? How was he going to feed himself? He was too young to get a job, though Pops Trotter sometimes joked about sending him out to clean chimneys. He liked to draw pictures of sharks, and Hailey Overson's dad had a job drawing designs for the council, so maybe he could do that?

Jonathan knew he was avoiding the real concern that his parents *had* gone missing. If they disappeared, he would be, as Brendan liked to say, *rooted.* He didn't know what that meant, exactly, but it sounded final and it sounded right, and he knew from the way teachers yelled at Brendan when he said it that it meant Trouble. *Rooted.* Like trees. Stuck. He'd played Stick in the Mud and had wondered—what if the people who got caught had to stay standing in that spot forever? They wouldn't be able to get food or get changed and they'd have to go to the toilet right there without any paper or anything. That sounded like *rooted*, all right.

"Mum?" he called, and then, "Dad?" No distant voices rose in reply, so he tried again. The trees stood stolid and whispered amongst themselves, ignoring him.

Jonathan decided that Optimus Prime would do something in this situation. He'd probably send Jazz and Cliffjumper to search for the missing parents, but since that wasn't an option, he decided he'd have to go himself. Luckily, there was a clear path to follow; unluckily, night had fallen, and Jonathan had no torch. He left the car door open so the interior light remained on like a beacon and cautiously made his way onto the almost-invisible trail that led into the trees.

Oh, now this was a bit scary. Jonathan knew he was a big boy, all of seven years old and ready to start ninja training, but the shadows made him feel like a baby again. It was like he'd opened his closet in the middle of the night and stepped inside and just kept walking on and on into the darkness, while the monsters he'd been told not to believe in watched and laughed and crept closer by the second. Why had he done this? If Mum and Dad came back to the car and found him gone, there would be *ructions*. That was a Pops Trotter word, and it meant Trouble. But maybe Trouble was already here, and that's why his parents were gone. Maybe they needed help. And Jonathan had watched enough cartoons to know that when Trouble called, heroes answered.

The wind whispered through the trees like distant laughter. Jonathan picked up a stick so he could pretend he had a laser rifle, but he didn't feel any more heroic for doing so. He was more and more certain that this was one of those situations he didn't understand, one of those times when he did the wrong thing without knowing it and got yelled at and sent to his room; and he was more and more certain that on this occasion, he would welcome such a familiar result if it meant everything went back to normal afterward.

The trip through the bush was nerve-wracking, but it didn't take long. Soon Jonathan was out of the trees and back at the meadow where they'd had such a lovely dinner. Still no sign of his parents, though they'd surely come this way. So where were they?

He remembered what he'd seen during his battle against the Decepticons. Off to one side of the meadow were two trees that stood a little further apart than the rest as if framing a doorway. Could that be where Mum and Dad had gone?

Running across the meadow felt like being on a football oval alone after dark when the crowd had gone home, or a battlefield when all the debris and dead bodies had been carted away to leave behind only the atmosphere of big Trouble. Jonathan was glad when he reached the other side, though it meant he was about to go back into the trees.

Sure enough, there was another trail here. And this one was shorter—it wasn't long before he hurried back out of the trees into another clearing. And then little Jonathan Trotter was stumbling to a halt, staring at the cave.

He didn't like it. It looked like a hole punched into the very Earth, like a Decepticon laser had burrowed deep in search of its molten core, and that meant it was bad news. Surely Mum and Dad hadn't gone in *there*?

Perplexed, Jonathan tried to think what he should do next. He really, really did not want to go in the cave, where the moon could not follow to light his way. But waiting here felt useless, and worse, *wrong*—like he needed to be doing something to help, *right now*.

"Mum? Dad!"

Nothing. He threw his stick to the ground in frustration, tried not to burst into tears like a baby. And that was when he heard something other than the wind at last. That was when he heard the bad thing coming.

It slithered and dripped and moaned.

Maybe he was still asleep in the car, and this was a nightmare! But no, this looked and smelt and felt very, very real.

It moaned and dripped and slithered. Closer now.

Jonathan thought of the film Dad had been watching on TV one night when he'd woken and peered into their bedroom to see what the creepy noises were. There was a walking dead person in the movie, and when they moved, they sounded *just like that*. This was no film though, unless Mum and Dad were hiding in the trees with cameras and just about to jump out and say they'd made him a movie star, and he knew that was too silly for words. What was coming was far from silly, though it might laugh at him if it had a mouth. And if it had a mouth, he knew what it would do next.

Jonathan told himself to run, but the approaching sounds kept him stuck to the spot—*rooted*. His bladder twinged and managed to muster up a couple of forgotten drops. They instantly turned cold against his skin.

The thing that was coming—

Was here.

It lurched over the rocky ground to the right of the cave, moonlight glimmering on its wet skin, staggering like something that had forgotten how to walk. Jonathan shivered on the spot, hoping it wouldn't see him, knowing it would.

The thing came off the rock and fell to the ground like a drunk he'd once watched leaving the pub. It staggered to its feet again, sobbing, then paused.

It had seen him.

"Jonno…?"

The voice sent a shock of ice up his spine. He knew it so well, and yet it couldn't be coming from this monster.

Dad?

His feet unfroze and allowed him to stumble forward as if mimicking the gait of the creature that approached him. And the closer he got, the more he became convinced that this thing *was* his father, that he wasn't dead or a monster at all. But the whining tone of his voice…that was bad, very bad. He had never heard Dad sound that way before, not even when Nanna Trotter had gone away.

"Dad…?"

"Jonno! Jonno. Jonno. Oh, my boy…"

Dad fell to his knees, still dripping all over the ground, and Jonathan drew up before him, uncertain. Was he supposed to touch his father when he was all wet and messy like that? The choice was made for him when Dad pulled him into his arms and held him like one of them had died a long time ago.

"Oh, my boy…my boy…oh, no, no…*Daisy*…"

The use of her adult name prompted the obvious question. In a small, shaky voice, Jonathan asked, "Where's Mum?"

Dad let out a splintered cry of hurt and loss, and Jonathan knew his life would never be the same again.

"Oh, son…I'm so, so sorry. My dearest Daisy…she…she's…oh, Jonno! Forgive me, son. Forgive me!

"We found the Chapel. It's *real*! Oh, Christ…and we went in. And your mum…my *wife*…she…she's *gone*!"

the memory remains

"THEN WHAT HAPPENED?"

"I don't know." Jonno lifted his hands to his mouth, and they shook at the import of what he'd just recalled. "Dad must have taken me home. I don't know."

"Holy *shit*, babe." Jessica was staring at him, transfixed. "What does this *mean*? You told me she drove her car into the creek!"

"That's what I was told! That's what *everyone* was told. But...Dad must have lied about what happened. He made it all up! What the *fuck*?"

Jonno's voice rose sharply on the last word, and he realised he was close to tears. Jessica did too, for she immediately stepped forward and folded him into her arms. He went gladly into that embrace, keen to cling to something real and true. He could feel her heart touching his, reaching out to let him know he wasn't alone, and found he could no longer hold back the tears. He let them come, unashamed. She accepted him. He need keep nothing from her.

Perhaps a minute passed before Jonno felt he had regained enough equilibrium to raise his head from her shoulder and wipe away the burning traces of his tears.

"It was all a lie. My own father *lied* to me for eleven *years*! How can I trust him now, Jess? How can I trust *anything*?"

She shushed him like a puling baby. "You can trust me, J. I love you. And I swear, I'll never lie to you."

Jonno held her tight again for a few seconds, letting loose a turbulent sigh. "I know. I love you, too. But...what am I supposed to do now?"

He already knew the answer to that. He needed to get home and have a serious talk with the old man. For eleven years, Alan Trotter had let his son believe in a lie, let him think that these visions of a cave and a wet shadow were just vestiges of a childhood dream that still sometimes flared to dark life on the wall of his mind. The worst part was that Jonno should have realised by now they were not; hadn't he been aware each time that he was waking up, leaving the land of dreams? He had been complicit in maintaining his own ignorance. He was no better than his father.

"When you get the chance, I suggest you have a word with your dad." Jessica pulled away from the hug but placed one cool hand on his cheek, so chilly after the hot tracks of his tears. "For now…well…"

"What?"

"I kind of don't want to say it now. I don't want you to think I'm being selfish or callous. But…I think we should go in."

Jonno stared at her in disbelief. "After what I just told you, you *still* want to go into that fuckin' place? Jesus, Jess! After what happened to my mum—"

"And what *did* happen to your mum?"

Jonno grasped for words, but there were none. He couldn't remember what else Dad had told him eleven years ago; the revelation of Daisy Trotter's disappearance had stunned his little mind into incomprehension.

"Exactly. All we know is that she went into that cave with your dad, and only he came out again."

"He didn't come out of the cave, though!"

"Right. So where did he come from? What happened in there?" Jessica leaned close and pulled his face down until their noses were touching. "Please don't hate me for this, babe. I know this is the worst time to be talking about this…but we're here now. Maybe we can get the answers you're looking for."

She let him go, turned and took a few steps toward the cave, stood there gazing into its hidden depths.

"If we go in, maybe we can find out what happened to your mum."

There was a certain logic to that, but Jonno was still dazed by his revelation. He needed to sit down alone for a while and think, process this new data, work out how he was going to proceed from here. He did *not* need his girlfriend to be pushing her own agenda now that it had been lent further dimension by his tragedy. For the first time in their nine months together, he felt true anger uncurling in his guts and turning on her.

"This changes nothing for you, does it?"

"Hey," she said, sounding hurt as she turned to face him. "J—"

"My mother's just another reason for you to get your own way. Like you *always* do. I've just had my *life* turned upside down! I find out my nightmare is real, and the first thing you want to do is poke it with a stick. This doesn't even have anything to *do* with you, Jess! What the fuck is *wrong* with you?"

Jessica stared at him, taken aback, and then her eyes flashed with danger.

"Okay, first of all, *fuck* you. Don't you *ever* talk to me like that. Don't you ever talk to me like I'm a piece of shit." Her voice trembled behind its shield of anger, and Jonno realised his words had hit her hard—had slipped through her guard like a knife between the ribs. "I know exactly how I sound, all right? I already apologised for that. But we came here to do just what I suggested! And now we can do something to help your mum, to help *you*, by finding the truth. And that matters to me, Jonathan. This has everything to do with me because it has everything to do with you, and I'll do anything I can for you. Because I love you. So *fuck you*."

She glared down at the dirt, hand to her mouth, closer to crying than Jonno had ever seen her…and suddenly the dirt was right where he felt he belonged. His anger curdled as quickly as it had come, leaving only shame and the suspicion that he might burst into tears all over again.

"I'm so sorry," he said.

Jessica shook her head, either in denial of his apology or of its necessity.

"I shouldn't take my anger out on you, Jess. And you're right, because if the roles were reversed, I'd want to do everything I could for you, too. I'm sorry."

She didn't look up, and Jonno got the distinct impression his apology had not been taken to heart. He fumbled for words—never his strength—and felt as though he'd been thrown back into every situation where he'd said the wrong thing, hurt a girl's feelings.

The wrong thing, he thought, and had a sudden flash of insight.

"And most of all," he continued, stepping close to her, "I need you to know that there is *nothing* wrong with you. You're everything I want, and I wouldn't change a thing."

Now she looked up, but only long enough to plunge into his arms and press her face to his chest. She held him with a strength that implied not only love, but relief—and that made a lot of sense to Jonno and his freshly descaled eyes. Jessica Grzelak was a girl who believed in ghosts so much she wanted to be one, a girl with strange thoughts buzzing through her head every minute of every day—a girl who'd been banished to the country by parents who couldn't get a handle on her. Was it so unlikely that she'd doubt herself, that deep down she might believe herself to be fundamentally broken? Was it possible that this notion was, in fact, her worst fear?

Jonno turned his sharpened eye on himself, and instantly saw his own deepest terror: that he would come to *bore* her. That his jokes would cease to amuse, his amorous tricks fail to arouse, that his very existence would begin to grate upon Jessica and push her away. And even if that didn't come to pass, there was another possibility—that in time, she would simply outgrow him.

Jessica was a complex person with a thirst for new experiences, new worlds—new people. How long before she realised she had evolved out of his grasp, that he was still banging rocks together while she reached for the stars? She seemed happy enough now, yes, but she'd already pushed them into having sex with other people, and he had yet to discover just how deep her waters ran in that regard. The last thing he wanted was to hold her back…and yet, if he was honest with himself, he couldn't see things ending any other way. And that day, when he turned and caught her looking at him with a speculative disappointment, or yawning when he spoke of things that mattered to him, or wandering through far-off fields behind her eyes as he worked his predictable prick inside her…that day would be so black as to make this one seem like cause for celebration.

But she loves you right now. She's moving in with you, she's taking you on that trip her parents promised her for flying straight—New Orleans, the place she most wants to be, and you're the person she wants there with her. Don't waste even one day of this.

The thought of parents brought him back to the big blow that still had his head ringing: Dad had lied about Mum's disappearance, to him and to the rest of the world. Why? And how had he gotten away with it for so long?

And what really happened to her?

The first notion was the worst: Dad had killed her.

No. No way.

That felt wrong on a gut level, flew in the face of all evidence other than the lie. Dad had always been firm but gentle; he couldn't even bring himself to stay on at his own father's farm because of the animals he'd have had to kill, and was the kind of man who'd take the trouble to catch and release an errant spider rather than squash it. He and Mum had been having an intense discussion that last day, but there had been no sense of aggression to it. Of course, people could always surprise you—Mum had always been a bit edgy, the kind of person who needed constant reassurance, and maybe Dad had pent up his frustration until it exploded. Maybe Mum had been unfaithful, and he'd snapped. Stranger things had happened.

No!

But if Dad hadn't murdered her, why would he lie about her disappearance? Most likely because he would otherwise be blamed for it. An accident, then? Maybe they'd gone into the cave and she'd fallen.

What the hell were they doing here in the first place?

It seemed obvious now. Mum had planned the picnic. She'd chosen the spot. And she had insisted that Dad prove something to her—something important enough that they'd left their son sleeping alone in a locked car.

Jonno took a deep breath as he realised Jessica was right. If he was to find any clue to Daisy Trotter's fate, it would be in his father's confession or in this cave—and only one of those witnesses could lie.

Jessica eased away from him, a rueful smile rising to her lips. "Well, there's something that doesn't happen too often."

"Only because I usually let you get away with everything," Jonno said, and kissed her forehead. "Are we cool?"

"We're cool." Jessica sighed and fished out her cigarette packet, finding a solitary smoke inside. "So, what do we do now, then?"

"I think you're right. If there's any chance, no matter how small, that going into that cave could tell me something about my mother…I should do it. I really don't *want* to, but I think I need to."

Jessica nodded. "Yes. And you won't be alone, J. I'll be right here with you."

They stood and stared at the cave for a minute as Jessica smoked her last cigarette. When the unnerving hole got too much, Jonno shifted his gaze up to the graffiti instead. The cross inside a love heart was the only detail that didn't tally with his young memory—someone must have been here since 1989, heard what this place was supposed to be, and left a knowing marker. It would seem the tale of the Chapel persevered throughout the generations.

And a lot of them, too. If Granny Mae was right, the story predates white settlement. And that was over two hundred years ago.

But why stop there? The cave itself would have been ancient by the time humans arrived in this part of the world. If Australia's first peoples had encountered it back then, the story of the Chapel could have been passing down through the generations for something like fifty thousand years.

Bullshit.

That was an instinctive reaction, but dismissal didn't seem so easy when one was standing right here and staring at something that was probably older than most continents.

"Imagine the life of a cave," Jessica said, on the same page. "A long, long time ago, this was a crack, worn into the rock by water. Drop by drop, that water made it bigger and bigger. And look it at now. All grown up, millions of years old. That's literally *awesome*."

"In cave years, it's probably barely legal." Jessica didn't respond to his jittery attempt to lighten the mood, so he pushed harder. "Trying to grow a cave moustache, going out to cave bars to chat up young holes in the ground…"

"*Patient.* That's the word." Jessica didn't seem to have even heard him. "So old, so slow, so patient. How must we seem to these places? Flashes of light and noise. Fireflies that live and die in a millisecond."

She matched these words with action, flicking the glowing butt of her cigarette toward the cave mouth. Its embers faded fast and went out.

"Ready, my love?"

Jonno braced himself, once and then again. "No. But let's go while we can. Are we going to tell the others what we're doing?"

Jessica glanced back down the path toward the meadow, where Brendan and Coralie were no doubt occupying themselves with more pressing concerns. "Do *you* want to go back and interrupt whatever they're doing right now? Never mind them. They know where we're going, they can wait outside for us."

She picked up her satchel, fished inside, dropped it again. Her pale fingers were wrapped around an orange torch about six inches long. She pointed the tube at Jonno and flicked it on.

"I *see* you," she cooed in a sing-song voice, and it was surely no accident that she sounded as creepy as she did playful. Jonno winced at the sudden brightness, frozen with one hand up, and couldn't help flashing back to a spotlighting trip he'd taken with Brendan and his dad. He'd aimed the spot from the back of the ute, picking out hopping figures that paused and stared back as if stunned, and Brendan had done the shooting. He missed more than he hit, thankfully, but Jonno had never forgotten the way those rabbits had stood transfixed by the light as rifle bullets punched into their flesh, the way their bodies twitched and fell into the darkness. And when Jessica flicked off the torch, he found he was still standing on the spot with one hand up, still waiting for the crack of a rifle and the brutal kiss of a .223 to put him down.

"That doesn't help," he pointed out.

"Oh, whinge, whinge."

Jessica turned the torch on again, this time aiming it at the cave. The first few feet of its innards were dimly lit, grey gums inside a toothless mouth.

"Shall we?" she asked, her free hand held out as if proposing a dance.

No, we should go, we should just go, Jonno wanted to say, and didn't. That would be safe, boring—and boring Jess would be fatal to their relationship. So he slipped his fingers into hers, shivering a little at the chill of her grip, and gave a squeeze of acquiescence.

Then, together, they walked forward and into the cave.

Jonno felt a cold hand tighten around his heart as he stepped into that open mouth, and the weight of the rock suspended above pressed down on him as insistently as gravity. He let out a long breath as the walls closed around them, and the echo of that breath sounded like the welcoming hiss of some subterranean snake. His fingers tightened around Jessica's hand and she squeezed back to let him know he wasn't alone.

The entrance to the cave was a short tunnel barely wide enough to allow them to walk side by side, a rough cleft in the rock that ran down at a gentle gradient for perhaps ten metres before the walls widened too far to catch the light. At this point, the rock gave way to a broad earthen floor, and Jonno paused to take in the sights as Jessica sighed in appreciation and sent her torch beam roving around the chamber.

The cleft had become a full-blown cave about as wide and long as a tennis court. The floor was dry dirt for the most part, punctuated here and there by lumpen stalagmites that thrust up a few feet toward the ceiling; from there, some four metres above, dozens of gnarled stalactites reached down in return like yearning fingers. In the centre of the chamber fell a twisted stream of rock, glistening with moisture, shaped into smooth tentacles by millennia of acidised rainfall seeping through the limestone above. If anything hid in the nooks and crannies thrown into shadow by the torchlight, it gave no sign of its presence. The cave held nothing but rough, nature-hewn rock, dotted here and there with shallow puddles of water amidst smooth, clay-coloured patinas of flowstone, and there did not appear to be any other exits.

"Is this it?" Jonno's voice echoed back at him, the only sound other than the slow dripping of water, and that was reassuring; he had been terrified of *this*? "Jess, is this the Chapel?"

"Can't be." Jessica did another scan of the cave with her torch, found nothing but the blunt spears of speleothems, cloaks of shadow, the glimmer of water. "You'd think there'd be some sign. Something...*more*."

Jonno was underwhelmed, but mainly he was relieved—the monster in his nightmarish memory had just been his father, and this mysterious cave was just an empty hole in the earth. He took a deep breath. The air in here was earthy, damp, with a hint of something he couldn't place—a chemical process, perhaps a touch of decomposition.

"Maybe it was just a story after all, Jess. A rural myth."

She shook her head as if bothered by a fly. "Let's go further in."

Jessica made to step over some flowstone, and her shoe slipped on the wet surface of the rock. Her leg shot out from under her, and only Jonno's quick reaction saved her from crashing to the ground.

"You okay?" he asked, and she nodded in irritation at herself, pulling free of his grip. "Be careful, Jess. I don't want to have to carry you back to the car with a broken leg."

"Yes, yes, I'm fine."

She stalked impatiently around the chamber, pausing only to gingerly step over puddles and slick rocky surfaces, and Jonno followed in the backwash of the torch. The light picked out knobby extrusions of dun-coloured rock, shone in the still mirrors of collected water on the floor, glistened on that ancient beard of molten tentacles that stood in the centre as if holding up the ceiling. It didn't fall upon anything out of place, but the wet glimmer did increase toward the back of the cave.

"Look at that," Jessica whispered.

Five feet before the back wall, the floor dropped away sharply and the hole left behind was abrim with water. It seemed to form a chute that ran diagonally down below the end of the cave, and it might have been ten feet deep or ten miles. The water looked black away from the light and impenetrable when shone upon.

"That must be what those divers found. They said it just kept going down and out until it got too narrow for their oxygen tanks—too narrow to turn around."

"I guess it runs out to sea," said Jonno, trying not to imagine being inside that chute, swimming down the tight throat of the world.

Jessica shifted carefully to the edge of the small pool and squatted, reaching out with her free hand, and every horror movie Jonno had ever seen came rushing back to remind him that something would surely grab her arm and pull her in. But she merely dabbed one finger in the water and raised it to her mouth.

"It's a little salty. *Brackish*. I've always wanted to use that word."

She rose to her feet and turned to face Jonno, who took her by the elbow and led her away from the pool. Her torch tilted up, illuminating a cluster of thin, straw-like formations that dropped down in dead-straight streams above them. To Jonno, the irregular pattern looked like an abstract depiction of a toothy maw with strings of saliva dripping from it, and though he was glad when Jessica lowered the torch, he remained very aware of that frozen mouth hanging directly above them in the darkness.

"Well?" he asked.

Jessica didn't look happy. "I don't understand. There must be something more than this. Why would the story have endured so long if it's just another fucking cave?"

"Because that's what stories do. They don't have to be true, they just have to interest people. Isn't that what you're always saying about religion?"

"Yeah, but…" Jessica frowned, caught out by her own words. "Shit. Good point. Maybe the Chapel *is* just a story with nothing real behind it."

"What else did you honestly expect?" Jonno asked, his voice gentle but massive in this natural echo chamber. "I thought you were a sceptic."

"I'm a realist," she corrected him. "Gods and angels and devils, all bullshit to me. But I believe in ghosts. I believe in things we can't yet explain. And I *hoped* this place would show me something like that."

"I guess not." Jonno cast another look about the cave. The landscape looked almost alien in its random formation, but nothing could be more natural than this. "And nothing to explain my mother's disappearance, either."

"Sorry, J." Jessica slipped her cold hand into his again. "I dragged you in here, put you through all that, for nothing."

"Not necessarily." Jonno pointed to the pool as Jessica shone her torch in the same direction. "Maybe Mum and Dad did come in here. Maybe they slipped and fell into that."

"It's possible. But then how did your dad get out?"

"No idea. But if that *did* happen, perhaps he thought he'd be blamed—especially if no body turned up. So he came up with something more believable? I don't know."

"You might be right. We won't find out until you talk to him." Jessica sighed, and the cave sighed deeply with her. "We should go back. What a fuckin' anticlimax."

Jonno started backing away, keen to get out into the open air again, and Jessica flicked her torch around the cave one last time. The light speared into the rear left corner, and her fingers tightened in his grasp.

"Hang on. What's that?"

"What?"

She didn't answer straight away. Jonno saw that the torchlight now fell on darkness instead of rock, and though it illuminated nothing beyond that, the shadows looked like another cleft carved out of the cave wall.

"I thought…" Jessica shook her head and thumbed the torch's power switch. "Hang on."

The cave plunged into total darkness, and Jonno flinched as the black became all. Something primal woke in the back of his mind and he was suddenly convinced this was no safe place to be.

Get out, get out. Go, now.

"Look," Jessica whispered.

At what? There was only nothing, and nothing else. But as Jonno tried to find her in the void—the light of his life, abruptly stolen away by the darkness—the edge of his vision picked up another light entirely. The faintest of glows could barely be made out ahead, and he realised it was coming through the apparent crack in the cave wall.

"I *knew* it." Her voice was a breath in the black. "There's a way through."

Only now did Jonno truly realise just how relieved he'd been to discover the Chapel was nothing more than a story, because this discovery struck a dire chord within him. The torch flicked on again, filling him with gladness, but it was only so Jessica could cross to the corner of the cave. The tug of her hand brooked no argument.

"How come the others didn't see this?" he asked, and the reverb of the cave lent his voice a sinister bass. "It's right there."

Jessica turned to him, and he cringed a little at the fascination in her eyes. She wore the look of a zealot. "Because we're special," she said. "Because we're lovers."

She raised his hand to her mouth and gave it an absent kiss, her eyes back on the shadowed cleft. Then she stepped forward as if her name had been called, and the sudden movement pulled him off balance so that he staggered into the darkness headfirst.

The torch cut out immediately. By the whispered curse, he knew that this time it had not been Jessica's doing. The darkness flooded in from all around, plugged his ears and stifled his breath. The narrow passage in which they stood felt like it was shrinking, the rock pressed against his shoulders drawing in almost imperceptibly to crush him. He hissed his lover's name, trying not to sound as panicked as he felt.

"It's okay, baby. Look."

Jonno's distress eased just a little as their eyes adjusted enough to pick up the faint glow they'd seen from without. It seemed to be emanating from somewhere ahead, diffused by a few turns of the passage. Unless he was mistaken, it held a bluish tinge.

Jessica must have tucked away the dead torch, for he heard her free hand slapping against rock. "It's a bit tight, but I don't think we'll have to go far. Come on."

Jonno really didn't want to, but he let Jessica pull him along through the narrow passage that felt like it might close shut around him at any moment, because that's how it worked. He kept thinking this was the worst idea she'd ever had, but her hand was in his, and that alone gave him the courage to keep on. Besides, if he backed out now, she would not follow—and he would never leave her alone in the dark.

The floor maintained a downward gradient a little steeper than the one at the cave's entrance, so that Jonno sometimes felt on the verge of falling forward onto Jessica's back. The passage swayed to one side, and then the other, and then back again. That blue glow grew a little brighter each time, until Jonno could see the silhouette of Jessica's head in the darkness before him. The slow return of light inspired an atavistic sense of relief.

"Here we go," Jessica whispered as they shuffled around one more lean turn. Then those looming walls fell away, and the cave opened up around them once more as they stepped out into another world.

came back haunted

"YOU'VE GOT ME HOOKED NOW," Sloane said, when Jonny's pensive silence threatened an end to his story. "And then?"

"I'm not sure," he muttered, staring over at the dying light that dappled the creek water, but a voice in his head whispered *liar*. "I know we found it. We found the Chapel. But…"

"But what?"

Jonny shook his head. "But maybe we didn't? I don't really know what happened. The next thing I'm absolutely sure about is waking up. I had the weirdest feeling. It was kind of like a hangover, only—different. I'd had some drinks, but not enough to feel shitty. This was something else. It was like a…a *psychic* hangover, if that makes any sense."

"So, what, you fell asleep in the cave?"

"No. When I woke up, it was five o'clock in the afternoon—about seventeen hours after we'd entered the cave. But it felt like *years* had passed. I had no sense of time, barely any sense of self. I actually struggled to remember who I was for a minute, and only then did I look around to see where I was. And what I saw was bars. I was in a jail cell."

Sloane's eyebrows shot up, and she pushed aside the cold pizza to shuffle a little closer. She'd listened intently to Jonny's story for the past hour or so, rarely butting in as was her usual wont, and he'd been able to tell when certain aspects had pissed her off (the truth about Mum), provoked her latent jealousy (some of the stuff involving Jessica), or intrigued her narrative sensibilities (the hidden path to the Chapel). But this was the first time she'd shown true concern, as if she'd only now realised he might be building up to something that would change the way she thought of him forever.

"Why?"

"I didn't know either, so I made some noise until Senior Constable Macklin showed up. I knew his son, had been over to his house, but he treated me like a stranger—professional detachment, I guess. He called a doctor to come take a look at me and refused to tell me what the hell was going on until the examination was finished. The doctor confirmed what he'd suspected upon first seeing me, which had been about one o'clock that morning—I'd come very close to drowning, and my mind and body had shut down to recover from the trauma. It was then that I realised my clothes were still damp, that I'd been draped in a blanket I shouldn't have needed at that time of year.

"Anyway, the doctor pronounced me fit for questioning, so Macklin led me to an interview room where Sergeant Connelly was waiting. I'd never had much to do with him, but I'd thought him a reasonable, easy-going bloke. Not today. He looked tired, like he'd been up all night, and my sense of dread got ten times worse. He switched on a tape recorder and asked me to explain what had happened on the night of December 9, 2000.

"I told him about the four of us leaving the formal at Jellicoe Hall, meeting up at the 49er. He started to look interested when I explained how we'd gone looking for the Chapel, how we'd found the cave. I left out the bit about Mum, though."

Sloane shot him a look that suggested they'd be coming back to that particular point before the night was through.

"I told him everything I just told you—how we went in, found a path that led us deeper, and how that was where my memory kind of went nuts and ended. And that's when I realised—so fucking late—if I'd nearly drowned…what the hell had happened to Jessica? I asked Connelly, and he shook his head. *We were hoping you could tell us*, he said.

"Apparently we weren't in the Chapel that long. We'd left Brendan and Coralie behind, remember, and then I'd told Jess about the night of my mum's disappearance, and then she talked me into going in—that was pretty much dead on midnight. Well, Brendan and Coralie ended up having sex there at the edge of the clearing while we were gone, and it wasn't until after they'd finished that I came staggering along, soaking wet and absolutely delirious. I collapsed on the spot and they freaked out, calling for Jess. Eventually they managed to drag me back to Brendan's car and he rushed me into town. The cops got a doctor to check on me while they sent men out to the Hunter property to look for Jessica. They searched the cave and the nearby area until dawn. And they didn't find her."

Sloane put a hand to her mouth.

"Connelly made me go over my story about the cave again, but this time he got impatient and stopped me when I explained how Jessica had found that passageway through to the Chapel. He didn't believe that for a second, because he'd been in the cave with the rest of the search party and they'd gone over the place with a fine-toothed comb. And according to him, the cave had just the one chamber. There *was* no passageway leading further in. There was no *Chapel*."

Sloane's eyes were wide, and she hung on every word. *You said on the way here that today seemed like the plot of a literary fiction novel,* he thought. *Well, the backstory is another genre altogether.*

"I was stunned. I knew what I remembered—I'd walked through that passage, touched its walls, come out the other end into…something. But Connelly not believing me was just the icing on the cake.

"Jessica was gone. When the reality of that sank in, I lost my shit. They had to get the doctor back in to give me a sedative, something to take the edge off my grief. Then they told me what *they* thought had happened.

"They thought we'd gone to the end of the first chamber, where that narrow shaft dropped down into the earth—the one filled with brackish water—and had somehow slipped and fallen in. They thought we'd been separated in the confusion and that I, by some lucky fluke, had hit a vertical cross-shaft and floated up to the surface. There's a pond back in the rocks behind the cave, and that's where I must have come out. But only me. Jessica…they thought she wasn't so lucky. That she was still down there."

Jonny shuddered as he imagined the scene—trapped in a narrow chute below the earth, blind in the darkness, rapidly asphyxiating with no way out. Sloane must have been doing the same, for her shiver had nothing to do with the summer air. Looking up at the sun where it hung low to the horizon, still an hour away from its departure, she fished out a cigarette and lit it. Jonny gestured and received one for himself. He barely smoked these days, but telling this story would require a goodly amount of fortification.

"I couldn't hack that thought, but now it was all I could see in my mind. I sat there bawling, and Connelly tried to assure me it wasn't over yet—they'd sent more parties that morning, all the way out to Tiny Point, in case Jess had been carried out to sea by some other freak channel they weren't aware of. They had people beating the bush flat for kilometres around in case she'd wandered out of the cave in shock and was sleeping it off under a tree somewhere. They even had cops checking the roads and the bus station in case she'd decided to do a runner for some bloody reason.

"I listened, but I didn't believe their theories. I didn't know exactly what had happened, but I knew it was none of those things. Jess, running away because I fell in some water? Fuck off. No way. That girl was in *love* with me! We were going to New Orleans together, finding a place in the city when we came back—she would never have left me by choice. Granted, the shock theory made some sense, and that was the one I pinned my hopes on, if anything. I was just so desperate to see her again."

Jonny blinked and realised his eyes were wet. A single tear broke free and streaked down his cheek into his beard. Sloane saw and took hold of his hand, her eyes once again full of the sympathy he craved but suspected he didn't deserve.

"So there's the police, doing their best to keep my hopes up, and there's me, now starting to believe this was all my fault. I figure I should have stopped her from going in, no matter how much it would have disappointed her and pissed her off, and I say so. Then Sergeant Connelly, who's ended the interview by now, pats me on the shoulder and undoes all his own work.

"*Jessie always got her own way*, he says.

"Now, he'd met her before, in a professional capacity—she was supposed to be behaving herself in Waterwich, but sometimes she just couldn't help herself, and she got cautioned a couple of times for stupid little things. I guess he figured he knew her to some degree, because that's part of being a copper, isn't it? You've got to know how people tick. But none of that really registered with me at the time.

"The thing that did? He used the past tense. *Jessie always GOT her own way.* And I realised that, for all his talk of search parties and cordons and holding on to hope, Connelly was just going through the motions. They'd try, but they'd already given up on her. Not one person out there looking for Jessica expected to find her alive."

Jonny blew out smoke with a strange sound that was somewhere between a sigh and a moan. He butted his cigarette out on a slice of cold pizza, and Sloane did the same before shuffling over to his side and laying his head down on her shoulder. She stroked his hair, his beard, her breath soft on his skin. He sighed and gave her earlobe a gentle tug of gratitude.

"And did they?" she asked in a whisper.

Jonny closed his eyes and tried to take what comfort he could from his lover's touch, but the warmth she engendered in his heart was not enough to stave off the chill his story had awoken there.

"No," he said.

summertime sadness

THE POLICE OFFERED TO CALL Dad in to pick him up, but Jonno turned them down—he wasn't ready to deal with his old man just yet. He left the station and stood on the footpath for a moment, feeling totally lost. Eight o'clock had come and gone, and the sun was hovering close to the horizon. *Fucking daylight savings,* he thought, his grief turning to anger and lashing out at anything it could reach. How could the sun still be showing its face on such a dark day?

He didn't know what to do, where to go. Sergeant Connelly had advised he head home, rest up, and be ready for further enquiries. What the fuck else did they expect him to say? Did they think if they kept interrogating him, he'd eventually change his tune and confess? *All right! I took Jess into the cave, bashed her head in with a rock, and dumped her in Brendan's trunk while he was shagging Coralie. It's a fair cop.* Idiots! He couldn't even take their advice and go home. Dad and Mick had been called when Jonno was brought into the station, and they'd already come and gone—he'd kept their lie from the cops, but Jonno was in no hurry to see them, not after what he'd remembered last night. So where now?

The caravan—

Jonno snorted out a bitter sound that barely tried to be a laugh. Right, because maybe Jess had stumbled home unseen by anyone and was waiting for him to come by so they could discuss what had happened in the Chapel. The thought was tantalising, but he could not afford such hollow hopes.

Brendan and Coralie.

Yes. They'd been out there too, knew things his stressed-out brain had been unable or unwilling to retain, and he desperately needed their company. Yes.

Jonno watched his feet carry him down the streets toward Brendan's house—it was closer, so he'd try there first. Now and again he lifted his eyes and looked around, half-hoping to see a familiar silhouette further down the road. He'd follow it, even if it were a spectre that led him to his doom. Because maybe then he'd be with her again, and who wanted to live a life like this, every tormented moment of it riven with despair and guilt?

Time had developed a strange elastic quality, so the trip seemed to take almost no time at all—yet Jonno was almost out of his mind with frustration by the time he arrived. The Swain house was one of the larger homes in Waterwich, but not in an ostentatious way; its owners weren't wealthy, but they had poured what they could afford into making their home a little castle. Jonno could see lights on in the lounge, in the kitchen, and figured that was probably the elder Swains; further down the patio in the rumpus room was where his friends would be, and a soft glow seemed to confirm his theory. He walked up the steps to the pinewood patio and knocked gently on its exterior screen door.

A few seconds later, the blinds were pulled back and Coralie peered out. Then she slid open the inner glass and outer screen door, her eyes wide and full of pain, and Jonno saw understanding in them for the first time all day. His face crumpling, he lurched forward and wrapped his arms hard around her as he broke down.

The tears felt like they would never end, not just because he'd let them build up for years without any kind of release but because his reservoir of pain seemed bottomless. He felt he might cry for the rest of his life, an image of Jessica burning in his mind every second like a religious idol, so hot with guilt that his soul ran like molten wax down his cheeks and dried there for all to see.

He'd never been so fanciful before he met her.

Coralie shushed and soothed him, sniffing back her own tears, her body soft and warm against him like a mother's breast. Her comfort was so welcome, but then a little pustule of memory burst open and the Coralie of four weeks ago was in his arms—a different kind of warmth there, no tears then but sweat, and instead of her heart opening to him in sympathy, it was other flesh that accepted him and held him close in its depths. Horrified by this recollection, Jonno squeezed open his wet eyes and found himself staring at the beanbag that had doubled as their bed. That didn't help.

He was glad when Brendan's hand closed firmly on his shoulder and prised him away from Coralie. That rough palm clapped him there, awkward, instead of inviting him into another embrace. The first hint of discord rang out in the back of his mind.

"There's no news?" Coralie asked, knowing the answer. Jonno just shook his head. "They'll find her, though. They will. They *have* to."

He shook his head again.

"What does that mean?" Brendan wanted to know.

"They're not expecting to find her," Jonno said, bitter. "Not alive, anyway. They're already talking about her in the past tense!"

Brendan let out a miserable breath and dropped his hand from Jonno's shoulder, stepping away to lean wearily against his mother's bookcase. "Fuck it," he said, softly. "Fuck it." Coralie backed up to the lounge until she fell into it, curling her legs up as if to protect her from the truth, and started weeping into her hands.

"What the hell happened out there?" Brendan wanted to know. "Jonno? What the fuck did you guys *do*?"

"We went into the cave," he said, and flinched as Brendan threw his hands up in frustration at their stupidity. "It was her idea! I couldn't stop her. She wanted to go to the Chapel."

"Wandering around in a dark cave, at *night*?" Brendan exclaimed. "Why would you do something so bloody *stupid*?"

"That's so her," Coralie pointed out in a tiny voice, but her partner chose not to listen.

"You were supposed to look after her, man! You were her boyfriend, that's your *job*—"

"Now *you're* doing it!" Jonno blurted, pointing at him.

"Doing what?"

"The past tense! You're talking about her like she's dead!"

"Well, she probably fuckin' *is*!" Brendan shouted, and a shocked silence fell over the room. "We've been looking for her all day, six search teams going over every place she could possibly have been, and fuckin' *nothing*. She's gone. And that's on *you*."

Jonno gaped at his best friend, his heart rent. "W-what?"

"She was your responsibility, mate! So she always got her way—yeah, I know that, but you still should've stopped her from going into that place. I don't care if you had to slug her on the jaw and carry her away, you should've *done* that shit, because at least then she'd be around to be pissed off at you!"

Stunned, Jonno turned to Coralie for support. She cut her eyes away, confused, and he realised with an agonising pang that she agreed with Brendan—no matter what the circumstances, Jessica had been his to mind, and he should have done anything and everything to protect her from herself. Worse, there was a third accuser in the room, the shadow that lurked inside his own head.

"I—I don't understand any of this!" he cried. "The police think we fell into that water at the end of the cave, and that I, I went up some other shaft that led up to a pond around the back..."

"When we found you, you were soaking wet," Brendan confirmed. "Babbling and sobbing like a psycho. Scared the crap out of us."

"But that's bullshit! Jess and me, we found another passage! It was near the back-left corner, in the shadows."

"What?" Brendan asked, his brow furrowing, as if this had been withheld from him, and Jonno grasped at these new straws.

"Yeah! We went in, man, and it was all bendy and shit, but there was something at the end of it. We *found* it, you guys! Jess and me, we found the Chapel!"

Coralie was staring at him with both hands to her mouth, and Jonno remembered that, after Jessica, she had been the quickest to believe such a place existed—had even tried to warn them off with a story from Granny Mae.

"No," she whispered.

"Yes!"

He had vague memories of the place, of what had happened there, but he couldn't seem to get a grip on any of them. The doctor who'd examined him had been of the opinion that Jonno's mind, traumatised by near-death and loss, had simply closed up shop for the duration—had claimed that the seventeen hours or so Jonno had spent sleeping had been for the benefit of his psyche, resting as it tried to heal itself. And how would it do that? By bandaging up some of the memories that had caused it so much grief. That time in the Chapel itself was not gone—he could almost see it, buried under layers of mental gauze—but his mind had decided it was best he not recall it properly for the time being.

Brendan stepped away from the bookcase. "No," he said, echoing Coralie, only firmer. "No, you didn't."

"What do you mean? Of course I did, I was right there!"

"Just stop it, Jonno, all right? You didn't find the Chapel, because there *is* no Chapel."

"That's what the cops said, too!"

Brendan let out a disbelieving laugh. "And why do you think that is, mate? Look, I don't know what you think you saw, but it wasn't the Chapel."

"Of course it was!"

"*It couldn't be!*" Brendan thundered, causing both Jonno and Coralie to flinch. "You fuckin' idiot. While you were sleeping, I was out there all night searching, and today, too. I was in the cave when they went over every square inch of the bastard, with floodlights and everything, and there wasn't so much as a crack in the wall, let alone a passage, okay? If there was anything at all, we would've found it. And there was *not.*"

He stepped closer again, punctuating each word with a stab of his index finger. "Jonno. There. Is. No. Fuckin'. Chapel."

Jonno floundered, stunned. How could they say that when he'd seen it himself? And then it came to him. *Of course.* Hadn't they talked about it just last night?

"Oh! But don't you remember the story? It can only be found by lovers!"

"Don't," Brendan said, his face grim, his eyes deadly. Jonno had seen him like this on only a handful of occasions—such as that time in Year 10 when he'd overheard Prickles referring to Coralie as a shit-skin. *You wanna see shit?* he'd said, low and dangerous. *It'll be flying outta you in seven different shades if you don't run like a motherfucker RIGHT NOW.* Prickles had broken a land speed record that day, and wisely so. But this was different. Jonno had nothing to fear from his brother.

"I know it sounds stupid, but that has to be it, right? You guys couldn't find it, but we did? The bloody stories were *right*!"

"That's just an urban myth," Brendan muttered through clenched teeth.

"*Rural* myth," Jonno corrected him, pointing one finger in his face. "The Chapel is—"

Brendan's fist caught him hard on the cheekbone and spun him around so that he staggered and fell to his knees with his back turned. Coralie shrieked, and by the time Jonno found where he'd left his feet and turned back to them, she had thrown herself onto Brendan and was telling him *no, no, no.* Brendan's eyes were locked on Jonno, and he was shocked all over again by the lack of empathy in them. The punch was one thing—they'd gotten worked up to the point of brawling once or twice before—but the blank rage in that stare was so much worse. It didn't recognise the eleven years they'd spent as best friends and confidantes; it didn't seem to recognise Jonno at all, or if it did, only as an enemy.

"Ow," he said, too stunned to cry.

"It's your fault," Brendan said in his battle voice. "You failed our Jess. If she's dead, it's your fault, Trotter. You killed her."

Those words were like a whole flurry of brutal punches, and Jonno folded under their force. He staggered back until he bumped into the TV cabinet, his limp hands scattering VHS and DVD cases onto the carpet.

"Brendan, *stop*!" Coralie cried, and finally, he did. He gave up trying to get past her, turned his back and stalked over to the lounge. He stared at it for a moment as if recalling the night Jessica had straddled him there, the love it had been meant to prove. Then, without turning, he said, "Go away. I don't wanna see you, and if she turns up dead, you better pray you don't see me. Now get the *fuck* outta my house."

Coralie flashed Jonno one last tearful glance before crossing to her boyfriend and laying a hand on his back. He grunted in warning and shook it off. That sight was so incongruous that Jonno felt like he'd slipped into an alternate universe. Brendan spurning the touch of his sweetheart, punching and threatening and abandoning his best friend, and all this because Jessica was gone? This couldn't be real. Maybe he was still sleeping in the cell. Maybe he was still in the Chapel, and this was part of the test.

In any case, this was no place he wanted to be. Feeling as weightless as a man in a dream, Jonno walked over to the sliding doors, pushed them open, and staggered out into the warm night air.

His head rang with the blows he'd been served, a low, sonorous tone that prevented thought for the moment. His cheekbone was tender to the touch and had begun throbbing in protest; no doubt there'd be a lovely bruise there tomorrow. His eyes were still streaming, and he relied on muscle memory to get him across the yard and back out onto the street.

Only one place he could go now.

Ten minutes later, Jonno stumbled to a halt outside the Cutters Arms. Though the sun was still peeking over the horizon, the pub looked dead to the world. It was always quiet on a Sunday night, but not this quiet. The Arms was closed. The Arms was in mourning.

Cutting around to the back of the building, Jonno was about to let himself in through the kitchen—meaning to go straight to the bar for a few stiff shots—when he realised that would only bring on an avalanche of Jessica memories. They'd worked side by side in that room for nine months, sneaking kisses between jobs, and they'd even done it on the workbench once just so they could say that they had. No, it had to be the accommodation entrance.

Jonno closed the door behind him and leaned against it. No sounds came down the staircase that led up to the rooms used by both guests and residents, but Dad and Mick were bound to be around here someplace. What the hell was he going to say to them? At least one of them had been lying to him about his own mother for *eleven years.* His father's life had been ruined by the Chapel, and thanks to his silence, Jonno had now suffered the same fate.

You could have stopped this from happening, old man.

Jonno felt his anguish, his betrayal and pain, alchemising into anger. Yeah, he was ready for this now. He walked out of the back hallway into the pub's rear corridor, past the kitchens and into the front bar.

Dad and Mick were sitting at a table in the back corner, a single light on overhead. A half-empty bottle of scotch held court before them, attended by two glasses in a similar state. Their faces were sombre as gravestones.

"Son," said Dad. "Grab a glass and come sit."

Jonno turned away from them without a word and ducked behind the bar. He fetched himself two glasses and a bottle of Jack Daniel's, then made his way back across the room. Dad pushed out a third chair with his foot, but Jonno sat at the next table over, slamming the bottle down as he did so.

"I'm sorry, mate," Dad said. "Jessie was a wonderful girl. We're all going to miss her."

Jonno gave a sarcastic nod and uncapped the bottle, pouring himself three fingers. Giving them a vague salute, Jonno raised the whisky and threw it back, then slammed the empty glass down on the table hard enough to shatter it. He picked a couple of splinters out of his fingers, grimly relishing the sight of blood, then dragged the second glass into the remains of the first and poured himself another triple shot.

"Take it easy, son." Dad exchanged a troubled glance with Mick. "I know you're hurting—"

"*Fuck* what you know," Jonno declared, enjoying the shock on their faces. "Shall I tell you what *I* know, Dad? I know that you've been lying to me for most of my life. I know that you've been keeping a secret from the whole town, the whole world. Would you care to comment on that little fact?"

Dad looked again to Mick. They had their poker faces on, but Jonno was sure he saw dread in their eyes.

"You're gonna have to be more specific, Jonno."

"Oh, really? So you have more than one life-changing secret, do you? For fuck's sake, Dad! You know where I ended up last night. Take a wild guess at what I remembered when I saw that place for what I *thought* was the first time."

Mick sucked on his teeth, avoiding Jonno's glare. Alan Trotter nodded slowly, never taking his eyes off his son.

"All right, then. So, you remember what happened that night, do you?"

"I remember you and Mum leaving me to sleep in the car. I remember looking for you. And I remember you scaring the shit out of me, all soaked in water and babbling about how you'd lost Mum. How's that for starters?"

Dad closed his eyes, sipped at his scotch.

"For some reason, you trusted me to forget all that and told me that Mum drove off the road into the creek. And that's what you told everyone else, too. So perhaps you'd like to finally stop bullshitting and *tell me what happened!*"

Alan Trotter nodded again, and suddenly he looked so old. Jonno had never realised how much he took his father's presence and health for granted, and this perceived frailty knocked another pillar out from under his life. He wasn't sure if he even had anything left to hold him up.

"It was your mother's idea," Dad began. "A picnic. She said she knew the perfect spot, out on the Hunter land. You know what she was like—once she got an idea in her head, nothing could budge it. It sounded nice, so I went along with it. And we had a lovely time that day, the three of us. It'd be one of my favourite memories, if it wasn't for…

"After we ate, you ran around playing, being a kid. Me and Daisy got to talking, and it turned out she had a reason for bringing us to that place. See, she'd got a bit…flighty, a bit insecure, since having you. She always needed to be reassured. And she'd got it into her head that with all the long hours, and us getting older, and other things, maybe the spark had gone out of our marriage. I told her we were fine, but this time she wouldn't listen. She had to know for sure. So there we are, having an after-dinner drink on the grass, and she tells me tonight's the night. We're gonna prove our love is as strong as ever…or we're gonna end it, and she's gonna take you and go live with her sister."

Jonno made a strange sound. He could have grown up in a different town, with Mum and Aunty Ellen instead of Dad and Mick! He could barely imagine the kind of person he would've been. No Brendan, no Coralie, no Jessica—

You don't have any of them now, remember?

"She said she knew how to do it. That's why she took us to that spot. Because she'd worked out where to find the Chapel."

The title sounded utterly incongruous coming from his father's lips, a familiar word in a foreign context. Jonno slugged some more JD.

"I'd heard about it, of course—that story's been doing the rounds in town for longer than anyone can remember. But I never thought it was real, so I played along. You were dozing off, so we took you back to the car and put you down. I always wondered why she didn't just leave you here with Mick, or at Mary's place. I reckon she figured that having you there would remind me of the stakes, what I had to lose.

"She led me to the cave. I still didn't believe there was anything to the stories, not until we went inside. Until we found the passage. And mate, there's not a day goes by I don't wish that I'd pulled the plug right there."

Mick closed his eyes, took a drink. Jonno swallowed, hard.

"What happened then?"

"Don't you know?"

"It's…it's a bit fuzzy."

Dad nodded. "Yeah, it's like that. Well, we went through with it, just like you did. And I ended up in that pond over the back, alone. Just like you did."

And gave me that horrible memory that I thought for so long was just a nightmare.

"Daisy was gone, and I was…I was a wreck. I didn't know what to do. You were chucking a right wobbly, but somehow we got back to the car. I drove us back here, put you to bed. Mick found me sitting at the bar, going out of my head, and wanted to know what was happening. So I told him.

"We figured there was nothing we could do about your mum. She was gone, and nothing was gonna bring her back. But if we told the cops what had really happened, they'd never believe us in a million years—they'd just figure I'd done her in. It was common knowledge by then that our marriage was…less than perfect. So Mick came up with a plan.

"We took the car back out, ditched it in the creek, and told everyone she'd driven off in a right state after an argument. We honestly expected to get caught out, but…it worked. And you were kind of in denial about the whole thing, so we lied to you, too. I'm sorry, Jonno. I just didn't know what else to do."

Jonno nodded, his fears confirmed.

"If I could take it back, do it different—"

"Stop," Jonno muttered, and his father looked down at his drink. Realising his own was empty again, Jonno poured himself some more Jack. The first two had gone to his head, and he found himself wearing an ugly grin at the sight of his bloody fingerprints smeared on the glass. They sat in silence for a full minute, the only sound that of the ceiling fan whirling away overhead.

"Jess told me how it's supposed to work," Jonno said at last, lightheaded as the booze sunk in. "It's a test, like you said. You have to prove your love is pure and true. Mum insisted on going in, but she's the one who failed. That's why she never came out."

Alan Trotter regarded his son with sad, heavy eyes. "No."

"What?"

"You've got it wrong. Yeah, it's a test. But your mum didn't fail it. I did."

Jonno stared at him. "But—"

"Maybe Jessie didn't hear the same stories we did. In any case, they're just stories. How many people do you think have actually *been* to the Chapel? How many would have bothered, based on a stupid old folk tale? And the tale used to say that if your love isn't pure and true, you lose it. I loved your mother, Jonno, I really did. But it wasn't enough. And so I lost her."

Jonno's fists clenched amongst shards of broken glass. "Then you…you let her down. You were supposed to love and protect her! How could you marry her and start a family with her and still not love her enough? What's *wrong* with you?"

Now there was fire in Alan's eyes, something Jonno hadn't seen for a long time. "Me? Yeah, I fucked up, kid, and I have to live with that. But aren't you forgetting something?"

Jonno opened his mouth, but suddenly his throat was locked tight and nothing could get out.

"That's right. What about sweet little Jessie, who was supposed to be the light of your life? Why didn't you love *her* enough?"

This new revelation had Jonno's head ringing worse than any punch Brendan could have landed on him. "I—I *did*!"

"*Then where is she?*"

"I—" Jonno cast about, lost. "I loved her more than anything! I *did*! I, I was even moving to the city with her next year!"

"Oh, right! And when were you gonna tell *me* that?"

"I only told *her* last night! I—no, *no*!" Jonno threw his second empty glass at the nearest wall and came to his feet, leaning heavily on the table. Horror consumed every cell of him. "Oh, God. Oh, no. Oh, no."

My fault. Brendan was right. My fault. I killed her. My fault.

The ground loomed below, threatening to swallow him up. He'd thought his love for Jessica was the best thing about him, the purest part—and even that was flawed. She'd put her trust in him, taken him to the Chapel knowing she loved him absolutely and without question…and he'd failed her.

"And you had the gall to come in here accusing *me*," Dad said, rising to his feet. "How does it feel, son?"

"Come on, mate," Mick warned. "Lay off."

"How does it feel to know that Kassie Rzepka is gonna be heartbroken all over again, only this time she'll never know what went wrong? What about Jessie's parents? Yeah, enjoy that feeling, kid, and know what I've been going through for the last eleven years."

"*Alan.*" Mick's voice cracked like a stockman's whip. "Sit down and shut up. *Now.*"

Jonno heard his father's weight collapse back into his seat, could almost hear the fight draining out of him. Another drink was poured. Silence followed, broken only by the heaving of Jonno's sobs.

"I'm sorry, son. I'm sorry I failed your mother, and I'm sorry I chose to lie to you about it. I'm sorry dear old Mick had to get caught up in all this. I'm sorry for poor Jessie, because she was a great kid and I really liked her. And I'm sorry this has all happened to you, too. Believe me, I wouldn't wish it on anyone."

Jonno managed to stand upright at last. He turned and stumbled away from the table.

"Jonno, please—"

He had no words, so he just screamed as he ran for the hallway. Chair legs scraped, and then came Mick's voice again: "Leave it, mate. Give him time."

He could barely see the stairs and tripped over at least half of them. When he reached his door, he fumbled for his keys and unlocked it with all the grace of a habitual drunk. He threw it shut behind him and staggered toward his bed. On a wall above it, Eminem sneered and flipped him a double bird. Jonno swung a punch at the poster and missed, the momentum carrying him onto the mattress. He collapsed face-first and screamed into his quilt, curled up into a foetal ball, writhed in torment that hell itself would be hard-pressed to match.

This night, he knew, Jonno Trotter would die. He didn't know who or what would take his place, but there was only one piece of advice he could give to his successor.

Forget. And run. Run, and just keep running until you can't remember why you started in the first place.

Never love again. And never stop running.

sooner or later you're gonna have to do something about me

JONNY FINISHED TALKING AND STARED down at the creek. All those words were out there now, running away from him like so much water, and he had just as much control over them. Sloane quashed her cigarette and watched along with him, for once choosing not to pipe up with a bunch of probing questions like his story was a manuscript that needed to be edited for clarity. The sun swung low to the horizon, leaving behind a sky that was dimming to grey and almost ready to give way to the night. A few frogs had already begun croaking out their throaty serenades.

"So that was it for Waterwich," he said eventually. "I couldn't bear to be here, so I just worked and kept to myself and saved every cent I could. I already had a couple grand in a savings account. I got through the last three weeks—man, worst Christmas *ever*—and as soon as the year was over, I just loaded up the XF and blew out of town. Said nothing to anyone except the old man and Mick, and that was pretty awkward. I stayed at a backpacker's hostel until I found a flat, and that was it—the beginning of my new life."

It hadn't been an auspicious start. The flat complex had been home to a loose-knit group of feckless party people around his age, most of whom were unemployed but always found money for weed and booze. He'd been quite happy to lose himself in a daze for a few months there, getting high all day and eventually indulging in hollow encounters with a female neighbour that left him in guilty tears as soon as she left, but soon he found himself having to sign on to the dole and sell a bit of pot to make ends meet. Scared into positive action, he'd scored himself a job at a nearby McDonald's—still following in Jessica's footsteps, despite everything—and moved to a new place, breaking free of his deadbeat social circle.

By 2003, Jonny had worked his way into the kitchens of a four-star restaurant and the affections of a young real estate agent with an unfortunate weakness for amphetamines. From there, things had slowly improved to the point where he barely found the time or inclination to think about the past. When he did, he found the edges of his self-recrimination dulling over the years and began to think that one day he might even be able to forgive himself.

And then, on the 10th of December 2005, he'd found a black envelope pushed under his door and realised the past was not so easy to escape. From his sporadic phone conversations with Dad, he knew that no trace of Jessica Grzelak had ever been found, so this development was deeply disturbing. But there had been no follow-up, so life had carried on as normal—until 2010, when another piece of black mail had marked the passing of a decade. The envelopes were just enough to keep him on edge, and he wondered if that was their intent. Whoever had sent them was clearly keen to ensure that he did not forget the worst night of his life.

Last summer, Jonny had gone out to a club on the seafront with the couple who owned the Hamburger Hilton and had still been able, at that point, to lash out on the odd night of careless largesse. Turning from the bar, he'd seen the setting sun shining through the hair and glass of a gorgeous woman laughing with her friends, and the vision had been compelling enough that he contrived a conversation when she passed him on her way back from the toilets. Her name was Sloane, and she acquired and managed manuscripts, and she had the most infectious laugh that spread to her rich brown eyes, and that night had been the first of the many they'd spent together since.

He looked up at her now. She sensed his gaze and met it with a resolute one of her own, and he knew she was ready to ask the obvious question.

"Thank you for telling me all that, Jonathan. I know it's not easy for you country boys to open up like that." She tickled the back of his hand to show she was joking. "But it does make me wonder. If being lied to about your mother's disappearance upset you so much, why did you lie to *me* about it?"

He nodded, owning his deception. "Well, now you know how well it went down when I mentioned the Chapel in the past. I guess I figured it would just be easier to go along with the accepted version of events. I mean, I'm still not sure exactly what happened myself."

"I understand, I do. But it does make me wonder what else you might not be telling me. It's not like I don't trust you, but…I guess anything less than one hundred percent honesty just doesn't seem enough. I want to be with you, Jonny, but I need to *know* you. I don't want any unpleasant surprises down the track."

"Don't worry," Jonny said. "This is the big one. The only other secret I have is where I'm keeping your Christmas presents, and that I will never tell you."

Sloane's smile was brief. "Okay. Because we've got some big decisions ahead of us. I know I keep pointing it out, but we can't ignore the Thing much longer."

"I know. I'm sorry. I've just been distracted with, you know, Dad. And the thought of having to come back here."

Sloane had announced her big news just one night before Mick had called with his. He knew he should have given her the answer she wanted straight away, but he'd wanted time to turn it over and work it out, and Dad's death had stolen that away. And then, on top of all that, there'd been the third envelope—

"Oh, there's something else. Consider this a part of my previous confession—I wasn't going to keep it from you."

Sloane rolled her eyes. "Okay. Go on. Just don't tell me you have a secret love child in this town or something."

Jonny reached into his jacket pocket and pulled out the three black envelopes.

"There's these. I've received one every five years since I left town, always on the same day. Always on the anniversary of…what I just told you about."

Sloane took them from him, her interest piqued, and turned them over in her hands. "Wow, that's…creepy. What are they? They're not stamped."

"No. They get pushed under the door of wherever I'm living, always in the early hours of the tenth of December. That one's from 2005, that's 2010, and that's the latest one."

"Didn't you say that night was the ninth? Oh, but then it was midnight when you—" Sloane stopped dead and glanced up at him, alarmed. "Hang on, that's two days ago! This came under our door? And you don't know who delivered it or why? And you didn't *tell* me?"

"I had no idea what to say."

"Well, what is it? A threat?"

"I don't know."

She opened the latest envelope, squinted through the dusk to read the card. "*You know where to find me*? What does that mean?"

"I'm not sure."

"It's scented." Sloane sniffed the card and frowned at him. "That's a woman's perfume. And this is a woman's handwriting."

"Yes. To be specific, it's Jessica's perfume. And, if I'm not mistaken, Jessica's handwriting."

"Ah. Geez. That's…a bit weird."

"Oh, yes."

Sloane slid the card back into its envelope and read the other two. The message from 2005 said *Home is where the heart is.* From 2010: *Bless you.*

"Bless you?"

"It was a private joke."

"Would anyone else know about that?"

"Possibly, but it's pretty obscure."

"Right." Sloane handed him the envelopes, looking glad to be rid of them. "Who do you think is sending these?"

That question was one he'd pondered many times, and he didn't like any of the answers.

"Is it possible that it's Jessica? That she survived, and she's taunting you?"

Jonny pulled a face. "I really don't see how it could be. This mysterious letter shit is something I could see her doing, but I don't think she'd spend her life in hiding just for this. She's too brash for that."

Sloane tilted her head toward him, and he realised he'd just used the present tense. "Was. Whatever. You can see why this was doing my head in."

"Well, if it's not her, who else could it be?"

"There is one other name that keeps coming up," Jonny admitted. "It would have to be someone close to Jess, someone who wants to keep reminding me of the night she vanished. Someone who still holds me responsible."

"Ah," said Sloane. "I'm with you."

"Yeah. I'm just really not keen on going there again."

"Well, you may have to if you ever want to get to the bottom of this." Sloane tapped a tooth with a fingernail, deep in thought. "It's the obvious connection, Jonny. Either she's sending you these cards, or she knows who is—and if it *is* Jessica, where else could she hide?"

Jonny nodded. "You're not going to let this one go, are you?"

"No, I am not. You came here to face your past. Let's do it properly."

Sloane closed the pizza box on its cigarette-studded contents, then groaned as she pushed herself to her feet.

"What, now?"

"You want to wait for midnight or something?"

Jonny sighed and stood up. The sky was almost dark. By the time they reached their destination, night would have fallen. For this, he would have vastly preferred broad daylight.

"You know where she lives?"

Jonny nodded. "Well, I know where she used to live, and I doubt she'll have moved. Nightingale Street."

"How far away is that?"

"About ten minutes' walk."

"Then walk we shall. You're probably still over the limit, and me, too. Come on, babe. Let's get this done."

She offered him her hand, and Jonny took it. A heavy weight sat in his stomach as they traversed the slope up to the road. Hadn't he always known he'd end up doing this one day? Or rather, hadn't he kept denying himself the opportunity to do so?

"Lighten up, sugar." Sloane put on a brave face for them both. "It'll be all right."

"I know. But think about who we're going to see. I wish we'd decided on this while the sun was still out."

"But now there's a breeze, and it's cooled down a bit." Sloane squeezed his hand and threw him a carefree smile that was almost convincing. "It's a nice night for a White Widow."

gloomy sunday

WHEN JONNO COULD NO LONGER bear the weight of grief that pinned him to the sheets of his bed, he rolled onto his feet and escaped the stolid walls of his room. He'd heard Dad and Mick tromping upstairs some time ago, but Mick's room gaped open and empty; Dad's door was closed, its foot limned with pale light, and low voices muttered within. Glad to avoid another confrontation, Jonno slipped down the back stairs and out into the night.

Sunday was drawing rapidly to an end, and Waterwich might well have been a ghost town for all the life it exhibited. Jonno followed his feet through deserted streets, knowing only that they were taking him somewhere Jessica still existed. Her loss had punched a hole in him, and he couldn't quite believe that the world was going on as if nothing had happened. There should be some sign, some universal acknowledgement of her passing—the sky blacked out, a moan of dismay from the pits of the earth itself.

Maybe she's not gone.

Jonno clung hard to that thought, knowing it was most likely false and not caring. Jessica Grzelak was too vibrant a soul to just vanish without a trace, he told himself, too important a character to be written out of life without explanation. There had to be more to her story, and that meant she was coming back. And if she did, where might she go first?

His feet turned him off the main drag, through a network of small and quiet roads onto Nightingale Street, led him to the house of her Aunt Kassia. The overgrown front yard obscured much of her home, left to annexe what space it would as she languished in depression, and he recalled Jessica telling him how she'd convinced a revitalised Kassia to leave it wild and warped because it lent the house an air of Gothic mystery. Jonno could see dim yellow light filtering through the branches that latticed the front windows, and his gut churned at the thought of facing Kassia now, trying to explain how he'd lost her darling niece. No, that wasn't why he was here. He had to go where Jess would go, where she burned brightest, and so he slipped down the side of the house until he emerged in the backyard.

The Chesney caravan she'd called home sat on flat tires in the middle of a yellowing lawn, slowly becoming jaundiced itself through exposure to the elements. Ranks of pots had been arranged on peeling plastic-coated wire racks along the front, most holding plants in various stages of health, one filled only with sand and dozens of crumpled cigarette butts. Jonno walked on soft feet to this display, picked up a flowerpot that held a single dead rose, poked his fingers into the dry soil until they wrapped around small steel teeth. He pulled out the spare key and let himself into the caravan.

With the door closed behind him, Jonno groped for the light switch and clicked it on. A soft glow suffused the interior; the curtains wouldn't keep it from being seen outside, but he barely cared now that he was safe inside this sanctum. The familiarity of the caravan flooded him with warmth as if Jessica's body heat still lingered in the atmosphere, and his next breath was deep and shaky as he fought not to burst into tears all over again.

Jonno had spent so many hours in here that he knew every messy inch of the place. Across from the door, the little sink and oven-top burners where she heated up soup on a winter's night, the old kettle she used for her coffee, the curiously decorated plates that must have come over to Australia with her family decades ago; to his right, a small table with almost every inch of its surface cluttered with books and papers and magazines; at head height, the storage compartments that gaped and dangled the sleeves of shirts, the studded tongues of belts, the empty skeins of black leggings; in the back end, the unmade bed where he had spent dozens of nights within her arms, inside her body, reflected in her eyes and thoughts and dreams. Pictures had been Blu-Tacked at random angles on the walls—Nick Cave glaring over a cigarette, Brandon Lee as Eric Draven, a black-eyed naiad of the night in PVC fetish gear—and Robert Smith stood over the bed like a guardian angel, reminding him that *Boys Don't Cry.*

Oh, but they do today, chum.

Now that he was here, Jonno stood still and numb and just stared. This space vibrated with Jessica's frequency, was as much a part of her as any limb or organ. He could almost feel the residue of her presence, and he soaked it in like sunlight. Eventually, he shuffled forward and began to touch things, stroking objects with bloodied fingers like they were much-missed pets.

Her stereo perched on the end of the kitchenette counter, balancing a precarious pile of CDs on its flat head, and whatever was on top was what she'd last spun. He picked up the case: Diamanda Galás, *The Singer.* Jonno found the woman's voice odd and a little disturbing, but Jessica seemed enthralled by it. Her favourite track was a cover of some old Hungarian song so depressing that dozens of people were rumoured to have killed themselves after listening to it, and that was so Jessica it hurt. She must have listened to this album whilst getting ready for the formal; a trace of her perfume lingered in the enclosed space, bringing a hundred intimate snapshots to the front of his mind.

Jonno returned the CD case to the top of the stack—a precarious tower of Placebo, Godflesh, Effigy, Deftones, hundreds of songs that would never be sung for her again. He slumped onto a stool beside the small table, letting his hands wander amongst the rubble of her life, pausing here and there to take stock. A visitor's guide to New Orleans had its pages marked with scraps of paper, plotting the tours she'd planned to share with him. A few scattered rectangles of black were revealed to be unused envelopes, the kind you'd expect to find sealed with red wax. A sheaf of pages photocopied from library books addressed the myths and legends of Poland, the uppermost featuring a painting of a sodden, long-tressed girl sitting in a tree beside a river, staring out at him with hungry eyes—some water spirit called the *rusalka.*

Another clutch of pages had been scanned from old newspapers. He understood their relevance when he found a copy of a black and white photograph of two youths dressed up to the nines in the fashion of their long-gone day. She clung to his arm like a happy bride, blossoming body flattered by a scalloped lace bodice and acetate satin skirt, her long dark hair twisted up into a tight bun as if to undercut a sensuality it only underscored; he had his hands stuffed into the pockets of black slacks as if to keep them restrained, looking like he wished his white sports coat was a leather jacket, his hair and cigarette-plugged scowl a self-conscious tribute to James Dean.

Billy and Poppy.

Judging by their outfits and the crepe-and-glitter décor behind them, this shot must have been taken at the 1964 school dance. Looking at the pair, you'd never know they'd slaughtered her family perhaps two hours before. How could you smile like that when those elbow-length gloves hid fingers that must still carry the blood of your murdered sister beneath their nails? Another time, Jonno would have been chilled; tonight, he sensed only the absence of that feeling.

He hid the couple beneath a poetry textbook, and in moving the detritus, he found a bent cigarette and a disposable lighter on its last legs. Jonno lit up and breathed in Jessica's most common scent as he stared around the caravan with eyes heavy and hard as stone.

What's going to happen to all this stuff now that she—if she doesn't come back?

Jonno imagined her belongings being dumped into thrift shops and second-hand stores, left to languish on shelves where they'd be incuriously ogled by people who had no idea of their provenance, and the thought appalled him. But what else should be done? Should the caravan be left intact as a shrine to her memory, then? Kept the way she liked it, in case she should somehow make a miraculous return from the darkness?

The darkness. For just a moment, Jonno was on the verge of remembering what had happened in the depths of the Chapel. Then it was gone, and he felt as much relief as frustration. Even if he longed to know the truth, perhaps a little ignorance was a blessing.

I know what she'd say to that.

No truth was beyond Jessica's interest, no fiction too bizarre to be discounted solely as such. The cairns of battered books littered around the caravan were testament to that—everything from Fiona Horne's *Witch: A Personal Journey* to a Colin Wilson tome on serial killers to a collection of Goya prints, novels by Ramsey Campbell and Tanith Lee and Anaïs Nin, a *Choose Your Own Adventure* he remembered reading in primary school. Jessica would have argued that each was as valid and true as the next, that each had something to teach about the world; but then, Jess had always loved a good argument.

Jessica…

Jonno left the cigarette to burn out in a used coffee mug and dragged himself to the end of the caravan, where he collapsed into the disarray of her unmade bed. The sheets were cool, but they smelled of her hair and sweat. This bed was the centre of the world they'd built together—it was where they'd so often dozed, cuddled and giggled, fucked like wildcats in heat. It was comfort and contentment and come, the heat of her beloved cunt, the dark and dozy green of her sleep-dusted eyes, the undignified snort of her snores, the crucible of their dreams. A grey oversized top she'd sometimes used as a nightshirt had been thrown aside to rest on her pillow, and Jonno clutched it to his face as tears blurred his world into something unrecognisable. He clung tight to all that was left of his rock as the waters swallowed everything he held dear.

He'd lived a nightmare today, and that must have been why his mind allowed itself to slip off again, trying to escape the grief that rocked it in relentless waves.

He wasn't so far down that he didn't know he was dreaming, but he wasn't all that surprised to find himself transported to the car park of Jellicoe Hall. The building wore a large glittering sash that simply said PROM. The music bleeding out from within was some doo-wop ballad at least forty years older than anything by the Baha Men. He was arrayed in a nonchalant sprawl on the front seat of a Plymouth Fury convertible, the collar of his leather jacket popped up, and the girl beside him in the polka-dot dress fixed her lipstick in the rear-view mirror before racking the slide of a pump-action shotgun and blowing him a kiss.

"Me and you, sugar," Jessica said, and got out of the car. He followed, shoving his hands into the pockets of his jacket to discover that they were large enough to hold pistols. He pulled them out and grinned, accepting everything. Then the doors of Jellicoe Hall opened to admit a stream of teenagers in '60s dresses and tuxedos, and he didn't recognise most of them, but some he knew from school and the two right at the front were Brendan and Coralie. He shot Jessica a glance to say, *You sure about this?*

"Wouldn't you do anything for me, baby? It's me and you, me and you. No-one else."

Jonno shrugged and raised the handguns like some John Woo gangster, and the two of them opened fire. He didn't see his best friends go down, but the other kids screamed and erupted into geysers of pixelated crimson like the zombies in *Resident Evil 2.* They fired and fired without pause until the ground was littered with the corpses of their classmates, the doors of Jellicoe Hall washed red with their blood.

More scarlet flashed behind them, and they turned to see a row of police cars blocking off their escape. A dozen cops aimed rifles at them, waiting for the word.

Jessica squeezed his fingers, the shotgun gone. "Just hold my hand and we'll be fine, my love. We'll be together."

He nodded, but somehow this action caused his hand to fall free of hers and gunfire erupted all around him. He held his arms over his face, bracing for the hail of bullets, but when the storm ended, he was still standing. He lowered his arms and saw the car park was empty, no cops, no bodies—no Jessica. The night was ending, sunlight peeping over the horizon, and he was alone.

He started walking, and then he was at the creek. Hours passed fast like time-lapsed video footage, and the sun's position in the sky indicated late afternoon. He stumbled down to the water, catching a glimpse of something tumbling by in the current beneath the surface. He didn't see its face, and when he turned to see the silhouette of a girl sitting in the nearby tree, he couldn't make out hers, either.

"Where do you think we all end up?" she asked, her voice dark and wet.

"The sea, I suppose."

She shook her head and slipped to the ground, jerky and awkward as if she'd long since forgotten how to use her limbs, and advanced on him like a broken vampire. She was sodden, dripping, just like his father in the memory he'd thought a dream, but it wasn't water that ran red from wet wells in her body.

"You didn't hold my hand," she whispered, and the voice didn't even sound like her anymore, unless it was the darkness in her magnified and showing its true face. "You let me go. You didn't love me enough, you fucking coward. *You let me go.*"

Jonno could feel his heart trying to tear its way free of his chest, unable to escape the pain even in sleep. She raised one hand to point at him, and her finger became the barrel of a gun clutched tight in slick, bony digits. He closed his eyes and waited, accepting the guilt and the punishment, and the gun went off with a loud *bang* that blasted him right back into consciousness.

Jonno flinched up out of Jessica's nightshirt, his hands scrabbling for support on the messy bed, and the banging continued. Someone was rapping fast and loud on the caravan door, desperation evident in the rhythm.

"Jessie? Jess, is that you?"

Her aunt must have seen the light inside the Chesney and gotten her hopes up. Jonno was sick to the stomach at the thought of dashing her dreams, but he couldn't hide from her forever. He'd let Jessica go, one way or another—this much was irrefutable. This responsibility was his to bear.

"Jessie, it's me, it's your *ciocia*! Please, open up! Jessie?"

The knocking continued until he'd dragged himself off the bed and opened the caravan door to the night outside. The subsequent silence should have been a relief, but it felt to him as much a judgement as the look in the wet eyes of the woman standing before him.

Kassia Rzepka had the same dark colouring as her niece, but with none of the generosity of figure. She was scarecrow-tall, only a few inches shorter than Jonno, and the black clothes she wore day in and day out emphasised the lean stretch of her figure, the gaunt cast of her features. A life of sorrow had lent hard edges to her face that were emphasised by this fresh grief. Now Jonno watched as the fledgling light of hope died in those familiar green eyes, leaving them dull and flat as coloured glass, and he could see why some of the townspeople called her the Black Widow. The longer she stared in silence, the more it felt like she was concentrating a hex upon him.

"You," she said at last, her voice quiet but firm, sharp as a blade. She'd always been at least civil to him, sometimes even warm, but there was no sign of that now. "What are *you* doing in there?"

He gestured around at the caravan, gave a limp shrug. "I…I had to be around her, Kassie. I needed to feel her."

The disappointment had fled her eyes entirely now, and the green flame that replaced it grew stronger by the second. "Where is she, Jonathan? What happened to my Jessie?"

He shook his head, fought back the helpless tears that threatened to spill free yet again. "I don't know. We went into the cave, and then…I don't know."

"The police said you both fell into the water. How did that happen?" Kassia's voice was thin, sharp-edged, cutting through Jonno like a razor-wire garrotte. "She loved you so much. How could you let her fall?"

And there it was again—the past tense. Even Jessica's family had written her off already.

"I love her too!" Jonno cried, slamming one hand against the jamb of the caravan door. "I love her more than anything!"

"Then why are you here? Why not her? Why did *you* come back, coward?"

"I don't know!" Jonno felt the tears pushing through again, leaking out of the corners of his eyes. "Kassia, I'm so sorry. I didn't even want to go in, but Jess…she always got her way, you know that!"

"*Dupek*," she muttered, clenching her thin fists so hard Jonno expected to hear bones splintering. "If I had *my* way, it would be *you* that disappears, and tomorrow my Jessie would be here again."

"I know. Me too."

Kassia made a disgusted sound that might have been a spit if she wasn't dry-mouthed with rage. "Get off my land, Jonathan Trotter. If you come here again, I will call the police, and if you are lucky, they will arrive before I get my hands on you! *Spierdalaj!*"

She stepped back, one arm stabbing toward the driveway. Jonno slowly nodded, then dropped one leaden foot onto the caravan's single steel step.

"Faster! You are not welcome here. *Morderca!*"

Oh, how well he knew that now. Yesterday he'd felt like the king of this town, so above it he could leave without a backward glance; today, it had turned on him and cast him out first. He'd spent eighteen years not even noticing the warm arms of Waterwich and then resenting the cloying cling of its embrace, and only now did he realise how much he'd taken that comfort for granted.

Jonno walked with his head down, feeling Kassia's furious eyes and rapid breath lashing across his back like a whip. He bore it without a whimper. After all, she was right. Jessica had insisted on going into the cave, had beaten down his resistance, but this one time he should not have bent to her will. This once, he should have been strong enough to say *no*. He was weak, an embarrassment, a disgrace. It was right that he should leave, and not just this house—he should maintain that trajectory until he was out of the town's sight for good and they had only the memory of him to keep their grief and rage alive.

You won't see me again, he almost said, but dared not in case it didn't sound enough like a promise. Maybe those words would come off more like a boast—that he would run away only because he was still able, leaving his shame behind to linger like a green-eyed ghost as he fled to keep his crimes from his heels. But he knew the truth of it already: run as he might, so fast and so far, he would always look down to see this shackle around his ankle. The chain might stretch a million miles, but one end would always be with him—and the other would always hold him fast to this town, to last night, to the spectre of what he had done and what he had not. Home was where the heart was, after all. And though his heart was lost, it would always be here, waiting for him to return—to follow it into the darkness.

suspicion bells

NOT FOR THE FIRST TIME today, Jonny felt the dread thickening in his gut with every minute that brought him closer to his destination. He didn't notice that he'd slowed down as they turned onto Nightingale Street until Sloane pulled ahead, and he started to feel that she was dragging him along like a temperamental child. How was this her call, anyway? Hadn't he learned enough hard lessons from letting women drag him into the dark?

"It's that one," he muttered, raising his free hand to point out Kassia's house. Whatever weird Colin's role might have been, it clearly didn't include yard maintenance—the garden was even more overgrown than he remembered, left to run rampant so that tree branches drooped almost to the ground and the lawn reached up long fingers to meet them. Morning glory hung heavy on side fences that hadn't seen the sun for years and unkempt bushes conspired to deter curious passersby. Beyond all this lurked the shadowy bulk of the house, as much a recluse as its owner. Its roof cut a sharp black line against the lesser dark of the night sky, and a dirty lemon light shone through front windows from distant rooms.

"Wow, Miss Havisham all up in this bitch." Sloane gave him an encouraging smile, but his feet dragged to a halt on the footpath. "Okay. I know I'm being a little too flippant about this whole deal."

"Yeah, no shit. Tell me again why this is such a good idea?"

"Well, look at your options. You can get to the bottom of this, or you can turn around and go home and try not to think about it. And that's fine, but what happens five years from now when the next envelope appears? You said it yourself, they've been doing your head in. Do you really want to go through life wondering and worrying about this?"

"No," Jonny sighed. "But I'm not sure the alternative is any better."

The Rzepka house stared back at them through the trees like a mad old woman through laced fingers, and Jonny could see why the local kids dared each other to approach it. A mild breeze shushed through the untended glade of its garden, but beyond that the summer night was almost silent bar the low throb of an approaching car.

Come on. It's just an old house, just an old lady. After everything you've been through, you can handle this.

Dealing with the Kassia Rzepka he remembered would have been daunting enough—Jonny remembered her rage and grief from their last meeting all too well. But thinking of the woman now, a Black Widow turned White, a ghost in all but the most literal sense, kept his shoes glued to the footpath. If that was the way she presented herself, what must be going on inside her head? If she was responsible for the cards he'd received, what else might she be planning? She'd had a decade to mould Colin Perkins into Mr. Dogsbody, a willing servant to her wicked whims. Was he dedicated enough to kill for her?

Yeah, right. That'd be the easiest murder case the Waterwich police could ever ask for: the butler did it.

"Jonny?" Sloane prompted, tugging at his hand. The car they'd heard turned onto Nightingale Street and rolled slowly by as if it, too, was staking out the Rzepka house. "The sooner begun, the sooner done, and all that. Don't worry. If the old bat tries to mess with you, I'll kick her arse."

He couldn't resist a little smile at the thought. "Okay, okay. But, fingers crossed, it won't come to a fight."

Jonny was given a moment to reflect on the timing of his words as the passing car lurched to a halt just beyond Kassia's house and spilled two men out into the night. The streetlight above threw a spot onto the unwelcome arrival of Corey Hamble and Prickles O'Hanlon.

"Oh, come on," he muttered.

"You think we were done with you, dickhead?" Corey tossed an empty beer bottle across the road, and the sound of shattering glass presaged further violence to come. "Let's see how tough you are without Brendan around, eh?"

"Yeah, faggot," Prickles added.

"Go home, guys," said Sloane, putting on a brave face. But Jonny heard the subtle tremor in her voice, felt the queasy clutch of her fingers, and hated these bastards for ever casting a shadow of fear over her heart.

"Sorry, love, but we got unfinished business." Corey swaggered closer, just a few metres away now. "This prick tell you about his other girlfriends? Did he tell you what happened to Jessica?"

"Yes, he did. And I know it wasn't his fault."

"Of course it was!" Corey dismissed her, turned his heavy-lidded glare on Jonny. "You gonna let your missus do all the talking for you, Trotter? You that much of a pussy?"

"Fuckin' pussy."

"You gonna drop her in a cave too, mate? Maybe it'll be so deep she'll end up back in China where she belongs."

Jonny pulled his hand free of Sloane's grip, their mutual sweat aiding his escape, and stepped forward. The dread within his stomach found a new purpose, raising its ugly head anew as it contorted into a righteous fury.

"Right, that's it. Come on, cockheads. Both of you, right fucking now."

"Jonny, no!"

He ignored her plea. Today's tensions had been aching for some kind of release, and this would do nicely. Jonny's body trembled with adrenaline, ready to purge, and even the thought of Sloane's horror at his violence wasn't enough to quell the grim excitement he felt when imagining his fists bludgeoning that mocking light from Corey's eyes.

"What the *fuck*?" Prickles exclaimed then, and his startled tone got everyone's attention.

Whilst they'd all been focused on the impending brawl, another figure had appeared on the footpath as if out of nowhere. His suit cut a blacker hole in the darkness, but his pale face glowed white, a morbid smile stretching from ear to ear. Prickles stumbled away from the man, bumping into Corey, who shoved him aside and sneered at the new arrival.

"Perkins. You want some too, arsehole?"

Mr. Dogsbody said nothing, his grin not slackening a jot. He took a few slow steps off the footpath and onto the road, his dress shoes slapping against the bitumen in a rhythm all the more ominous for its dread patience.

Prickles puffed up his chest like a threatened rooster, not wanting to lose face in front of his mate, but Corey seemed a little less sure of himself now. Hands hanging loose at his sides, Mr. Dogsbody stopped and stood smiling at them from a metre away. He appeared slight in comparison to the bloated figures of Jonny's old classmates, but there was something in his demeanour that implied they were the ones who should be worried. The red glow of Corey's taillights seemed to warn all present of imminent danger.

I wouldn't want to mess with this creep, Jonny thought. He was glad Mr. Dogsbody had chosen to step in, but less so when he remembered this man was one of the things he and Sloane had come here to face.

The standoff dragged on, Mr. Dogsbody's grin fixed fast to his thin jaws even as the aggression in Corey and Prickles seemed to evaporate. And then Kassia's servant took one more step, his smile twitching as he whispered something that Jonny couldn't catch over the rumble of the idling car engine. Whatever he said, it seemed to have the desired effect. Corey nudged Prickles and backed up around the rear of his car, keeping his eyes on Mr. Dogsbody; Prickles gave a huff of relief and followed, choosing to walk all the way around the front end to the passenger side rather than brush past the man.

"You'll get yours, Trotter," Corey called, throwing Jonny a look that was markedly less threatening than it had been half a minute before. He dropped into his car and slammed the door in a half-hearted attempt to retain his edge, something Prickles didn't bother to copy. And then they were moving off, the red eyes of their taillights shrinking into the night, and Jonny and Sloane were left alone in the street with Mr. Dogsbody.

"Uh…thank you." Sloane stepped up and grabbed Jonny's hand, and he knew that she was wondering, like him, if the frying pan had just disappeared and left them to the fire.

Mr. Dogsbody turned and bestowed a shallow bow upon them, gesturing with one hand toward the house they'd come to visit. He was still smiling.

"Looks like we're expected," Jonny said, the adrenaline keeping him on edge, and Sloane gave him a look that said she was beginning to regret her insistence upon coming here. "Well, let's not be rude, then. After you, mate."

Mr. Dogsbody tipped them an as-you-like-it nod and led them along the footpath to the driveway, where Jonny noted a parked car with a Handicapped sticker on the back window. Then they stepped onto the lawn and into the jungle.

The grass grew strong in the shade, unyellowed by the gaze of the summer sun, and reached almost to Jonny's knees; with every step, he half-expected a snake to turn under his foot and lash out, and he'd seen enough deadly browns whilst growing up to know that fear was well-founded. Ducking under the hanging claws of the trees that edged the lawn, he glanced up through their branches into their shadowy hearts and wondered what might be up there looking back at him. Sloane's hand gripped his with the force of a woman in the throes of childbirth, and he knew her imagination must be throwing up all kinds of sinister possibilities.

He found it a little easier to breathe when the three of them stepped out from under the canopy of branches and onto the front porch of Kassia's house. Blind windows looked out onto a dizzying array of potted plants, palms and cacti and flowers and all sorts, and what little of the tiled space that remained clear was stained by the dim yellow glow that crept out through the open front door.

Jonny remembered the first time he'd walked into this house, a few weeks after he and Jessica had started dating. He'd been anxious then, too, hoping he'd make a good impression on the strange woman in black who lived here, but he'd survived the encounter. *Let's hope it goes that well tonight,* he thought, with a kind of hopeless bravado.

The front hallway was lit only by the pissy glow that spilled from deeper inside the house, but as Jonny followed Mr. Dogsbody in, keeping Sloane behind him, he found it chimed almost exactly in tune with his memory of it. Bookcases and shelves loomed to either side, enforcing single file down the length of the hall, and they were near to overflowing with knick-knacks and ornaments. Old dolls sprawled splay-legged against vases like dead little girls who had fallen prey to a Victorian taxidermist; grim, sepia-toned faces stared out at the future from behind smeared glass; china animals pranced and posed on the spot, happiness ringing hollow in their painted-on eyes. Everything wore a coat of dust, exhibits in an abandoned museum. Whatever Mr. Dogsbody did here, it rarely involved a can of Mr. Sheen and a damp rag.

At the end of the hall, the light filtered through a beaded curtain that would admit them to the sitting room. A doorway gaped open to either side, and Jonny recalled that one was Kassia's bedroom whilst the other had been a spare she'd used for storage. He glanced at both as they passed.

Kassia's room was dark and musty, showing nothing but one bedpost that stretched up higher than his head, and he found it all too easy to imagine a rotting bed draped in cobweb curtains; that doorway was a mouth he didn't dare approach. The storeroom, on the other hand, contained a single candle burning in an antique holder, and by its glow he could see the chamber had been emptied of junk and given over to Mr. Dogsbody. A rolling clothes rack in one corner held half a dozen black suits identical to the one he wore now; they might well have been another six Dogsbodies on coathangers, one for each day of the week, patiently awaiting their turn to serve. A single mattress lay face-up in the middle of the bare wooden floor, and beside his sleeping place, this strange young man kept nothing but a glass of water, a box of tissues in a knitted doily holder, and a splayed-open paperback thick enough to be used as a bludgeon.

Mr. Dogsbody stepped through the beaded curtain and stood to one side, holding a fistful of strings with one hand and beckoning them in with the other. Jonny glanced back and saw Sloane's worried gaze, and beyond that, the night-coloured cut-out of the open front door. At least they had a ready exit if things got a bit too intense.

Bracing himself, Jonny stepped through the curtain and into the sitting room. This too was much as he remembered it, but even more densely packed with things—the ornate coffee table was stacked a foot high with old fairy tale books, sideboards sagged under the weight of chintzy plates, the walls were populated with framed faces both photographed and painted, and an archaic spinning wheel sat to one side of the velvet-draped settee. The thick carpet was mould-pale and breathed out puffs of dust at every step. In each corner of the room sat an antique lamp, four coloured-glass sheaths with candles burning within them like hooded eyes.

The White Widow sat in the middle of the couch, one hand resting on a gnarled cane that looked like it might have been yanked off one of the trees outside and pressed straight into service. The veil still hung over her face, shifting almost imperceptibly with every breath, and the same white dress cloaked her crooked figure. Since the wake, she'd added a garland of flowers around her neck, and Jonny could smell their fresh-cut scents over the musty miasma of sandalwood and dust. He could see nothing of her eyes but felt them burning into him like irons that had been kept in the fire for many, many years.

"Jonathan Trotter." Kassia Rzepka's voice was thin, creaky, as if under- or over-used. "I once told you never to come back here. Are you surprised that I have now invited you?"

Was that a confession, straight off the bat? Jonny licked lips dried out by the beer and cleared his throat.

"Not especially, no. This feels like something that's been waiting to happen for a long time."

"Yes. You were always going to come back here. And I was always going to be waiting."

Jonny cast a glance at Mr. Dogsbody to make sure the man hadn't produced a knife to enact Kassia's long-delayed revenge. But he was simply standing in the corner with his hands folded before him, eyes down, a distant smile aimed at the carpet. Maybe Kassia guessed what Jonny was thinking, for she addressed her companion next.

"Mr. Dogsbody, kindly leave us to our reunion. You have plenty of things to be getting on with."

The strange young man bowed and backed out of the lounge, still smiling in a way that made Jonny wonder if he was going back to his room to dissect a cat or something.

"I know what you must be thinking, Jonathan. Yes, I've had much time to mull over what happened to my Jessica, *o a od a yre a*. For fifteen years I have been sitting in judgement of you, as I judged my husband before you, and like that faithless *w a*, you have been found wanting. But I will not lay a finger on you. That is not why you are here."

"Then why?" Jonny asked. He couldn't help imagining that, beneath those white gloves, the fingers she'd mentioned were nothing but bone—that at any moment Kassia might lift that veil to reveal a dry, grinning skull.

"Did you ever hear about my husband?" she carried on, as if he hadn't spoken. "Did Jessie tell you what happened to him?"

He nodded. Of course she had—a story like that was right up Jessica's alley.

Aunt Kassie married a guy called Gerry in '95, she'd murmured into his ear one night as they lay in her bed, one hand propping up her head and the other toying idly with his stomach hairs. *Never liked the dude much from the couple times we met. Got a sleazy vibe off him, so I wasn't surprised to find out he'd been cheating on her. Some girl from his work, young, chubby, and keen—just another dumb bitch who fell for empty promises, cheap trinkets, and sordid nights in hotels the next town over. One night in '98, they were out driving along the coast when BAM!—they ran head-on into a ute with a big-arse bull bar. I heard that she wasn't wearing a seatbelt, so they found her body ten metres down the road…and her head on the passenger seat. She'd been going down on Uncle Gerry when they crashed, you see, and when they opened her mouth, guess what they found?* Her playful fingers had tightened suddenly around his cock and balls, causing him to flinch. *Now THAT, baby, is one hell of a head job.*

"Then you know he was punished for his mistakes, and not by me. You will be called to account for yours, but I will play no great part in that. I'm just here to show you the way home."

"Did you send those envelopes to Jonny?" Sloane blurted, like she'd been carrying that burning question in her mouth all day. "You did, didn't you? You wanted him back here."

"Ah," that dry voice croaked, the veiled head turning to regard the younger woman. "Sloane, isn't it? Tell me, *h a lal a*—what is your last name?"

Kassia's question had a teasing lilt that implied she knew full well, but Sloane paused only a moment before giving her answer.

"It's Nowak."

"Another old Polish name—interesting. The circle closes, and we find ourselves right where we were back then, yes?"

"How did you know about Sloane?" Jonny asked, not liking this new wrinkle. "How did you know her name?"

Kassia flexed her gloved fingers on the handle of her cane. "We have…ways. I simply had Mr. Dogsbody consult the Book of Faces."

Jonny frowned. "What's that supposed to be? Some occult shit? You really have lost it, Kassia."

The White Widow let out a scraping sound that he took a moment to recognise as laughter. Sloane shook her head, unimpressed.

"She means Facebook, Jonny."

"Oh. Well, to be fair, I wasn't expecting jokes."

"You know some very strange people, babe."

"Tell me about it."

"*I* shall tell you," Kassia announced, bracing herself on her cane to sit up straighter. "Our blood is in your veins, Miss Nowak, so you should know how things came to this. Do you recognise that painting there?"

Jonny and Sloane followed her finger to an eight-by-ten framed reproduction on a nearby shelf—a dour woman in a *fleur-de-lis* robe, two cuts carved into her cheek.

"No."

"That is the Black Madonna of Częstochowa. After Hussites damaged the painting, slashing her face with their swords, an attempt was made to repair it. This failed, so the Madonna was recreated, painted anew—the same, but not the same. That is me. I have suffered, tried to heal and remake myself, only to suffer and heal again. I am more scar tissue than woman. But pain is our lot, is it not, Sloane? Always the man who brings the ruin down, the woman who pays the price. My own family taught me this.

"My father fought in the Home Army during the second Great War, and having somehow survived that, he was then arrested and imprisoned by the NKVD in 1950. He was not released until Gomulka's Thaw, six years later, and it was another two before he met Danuta—my mother. I came along quickly, and then my sister, Marlena. My parents decided to leave Poland for safer lands and chose Australia. We travelled until *tatu* decided on this town, because he wanted peace and isolation after all he'd been through. That was in 1964."

Kassia pointed to one wall, where an age-browned sheet had been framed and hung—Jonny had noticed it in the past but never bothered to read it. It was the front page of a paper called *The Coastal Courier*, busier than the streamlined covers of its modern equivalents; there were at least five different stories leading off the issue, and, cued by Kassia's tale, Jonny's eyes cut to one in the bottom right corner: WATERWICH WELCOMES THE RZEPKAS. A serious-looking couple with Slavic cheekbones stood to attention, two young daughters at their feet—Kassia and Marlena, before time and trouble had taken their toll.

Jonny made to pull his eyes away, only to find himself caught by the other photograph on the front page. It was a picture he'd seen in Jessica's caravan the night after she'd disappeared: the surly James Dean wannabe and the bright-eyed Greek princess. TEENAGE RAMPAGE ENDS IN GUNFIRE, their headline declared, and beneath: *One Dead, One Arrested—An End to the Senseless Slaughter.*

There was a kind of sinister sense to the way these threads twined together. Jonny was starting to feel that he was a tiny speck caught in a massive, unseen web of causality, thousands of seemingly random events woven into a pattern too vast for him to comprehend.

"My father did not live to enjoy his peace and freedom for very long. He died in a farming accident the next year, and my mother had to raise us alone. Many times we almost starved, but for the generosity of our neighbours. Yes, Waterwich was kinder to us than Warsaw ever was, but the struggle did something to the mind of my mother, I think. *Matka* became…strange. Marlena, she was always the troublesome one, fighting and drinking and sleeping around, and eventually she ran away to the city. That is where she met her husband and they had their daughter, while I stayed here and looked after the crazy woman and watched my own life dribble away."

Poor you, Jonny thought. *Get to the fucking point.*

"But I bore you. I tell you this only to show you how lucky it was that Jessica Grzelak was born at all. Her grandfather was shot at, imprisoned, tortured—her mother impoverished and reckless, self-destructive. Jessie was a miracle. She always will be. You knew that once, Jonathan, and it meant the world to her. So that is why I have helped to bring you back home. I have done it for her.

"Because all this time, while you lived your life and forgot about the past you left behind…Jessica has been right here, waiting for you to come back to her."

Jonny felt a shiver ride his spine from one end to the other. "What?"

Kassia gave that horrid little laugh again. "That's right. Didn't you know? Didn't you *always* know?"

"What are you saying?" Sloane demanded to know. "Is Jessica *here*?"

"Bullshit," Jonny declared, shaken. "There's no way. Jessica's gone. *You* sent those cards to me every five years, didn't you, Kassia? You're the only one with access to Jess's handwriting, her perfume. You faked those cards and then Dogsbody drove you to town and you put them under my door."

Kassia laughed again, and Jonny snapped, "Don't deny it! It was you!"

"I deny nothing," the White Widow croaked, back to seriousness in a heartbeat. "I am only an instrument in this symphony. Jessica haunts you through me, through your memories. And she has been waiting here all along for you to come home."

"Fuck this." Jonny grabbed Sloane's hand. "She's crazy. We're going."

"But don't you want to see the truth for yourself, Jonathan? It's simple. All you have to do is open that door."

Kassia raised one long finger and pointed to a spot across the sitting room. Jonny realised that what he'd thought was a drape was actually a door, then remembered it had always been there—though in the past, it hadn't been painted black.

"The kitchen?" he asked, shaking his head in confusion.

"Go through that door," the White Widow said, "and know the truth of it."

Sloane squeezed his hand in either encouragement or its opposite. He wanted nothing more at that moment than to be back at the Cutters Arms with Brendan, knocking back some pints and remembering the good times—shit, he would have been happy to trade this insanity for another encounter with Corey and Prickles. But as Sloane had reminded him a few times today, he'd come home to lay his demons down, and if he didn't do that, he'd carry them on his back the rest of his life. He let go of Sloane's hand and crossed the sitting room to the kitchen door.

"Jonny," his partner muttered.

"It's okay," he said without thinking. "It's just a—"

His lips stopped working as he reached the black door and noticed what else had been changed. On the lintel above the door itself, someone had drawn a mash-up symbol in white paint: a cross within a love heart.

"Fuck's sake," he breathed. And then he reached out, turned the handle, and stepped into the darkened room.

Nothing stood out, or jumped out, or whispered his name—it was the same kitchen he remembered from 2000 lurking in these shadows, now dusty and disused. What caught his attention was the door to his left, open and allowing light in from that direction—and not just light, but sound as well. Music.

What is that?

A chill down his neck implied some part of him had already recognised those faint strains and was waiting for the rest to catch up. He strode across the kitchen to the open door, which led out into a cement-floored passage that ran along the back of the house; to the left were the bathroom and toilet, to which he'd snuck many a time from the warmth of the Chesney, and ahead was the door that led outside. This, too, was open, and an exterior light had been left on. Not only that, but the music grew louder as he approached the back yard.

"I know that song," said Sloane from behind him, and from beyond her came the sounds of Kassia shuffling after them through the house.

"Me too," he said through numb lips. And with that, he crossed the passage and strode out the back door into the night.

Jessica's caravan still squatted there in the back yard on flat tires, another abandoned relic. Its door, too, was open, its internal lights switched on—and so was its stereo, pumping that familiar song out into the night like a siren's call meant for him alone.

Joy Division, "Love Will Tear Us Apart". One of Jessica's all-time favourite tracks. She'd told him once that if she ever decided to kill herself, the deed would be done to this song—much as Ian Curtis had died with Iggy Pop on the turntable, she'd decided she would go out with *his* sonorous voice as the last thing she ever heard.

Don't you ever do that to me, he'd said to her, upset that she found his earnestness amusing. *Jessica, don't you ever die.*

Jonny shook, his breath coming fast. Sloane appeared beside him, her eyes wide.

"Is that…?"

What if it was? What if Jessica had survived and lain low all these years, waiting for him to come home and face what he had let fall into the darkness?

He steeled himself, let anger mix in with the fear. How could she have done this to him? Just one word could have let him know the truth, would have lifted the weight of guilt off his back. Before he could think twice, he strode across the overgrown lawn to the caravan. The music swelled around him as he placed his foot on the steel step to push himself up and inside.

Like the house, little had changed here since his last visit. The same posters hung ragged from the caravan's walls, the same stacks of books and CDs and detritus teetered on every available surface, the same clothes dangled from compartments and lay strewn across the bed. And it was the bed Jonny was staring at as his breath caught in his throat.

The caravan was empty.

More fucking games!

Jonny stepped across the caravan's floor, as if he needed further convincing that his erstwhile lover was not hiding somewhere in this mess. His eyes flicked to the table as he passed it, and the photocopied faces of Billy and Poppy stared back at him. Something squelched beneath his shoes.

The floor was wet, small puddles gathering at the edge of the bed—and something caught his eye there, too. Leaning forward, he placed one hand on the cold, stale sheets. They were damp.

What is this?

An image came to mind then. He banished it immediately.

Jonny turned and saw Sloane leaning in through the caravan's door. She realised he was alone and threw him a confused look.

"Let's get out of here," he said, and hurried toward her. She stepped back and let him out of the caravan. Kassia was standing in the doorway of her house, her shoulders shaking as she let out that awful laugh. For one brutal moment, Jonny was tempted to dash across the yard and strike her down, kick her old bones into powder, anything to stop that mocking sound. It might have been his conscience that prevented him, or Sloane's presence, or it might have been the daunting figure he glimpsed behind Kassia, rust-haired and black-suited and grinning.

"What the hell is this?" he demanded of her. "There's no-one there!"

"Of course not!" the White Widow cackled. "You know where to find her. You know where she is—right where you left her. Waiting, Jonathan! Waiting for you to come home and prove your love!"

"Fuck you!" he seethed. "You crazy old bitch!"

For the first time, he saw the smile drop from Mr. Dogsbody's face. The young man made to step forward, cold iron in his eyes, but Kassia raised a thin arm and held him back.

"Go to her, Jonathan. Make amends to the woman you betrayed. But be careful! Time changes a person. Perhaps Jessica is a Black Madonna now, too."

Sloane grasped at his arm. "Jonny—"

"We're going," he declared. "Come on. We're going back to the car and we're getting the fuck out of this town and I am never, *ever* coming back here again."

Sloane was pulled along in his wake as he stalked away from the caravan, away from the house, away from the mocking laughter in Kassia's voice—down the driveway, past the parked car, back out onto Nightingale Street. The music from Jessica's stereo faded as they went, as if it were falling deeper and deeper into the dark.

"Jonny!" Sloane plucked at the sleeve of his suit. "Slow down! What the hell just happened?"

"I don't know!" he cried, not slowing his pace. "Doesn't matter. I'm not sticking around this place a minute longer."

His black mood must have discouraged any further questions, as Sloane remained silent for the duration of their walk back to the car. When they arrived, the Cutters Arms looming on the other side of the road and funereal celebrations still going on inside, Jonny fished out his car keys and thumbed the unlock button. The Clubsport's lights flashed and Sloane spoke at last.

"Give me those," she snapped, grabbing the keys from his hand. "You're not driving."

"Fine," he replied, crossing to the passenger side and opening the door. "Just get me out of this shithole."

Sloane poked the key into the ignition and adjusted the seat, not looking at him. Jonny slumped forward and rested his face in his hands, wondering how this day could get any more fucked.

"What about Mick's room key?" Sloane said eventually.

"We can mail it to him. Come on, let's go."

"No. We'll hang onto it. Because we're not leaving."

Jonny raised his head and stared at her. Sloane matched his gaze, resolute.

"What are you talking about?"

"Listen to me! I know, okay? I know. But what I said on the way to that house? Nothing's changed. If you run out now, this shit's going to haunt you forever."

"Sloane—"

"And I won't stick around to help, okay?" She paused for a moment, biting her lip at the stunned surprise on his face. "It's bad enough that you can't make up your mind about the Thing, which should be the easiest choice in the world if you love me...but if you run away from this, how can I rely on you, Jonathan? I need you. I need your support, your strength. So prove to me you're that guy. Prove to me you're *the* guy. Finish this. Tonight."

Jonny fell back in his seat, close to tears for what felt like the hundredth time this week. Didn't she see what this was doing to him? Every time he thought he was close to closure on this, the torment was extended. He'd just put his dad in the ground today, for Christ's sake!

And what do you suppose he'd think of you running out now?

He could see Alan Trotter shaking his head, weary, disappointed. But how did that matter? He was dead. Not blissing out in Nirvana, not rolling around with seventy-two virgins, not on a cloud somewhere plucking out "Stairway to Heaven" in some fucking harp ensemble. He was fertiliser. He was giving back, becoming a part of the land he'd loved so much. He was dead.

So do this in his memory. Make him proud in your own mind. Time to stop running, because it never helped before and it won't now. Face this. Fight it—and win.

The engine rumbled to life, and Jonny busied himself by fumbling with the iPod and setting it to random. The device chose a morbid minor-key ballad by Chelsea Wolfe as if attuned to the mood in the car. They sat and idled and said nothing.

When Sloane looked over at Jonny again, it was not in anger but sympathy. Of course; she was a saint. Didn't he owe a resolution to her, too? After all she'd done for him, coming here today, accepting that he'd lied to her and kept her locked out of the darker compartments of his life?

"Well?" she prompted, her voice gentle.

"I think...I think you're right. No. I *know* you are."

She nodded, tried to interject a little levity. "Yeah, me too, but it's always nice to hear someone else say it. And I know you'll roll your eyes at this, babe, but doing this is the only thing that makes narrative sense. I know life isn't a story...but it is, too. You can't set up a big old mystery and then shy away from it at the last minute, it just doesn't work. You need closure on this."

"You've been so amazing today," Jonny told her. "I'm so hopeless without you, Sloane. But there's something else we need to talk about."

She closed her eyes; even saints had a limit to their patience. "What now?"

"I told you that no-one believed me when I said Jess and I found the Chapel—that there was no other passage through the cave when everyone else looked. And you didn't push me on it. So...do *you* believe me? Or do you think I just imagined it?"

Sloane nodded at his seatbelt, and he buckled up. "I honestly don't know what to think about that, sweetie. But I think there's more to that story. Things you haven't told me. You *do* remember what happened, don't you?"

He nodded. "But it seems…strange. Like a dream. I'm not sure I even believe it myself."

"You can tell me. I'll listen—I will *always* listen, Jonny. You know that, don't you?"

"Yeah," he said, and he did.

"Right. Well, you better tell me how to get wherever it is we're going now. And while we're on our way, work out what it is you have to say and how you're going to say it. Because when we get there, you're going to tell me what happened the night you and Jessica found the Chapel."

chapel of love

JONNO SUCKED IN A STUNNED breath, and Jessica echoed it beside him. "Oh, *wow*," she whispered, a note of almost religious reverence in her voice, and he couldn't help but agree.

This new chamber they'd entered was vastly wider and deeper than the first, but that fact registered in an almost subliminal fashion—their eyes were drawn to the thousands of soft blue lights scattered across the cave ceiling some twenty feet above, spread across the darkness like countless stars in a night sky. In some parts they hung closer as if falling to earth, and Jonno realised these lights had clung to stalactites stabbing down from the ceiling; he spotted other speleothems that were bare of glowing points, and they stood out against the backdrop of blue like the shadows of teeth. Beneath this strange new galaxy lay a still mirror of water, reflecting the azure glow back at its source. It ate up most of the floor, but he didn't think it ran deep—perhaps a couple of feet. On the other side of the pool, an ominous hump of rock rose before the chamber's back wall and squatted there with a sense of self-importance like a pulpit. The other walls scooped and swelled in abstract patterns, some of the sapphire glows spreading out across those surfaces too like a beautiful rash, and Jonno failed to get a sense of the cave's shape. He could see no clear angles or corners, yet the space folded around him. He put that down to disorientation and lack of bright light, but it still bothered him.

"This must be it," Jessica murmured, her hand shaking in his. "We found it, J. We're here. This is the Chapel."

"What are those lights?" he asked, his voice hushed.

"Glow worms, I think."

"Wish I'd brought a camera."

"Don't need one. I'll never forget this." She gave an odd little sigh that made Jonno think of a fleeting, non-sexual orgasm. "It's like standing outside the universe."

They shifted on the spot and stared around for perhaps a full minute, trying to process the vista laid out before them. Jonno couldn't shake the feeling that although this cave was beautiful, it was not necessarily benign. The natural world was brutal, impartial; whatever this was, it surely cared even less for ephemeral things. And why should it? *Flashes of light and noise,* Jessica had called them, *fireflies that live and die in a millisecond.* Should he be expected to take an interest in the bacteria that coated his skin, and individual ones at that?

"What now?" he asked when he could bear the silence no more.

"We take a closer look," Jessica replied, still rapt. She hadn't so much as glanced at him since they entered the Chapel, though her fingers were tightly bound in his. "See that rock across the water? I think it's got markings on it."

Jonno peered through the gloom at the stone he'd thought of as a pulpit. He could see some kind of pattern or discolouration on its surface, but when he focused on that, the shape of the rock itself seemed to loom larger in his peripheral vision as if shifting and growing whilst he was distracted. It was an odd and disconcerting sensation.

"Let's go see," Jessica whispered, stepping up to the water's edge.

"Really?" Jonno winced at the whine in his voice. "You want to go in there?"

"It's just water. I think it's shallow." She ducked and dipped a finger into the still surface. "Oh, and it's *cold*."

"It was hardly going to be a heated pool."

"It could've been. There might have been warm springs beneath us. Oh well." Jessica rose to her feet and looked at her lover for the first time since they'd entered. "Ready?"

No!

"Uh…"

She grinned her devil-may-care grin, and Jonno knew he would follow her anywhere. "Come on. Me and you, my love."

Jessica stepped forward and sank her foot into the pool. The water swallowed her leg up to the calf, and she shuddered in a way that made Jonno even more trepidatious…but then her other foot was in, and he was lowering his own through that glowing blue mirror.

The water was icy, and it stole Jonno's breath in a heartbeat. He told himself it was no worse than wading out at the beach on a cold day and stepped in with his other foot. He lost feeling in both, and when he glanced down, he was half-convinced that his legs would now end where the smooth surface began, that he would never see his feet again. But no, there they were; the water was pure, so clear as to be transparent.

Jessica began wading forward, the pool parting quietly around her legs as its echoes slapped and danced between the rock walls above.

Jonno moved alongside her, wondering just what they hoped to find. He doubted he'd discover any sign of his mother's presence here, unless—and he shuddered hard at the thought—unless she lay beneath the still waters ahead, her eyes open and staring up at the lights above as though transfixed by heaven. But nothing touched their feet as they waded on, and the floor of the pool appeared to be plain rock beneath their soles as it gradually sloped away. By the time they reached the middle of the cave, the water had risen almost to his knees.

"Think how lucky we are," Jessica murmured, and he focused on her. "Millions of years, and hardly anyone's seen this place."

Jonno was reminded that many people had entered the first cave and found nothing more than that. "So why us?"

She squeezed his hand, rubbed his thumb with hers. "You know why."

Jonno stared up at the ceiling as they waded onward. He was reminded of Michael Gregson's bedroom that one time Mike had hosted a sleepover with himself, Brendan, and the Ronson kid; Mike's dad had glued glow-in-the-dark stars to his ceiling, and it had seemed like they were camping out under some magical night sky. The Chapel was like that on a grand scale, and Jonno could almost believe the countless points of light above were not worms at all but the stars they resembled. Like the age of the cave, the view reminded him that he was merely a tiny, short-lived speck of carbon in a universe of unfathomable breadth. He was humbled, awed, and more than a little terrified.

"Look," Jessica breathed, and he brought his gaze back down to see that they had almost reached the far side of the pool. The crystal-clear water was above his kneecaps now. "You see that?"

The rock that loomed before them was at least twice their height, its shape appearing to be random but hinting at a design they couldn't quite comprehend. The cryptic colossus did indeed have markings, and now that they were close, he recognised them: pale handprints, dozens or more, all overlapping and angling off on variations of upright. Jonno realised the markings on his side were all of right hands, those before Jessica all left, and a space of bare rock at least a metre wide stretched between.

"What *is* that, some kind of…indigenous art?" Jonno peered closer, turned to her. "Is that ochre or something?"

Jessica smiled and gently shook her head.

"What, then?"

She shrugged. "I'm not sure. But I think I see how it works."

Jessica raised her free hand, her left. When Jonno mirrored the action with his right, he knew what she was getting at.

"You think we're supposed to touch it?"

"Yes."

"And then what?"

For the first time tonight, he saw a hint of the nervousness behind her bravado; for the first time tonight, her smile looked forced. "According to the stories...there's a test. If our love is pure and true, we pass."

He knew there was no point to asking what this test might involve—she was as in the dark as he. "What if we don't touch it? What if we aren't tested?"

Jessica shook her head. "Then I'm not sure we'll be able to leave."

"That doesn't make any sense!"

"Not to us. Look, it's just a feeling. Don't you feel it, too?"

"I don't know." Jonno was a conflicting mess of emotions right now. "I'm a bit...I'm freaking out here, Jess."

"It's okay, baby. I'm here with you. Don't be afraid." Jess took a step closer to the rock, and now she was within arm's reach. "We're going to be fine. Me and you, remember? Just think about me—about *us*. Think about how much I love you, and how happy we are, and how happy we'll be. Because that's what this is all about, J—love. That's why we found this place. Think of me, and love me, and everything's going be all right."

She moved her hand closer to the rock, glanced over to make sure he was doing the same. She met his eyes for one last long and lingering look, and though there was only the azure glow to light her face, he could read everything in that gaze—all she felt for him, all she'd ever been, all she hoped for and dreamed. The enormity of her engulfed him, pushing back the shadows, and he lost himself in her. How could he fear anything with her at his side?

"Me and you," he said. "Forever."

Then, together, they reached forward and placed their palms on the damp stone.

stranger than kindness

JONNY FELL SILENT AND LEANED his head back, letting out a long breath. That was the first time he'd ever told anyone what he remembered about the Chapel, and oh, the *relief*—like letting go of a stone that was dragging him down into the deeper dark. He'd carried this shameful burden alone for far too long, and Sloane's offer of a slender shoulder to share that weight left him awed by her support. But sympathy could walk hand in hand with judgement, and he was worried her investment in uncommon narratives might not be strong enough to suspend the weight of her disbelief. Still, she'd asked for this information, and what she did with it was entirely up to her.

She didn't say anything at first, just passed him a cigarette and lit them both up. Leaving the street near the Cutters Arms, they'd taken the Clubsport out to Mermaid Drive, Jonny giving grim directions to the wild end of Gavin Hunter's property where generations of teens had come to explore their options. They'd passed between the red eyes of the reflectors still mounted at the opening of the unnamed track, run the gauntlet of trees that loomed over the trail like storybook phantoms, parked in the same spot that had once held his XF panel van, marvelled at the broken bulk of the school bus hunched in the corner of the clearing. And now they sat within its belly the way he'd often done fifteen years ago, a picnic blanket spread over the torn vinyl of the back seat, Jonny bunched up in the corner and Sloane by his side with her foot trailing into the aisle.

The bus, like many things in and around Waterwich today, was not quite as Jonny remembered it. During his conversation with Brendan, Jonny had learned that the 49er had continued to rust and degrade until it was too derelict for any further use, and after a kid had fallen through the floor and cut himself, it had finally been hauled away and junked. And that was the end of the 49er, the end of an era…but what no-one had expected was that over a decade later, someone would dump another bus in its place.

This one had appeared a few years ago, a newer model than the last but likewise at the end of its operational capacity, and it was going the same way as its predecessor. Its fading, bone-white hide was coated in colourful tags and misspelled coarse graffiti, its windows smashed or removed entirely, its seats slowly falling prey to the ravages of time and the elements. The new bus was shorter, its interior lines different, but by moonlight it might well have been the 49er itself—it even bore the same warning, CAUTION branded on its forehead above the broken glass of its eyes. Jonny wondered if some nostalgic adult had brought the vehicle here so that future generations of Waterwich teens could share the debauched environment of their forebears; and then he wondered if Kassia hadn't somehow arranged its placement, keen to keep the stage set the way it had been fifteen years before.

He sat in silence and smoked, the summer breeze blowing through empty windows to carry their wisps of grey off into the night. Sloane played with the hem of her summer dress—upon arriving here, she'd changed back out of her black funeral outfit as though sick of mourning for someone she'd never known, and Jonny wondered whether that might be Alan Trotter or his ever-dissembling son. Crickets sang them songs of longing, and the trees whispered sweet nothings to each other, and maybe that was why Jonny flashed on the memory of another night he'd spent out here so long ago: high and horny with Jess on the back seat of the 49er, her wicked grin flashing as she ducked down and took him in her moist mouth, his semen arcing into the darkness like shooting stars stained silver by the moonlight.

Not now, please.

"So," he began. "There it is. That's really everything this time. At least, everything I remember."

Sloane nodded, still digesting the tale.

"It took a while to come back to me—at first, I guess I didn't *want* to remember. But over time, it started bleeding back into my memory. I'm not sure if that's a good thing."

His partner smoked and stared up at the bus ceiling, silent.

"Do you believe me, then?" Jonny desperately needed an affirmation, but he pressed on. "Frankly, I understand if you don't. It feels real to me, but it also seems…*otherwise*. That's the only word I can think of. Like it happened, but not here, and maybe not even to me."

Sloane nodded again, and now she turned to regard him.

"I believe you. Which is to say, I believe that *you* believe it happened, because that story was too detailed to be some random delusion. You wouldn't make something like that up, so…either you stitched together a scenario from dreams and other fragments that you slotted into place to plug the gap where the truth had been, or it actually happened."

Jonny mused on the possibility. "I suppose that makes sense—I erased what really happened because I couldn't handle it, replaced it with something I could create and control. But if that's the case, babe…what did I do to Jessica? What could be so horrible that I couldn't bear to remember it?"

Perhaps I did kill her.

The thought was a thorn in his mind, stabbing deep, numbing him. He didn't realise he'd spoken the words aloud until Sloane replied to them.

"No. Jonny, no. You're not capable of that. You're a gentle man, a kind man."

He recalled how eager he had been to fight Corey and Prickles, his atavistic impulse to wipe their faces clean of mockery and wash them with their own blood, and his head shook as guilty tears once again pricked his eyes.

"Do you want to know what's really been bothering me today?" Sloane dropped her cigarette on the bus floor, plucked his from between shaking fingers and did the same. "Everywhere we go in this town, someone seems to be accusing you—blaming you for what happened to Jessica all those years ago. Even *you're* doing it! And you know what? They're all wrong—and you, my love, most of all. Because what is it you're actually supposed to have done? Did you push the bitch down a hole or something? No! Jonny, the only thing you're guilty of is going along with your headstrong girlfriend, and hindsight is the only reason that looks like a poor choice. You couldn't possibly have known what would happen, and you did absolutely nothing to *make* it happen."

Jonny avoided her eyes, trying to believe her.

"You know who's to blame in all this? *She* is. Jessica. She was reckless, and she forced you into a situation that ruined both your lives. I know you loved her, Jonny…but the more I hear about that girl, the more I hate her. Everyone holds her up as some kind of dark angel whose wings were clipped too soon when really, she was a selfish and dangerous young woman who never thought about the consequences of her actions until it was too late. It's *her* fault, and if we happen to find her out here tonight, I will tell her that myself. So please, babe—stop thinking that any of this should be blamed on you. You did your best to love her, but sometimes it's just not enough, and that's just life. Let it go."

Her kindness cracked him open, tapped the inexhaustible well of tears at the heart of him. Sloane slid across the blanketed seat and took him in her arms, stroking him, shushing him.

"Come on, honey. It's okay."

Was it? It never had been before, not really—not since Jessica had vanished off the face of the earth. Every day since then had been a struggle to accept his survival, his loss, his lack of worth, even when that day passed without a single conscious thought to what had happened out here. He blamed himself for being the one to make it through, for not loving Jess deeply or truly enough despite his best efforts, and at his core there burned an unquenchable self-hatred that was only fuelled by the blame others pinned on him.

So to hear these exonerating words now, from a source as unimpeachable as Sloane Nowak? Jonny couldn't even begin to explain what that meant to him. These hot tears were washing him clean, and splinters of the black ice he'd carried in his heart for so long were calving away from the mass, breaking up in the warm waters of her regard. For the first time, he began to believe that he could truly leave the past behind.

"Thank you," he whispered.

"It's okay, baby."

"You're just…*amazing*."

And to think that he'd imagined himself in love before this! There'd been half a dozen women between Jessica and Sloane, and a couple of times he'd found himself saying the words…but no-one had touched him as deeply as those two. He'd learned to love with Jess, and that had been so important to them both—but Jessica had been a dead-end girl, and Sloane was a woman who had her shit together. Jess had been the first, but Sloane could well be the last, and lasting, love of his life. Wasn't there something he could do to show her his gratitude?

Jonny pulled back from Sloane's embrace, wiped his eyes clean, then held her hands in his.

"I've been so selfish lately," he began.

"Hey…"

"I know I have, and I've given plenty of excuses why, but that doesn't make it okay. This day's been about me when it should have been about us. I think it's time we talked about the Thing."

Sloane winced. "I know I've been on your case about it, but that's just *me* being selfish. It can wait one more day."

He shook his head, adamant. "No. You were right when you said it should have been the easiest thing in the world to decide. And it is. I mean, I haven't given it as much thought as I should, but my answer was always going to be the same."

Sloane stared at him. Were her eyes now shining in the starlight? "What are you saying, Jonny?"

"I'm saying *yes*. When you move to Sydney in February and start your new job, I'll come with you. Of course I will."

She threw her arms around him again, this time fast and hard like a tackle, and she held him to her with a ferocity born of relief.

"Oh, babe! I'm *so* glad to hear that. Thank you. Thank you."

Her lips found his, and they spoke volumes to each other. It seemed to Jonny like the deepest and truest conversation they'd had in weeks, and not a word was spoken. It didn't need to be—all the facts were already known. Sloane had been headhunted by a major publisher, and it was a huge opportunity; he'd just needed a few days to come to terms with relocation, working out how he was going to fit into his new life. Dad's death and the impending return to Waterwich had distracted him from that, but really, he was always going to make the move. There was nothing for him anywhere else—and certainly not here, now that his last family tie had been severed.

"I was so worried," Sloane whispered when their lips parted, her fingers stroking his beard.

"Well, you can stop that now. I'm not going to lose you, Sloane. You mean so much to me."

They sank into another kiss, and after that she rested her head against his and sighed in contentment as his hands glided up and down her back. The closeness was a vivid reminder of her vitality—her breath rolled in and out of his ear like the tides, her body was as hot as the summer against his, and he could have sworn he felt her pulse pounding through his skin. She was a marvel, a million-to-one shot, a universe wrapped in a mundane miracle—and she was his, and he hers.

Jonny's hands roamed lower, cupping her buttocks beneath the thin material of her dress and squeezing a giggle out of her. Then they wandered up her front, gently cupping her breasts as he moved in for another kiss. When she pulled back from this one, she was reading him loud and clear.

"Seriously? Here?"

"Yes." He kissed her again.

"But it's so…unhygienic."

"Don't care. I need you."

Sloane dropped one hand into his lap to gauge the sincerity of his claim. "So I see."

Her own happiness, combined with his arousal, seemed to be enough to sway her. She looked around to confirm they were alone as Jonny worked his hand between her thighs and stroked the heat he found there, and then she kissed him hard as she pushed her groin forward into his touch. His fingers worked her with urgency, and her own squeezed gently at the bulging head beneath his pants. But he needed more, and she knew it. Sloane pressed her legs together and lifted her rump so he could pull her underwear off, kicking it to the floor with her sandals, then sat there with her thighs apart and teased herself as he unzipped his slacks. She grinned at the bounce of his cock as it was freed, gave it a quick kiss as she crawled over his lap and into the back corner of the bus, watching him over her shoulder with an expectant glint in her eye.

Jonny knelt on the bench behind her, sat back on his feet, lifted the hem of her dress to reveal the glory beneath. He took hold of her hips and she reared back into his lap, grabbing at his hair with one hand as she reached down with the other to guide him up and into her. Sloane moaned at his entry, turning her head to gasp into his ear, and he wrapped his arms around her narrow waist as he eased deeper inside. The angle was uncomfortable, but he relished the feel of her around him—she was warmer than summer inside, wetter than winter. He pulled her downward as he drove up, pushing as deep as his trajectory would allow, trembling and yearning for more sensation as her excited exhalations egged him on. *This* was love; this was life.

As they ground away at each other, Jonny found himself staring over Sloane's shoulder and out into the night-cloaked trees. Was some curious possum looking back, wondering what these ridiculous animals were doing?

Was Jessica?

Jonny couldn't help imagining for a moment that she was, that she'd been waiting out here to play some kind of trick on him—Jessica at thirty-three, aged by a life in hiding, her hair tending toward grey without the sweeter lie of hair dye, crow's feet around deep green eyes that blazed at them out of the darkness. What would she think of this display, at this place, at this time?

She always did like to watch. Well, if she's really here, let her see. Let her rage. And let her realise that her grip on me has been broken.

Jonny blinked away these thoughts, focused on his current lover. His hands rose to the spaghetti straps of Sloane's summer dress and yanked them down her arms, dug under the cups of her bra and shoved them up. He kneaded her small breasts, kissing and nipping at her neck as he thrust. Sloane gasped and moaned and sighed, her fingers twisting in his hair.

Perhaps it was the angle, the spontaneity and raw passion, or the location—but Jonny found himself nearing the edge much faster than usual. He felt that sweet pressure building and flashed again on that time out here with Jess, the way his come had glistened in the moonlight as it shot past her hungry grin. But he didn't need to pull away this time, and he brought Sloane down against his thrusts even harder as he accelerated toward his end. His excitement always fuelled her own, and the realisation that he was close had her choking out hitching gasps that hinted at finality, and so Jonny pushed and pushed and pushed and leaned into her hard as he shot fire deep inside, her own orgasm ringing in his ears.

They hung together, gasping and twitching—two, but one.

Soon Sloane pushed back against him and he slouched on the centre of the bench. The picnic rug had been twisted into a comma of tartan disarray and the torn vinyl of the bus seat was coarse and ragged beneath his bare buttocks. He heard Sloane fossicking on the floor for her discarded knickers and pulling them on, her breath still heavy, and grinned to himself in satisfaction as his slick erection slowly succumbed to the forces of lassitude.

"Might end up with a few bruises from that one," she murmured, adjusting her bra and dress straps. "Worth it, though. Wow."

He rolled his head to the right to receive her kiss but couldn't lift a finger to do any more than that. The urgency of their coupling had drained him.

"Look out, coming through. I need to go and clean up." Sloane pushed by, giggling as she tapped the head of his drooping dick with one finger. "Aw, he's all tuckered out. Make yourself decent, man. I'll be back in a minute."

Jonny grunted and somehow gathered enough motivation to do as she said. Everything had caught up to him—the mental and emotional stress of this long day, the alcohol he'd consumed, the exertion and depletion of their sex. The night seemed to be creeping into the bus through those broken windows even as Sloane stepped out and made for the car. Its weight forced his eyelids down, blacked out his thoughts. And then, before he could argue or struggle, Jonny was dropping fast and deep into the dark.

the great below

THE ROCK WAS SO COLD beneath Jonno's palm that it burned, though he felt no pain as such. He wondered if he was leaving another handprint for future explorers to find—and then, as he turned to look at Jessica, his heart seemed to freeze between beats as he realised there was no longer anything beneath his feet.

He had just enough time to suck in a startled breath before he and Jessica dropped straight down into the pool and the chill waters closed over their heads.

Jonno was stunned for a second, his whole world suddenly black and icy cold, and then he kicked out in reflexive panic. His feet found no hint of purchase, and the flailing fingers of his free hand groped in vain for the surface, and all the while his gut informed him that his body was sinking like a stone. Jessica's hand was vice-tight in his, tugging wildly as she thrashed alongside him.

Drowning!

He had to see where he was, what he could do! Jonno squeezed open his eyes and they turned to ice in their sockets, the lids forcing themselves closed against the freeze of the water, and still all was black. He twisted and strained and managed to get his eyes open again, only to see that there was nothing to be seen. Yanking his head back, he saw the shimmering surface of the pool above him, three metres gone already and receding further with every passing second. The dim azure glow lit rising streams of bubbles as the air escaped their lungs in silent screams of desperation.

NO!

He couldn't see his own hand in the abyssal dark, let alone Jessica, but he felt her squeeze his fingers even tighter—once, twice. It might have been a spasm, or perhaps she was trying to tell him something. What was the last thing she'd said?

Think of me, and love me, and everything's going to be all right.

He might have laughed at such optimism now, or screamed. He flapped both arms and kicked his feet in an attempt to slow their descent, all to no avail. Their combined weight was dragging them deeper by the second, and how many seconds remained before they would have to open their empty lungs to the icy water? This was it. Here it was, so much sooner than he'd ever guessed, sudden and brutal and unforgiving—the end.

NO!

Jonno flashed on a thought for a second, and it was stone-cold and so inviting: he would shake his hand free of Jessica's grip and concentrate his efforts on swimming upward, and if he was fast and very lucky, he might just make it back to the surface.

Don't let go!

No. That thought was craven and shameful but fleeting. He would not sacrifice her to save himself, no matter how much that primal part of his brain pleaded otherwise.

She's going to leave you anyway.

Not true. Not yet. Maybe never—

You can't hold on to her forever.

But he had to—

Then you'll die. Because of her.

No. No. No.

She'll drag you down into the dark and leave you there alone forever.

But he was *not* alone. He pictured Jessica beside him in the dark water, terrified, needing him. Cuddled up to him in her bed, in the back of his panel van, her eyes sleepy and satisfied, content as a patted cat sprawled beside the fire. Riding him, under him, *his*—owning him, part of him, the best of him. Then throwing him that secretive look that always made him feel left out of a joke—atop Brendan in the rumpus room, so bare and open and raw as her reckless plan played out—the way she looked in his nightmares, scornful, walking away with strangers, bored of him, needing more, more, more.

NO!

He couldn't tell if it was their mutual struggle or the pressures of their descent or something else altogether—but Jessica's fingers began to slip through his, even as they both clutched for a firmer hold. He grabbed hard, catching her fingertips, hanging on for one long, frozen moment.

No, baby, please—

And then she was gone.

Jonno twisted his head in the dark, desperate for any glimpse of her as he swung his arms through the water in wild sweeps. Nothing.

JESS!

He caught a glimpse of the surface as he writhed in terror and anguish. That soft blue glow was so far overhead that the light was almost gone, too far to reach now no matter how hard he tried, and still there was no hint that his fall into darkness would ever end. He could see nothing, but he could somehow sense the emptiness around him, and it was so vast that he might as well have been dropping through the infinite expanse of dead space. This abyss was ancient, depthless, and this descent would continue long after Jonathan Trotter had given up the ghost.

He struggled against the downward trend, his lungs aching as his thrashing limbs used up the last of his oxygen, but resistance was a token effort. Not long now.

Where is she?

Gone, gone, gone. Had he ever really doubted it would end this way? Love was transient, loss inevitable—just look at his mother.

Don't leave me!

But she *had*, and she had already begun that journey long before setting foot in the Chapel. Jessica Grzelak would never have settled for him in the end; her world was too big for any one person to encompass. Oh, she loved him—but that was not enough. The first time they'd kissed had been the first step toward the last time, and he'd known it all along…known that one day, like his mother before her, she would disappear into the darkness where she belonged and leave him broken, bereft, alone. Only the circumstances were unexpected.

Jessica…

It was over. She was gone. And the only consolation was that his heart would barely have time to break before it stilled forever.

Jonno stopped struggling. Another blackness was coming over him now, and he felt sanguine in his final moments. No-one would ever find him down here, not in this illimitable gulf that might have been utterly empty or teeming with unseen horrors beyond imagining, but he made his peace with that. No-one would recover his body, cry over his coffin, bring flowers to his grave. And that was just fine.

Jonno's head drifted back in weary acceptance, his fall coming to an end even as his body continued to sink. His last thought was that maybe, just maybe, his beliefs had been wrong—that there was somewhere else to go and he would find love there, familiar feminine arms waiting to welcome him into an eternal embrace.

Far, far above, the soft sapphire glow of the pool's surface closed to a pinprick, and then the last of the light winked out and was gone.

the fireball at the end of everything

BLACK. JUST BLACK. DEPTHLESS, ETERNAL.

Jonny's eyes snapped open as if cued by a silent alarm.

"I remember," he said.

Something important, something he'd kept from himself until now, had resurfaced in his mind. He needed to tell someone before it slipped through his mental fingers like so much sand—needed to tell *her*. Where was she?

He was alone on the bus. How long had he been dozing? Jonny looked out into the clearing but couldn't see his car; its dark duco must be blending in with the night. He glanced over his shoulder, out the back window, and halfway down the subtle path into the bush he saw a retreating shadow. She walked fast and didn't look back.

What the hell was she doing, going without him? Jonny leaped up from the back seat, and then, not wanting to waste any time, he stepped up onto it and clambered through the back window. This was an emergency exit and the glass had popped right out, so there were no jagged glass teeth lurking in the frame to bite him. He hit the ground on bent legs and straightened, catching a flash of movement as she disappeared into the trees ahead.

"Don't leave me!" he called, and his voice was shockingly loud. He realised why as he began to hurry after her—the sounds he made were the only ones he could hear. The crickets had fallen silent and the breeze had died, leaving the woods feeling fake and empty. He was glad to hear his shoes pounding on the dirt and twigs beneath him, but could only wonder what sneaky sounds those footsteps might be covering.

The trail was just as he remembered it, an indistinct path that wove through the trees and was rarely straight enough to provide a clear look ahead. He caught glimpses of her through the branches, always just in sight, and she didn't turn to look back even once, though she must have been able to hear his cries in this eerie silence. He stumbled on, desperate not to lose her.

"I can't be alone again," he said, and caught a flash of movement to his left. He peered across, saw nothing.

And now again, to his right. Jonny stopped and glanced that way, caught a split-second glimpse of a woman stepping behind a tree trunk.

"Who's there?"

"Knock knock," said a voice to his left, and a head popped out from behind a eucalyptus. A young face set in a perennial scowl, cigarette jutting from its lips. Jonny recognised the man straight away, and somehow wasn't even surprised to see him.

"Oh, piss off," he said. "You're dead."

"Knock knock," Billy Ross repeated, stepping out from behind the tree. He hadn't been leaning around it; his head lolled loose and crooked on a broken neck. He was dressed in the same outfit he'd worn to the 1964 school dance, but now his white sports coat boiled with shadows and rejected the glowing touch of the moonlight.

"Sorry, I haven't got time for this right now," Jonny said, in the polite manner he reserved for friendly young people on the street with dangling lanyards and a charitable cause to pimp. He dashed along the scant trail, worried he might lose his lover in the darkness, and a slender shadow paced him in the trees to his right. Poppy Diamantopolous giggled, forever the corrupted child, seemingly oblivious to the blood that trickled out of her hair and ran down to stain her colourless bodice and satin skirt.

"Knock knock," Billy Ross said a third time, flickering through the trees to Jonny's left like an image in a flip book, never once breaking out of his slouching walk.

"Fine," Jonny sighed as he ran. "Who's there?"

"Nicholas."

Poppy tittered from the other side of him, poking a finger into one of the pulpy holes that dotted her body.

"Nicholas who?"

Billy took his cigarette between two fingers and butted it out in his left eye. "Nicholas girls shouldn't climb trees," he said.

Poppy laughed uproariously at this, a sound somewhere between an angry cat and a drain being unclogged, and Jonny shuddered to hear it. He forced his eyes back to the trail and managed to raise his hands just in time to keep from slamming face-first into a tree.

Startled, Jonny pushed himself back from the trunk. A drop of icy water struck his hand, and then another. He craned his head back and looked up.

The moon was casting little light into the bush tonight, and yet it loomed low and burned so bright through the branches that Jonny could barely look at it. He raised one hand to block it out and realised that this cold eye was backlighting a figure, silhouetting something against its pale mass. It might have been a person, sitting up there on a branch and looking down on him with unseen eyes. Wet hair hung long and lank, dancing as if stirred by a breeze that he could not feel, and drops of chilly water fell from those sodden locks to strike his cheeks like freezing bullets. As he squinted to make out its face, the shape shifted and gathered its weight above him.

She was coming down.

Jonny opened his mouth to draw in a breath, and then something cold and wet slapped his face. He recoiled, trying to gasp and choking instead, and though his eyes were already open, he opened them again and turned the world inside out.

"Jonny!"

Sloane was standing before him on the bus, one hand to her mouth, the other clutching the plastic drink bottle she took on runs and road trips.

"What—" He spluttered, coughing up water that had splashed into his mouth and down his throat. "Sloane?"

"I'm so sorry, but you were—you looked like you were having a nightmare. I tried to wake you, but you weren't responding, so I—"

"Yeah, I get it." Jonny pushed himself out of his slouch and sat up against the backrest of the bus seat. "Jesus, woman! You frightened the life out of me."

"Don't be so melodramatic." Sloane sat beside him, placed a hand on his shoulder. "You're okay now. Were you dreaming?"

"I—yeah, I was." Jonny frowned, tried to concentrate on what he'd just seen—but as dreams are wont to do, it was already fading away. "I was looking for you, I think. I remembered something—something I'd forgotten, and I had to tell you before I forgot it again."

"What was it?"

Jonny screwed up his face with the effort of trying to recall his dream, but the more he clutched at the it the faster it slipped through his fingers. "I don't know. It's gone. 'Knock knock'—that's all I've got."

"Fascinating," Sloane said, her voice much drier than Jonny felt right now. "No wonder it wasn't worth remembering."

She kissed his temple with a post-coital fondness, and he remembered that they'd coupled on this very seat before sleep had taken him. "How long was I out?"

"Half an hour, maybe? I left you here when we were done and went to the car to clean myself up. You were asleep when I came back, so I thought I'd let you rest for a little while. Then you started twitching, and—you know what dogs look like when they're asleep, when they look like they're dreaming of running?"

Jonny winced. "You flatter me."

"Anyway, you started looking a bit freaked out, like you were having a fit, and you didn't answer me. You can guess the rest."

"Yeah." Jonny wiped his face with the sleeve of his jacket. He felt worse than when he'd dozed off—perhaps a mild hangover had started to kick in. "Thank you so much."

"You're welcome."

"Got a smoke?"

Sloane raised an eyebrow but lit them up without complaint, and they sat in silence for a minute as she stroked the hair over his ear.

"So, now that you're awake…"

"What, you want to go again?"

"Ha ha. You know what I mean, baby. We should do this thing and get it over with."

The suggestion hardly filled Jonny with enthusiasm, but he knew she was right. It was time to face the cave again. That black mouth in his mind's eye was enough to make his soul cringe, but then, he was picturing it wrong—hadn't Brendan told him the cave had been boarded up? If that were true, how bad could it be?

Bad enough, if Kassia's right—if Jessica is waiting for me there.

And how would that confrontation pan out? He couldn't believe she would be glad to see him again, not after making him wait so long and taunting him from a distance—it wasn't likely she planned to make peace with him or win him back. He imagined Jessica and Sloane throwing down over his affections, a clichéd catfight with hair-pulling and all, and the thought lent him a grim smile to wear.

"Something amuses you?"

Jonny sighed and accepted his path. "Okay, we're going to need a torch. There's one in my toolkit, it's in the boot of my car. And you'll need some sensible shoes."

"Sensible shoes? What kind of woman do you think I am?" Sloane grinned and raised her foot. "Sandals are as good as it gets, I'm afraid. I didn't pack for this shit."

They finished their cigarettes on the way out to the car and Jonny fetched his torch from the boot. It hadn't seen active service in some time, but the batteries seemed up to the task.

"Stay close to me," he said, "and watch your footing. Coralie came a cropper last time we did this."

Not that she'd mind, really, since it seems she got her first child out of it.

Jonny took her hand and led her behind the bus. Though forewarned, Sloane was surprised to see the trail, as there had been no sign of one until now—he remembered reacting much the same way once. Then they shared a shrug of resigned resolve and stepped into the trees.

He kept cutting his eyes to the left and right, though he wasn't quite sure why. No-one else was likely to be around tonight—unless Jessica was stalking them through the bush, an image he found hard to shake. Keen to make sure everything played out differently this time, Jonny thumbed the torch on and picked out the path ahead, waving the beam around as if to sweep away any lurking ghosts. It marked him out to anyone who might be watching, but the light lent him a certain cheap courage nonetheless.

They didn't speak, but the bush around them was teeming with chirruping, feeding, mating life, and when the not-silence got to be a bit much, he asked Sloane to tell him about the manuscript she was currently editing. She ran off a short synopsis, and this harmless chatter kept him somewhat insulated against the dread building up in his heart. That apprehension really kicked up a notch when, a few minutes later, they stepped out of the trees and into the meadow.

"Nice," Sloane commented, her voice contriving to sound casual as she looked about. "This is where you had that picnic with your parents?"

"Yeah. The last time I saw Mum before—"

He cut himself short, and Sloane pressed herself against his side.

"Be brave, honey. This'll be over soon."

Really? Sometimes I feel like this nightmare will NEVER be over. That I'll just keep coming back here with every woman I ever love, and I'll just keep on losing them.

They cut across the meadow, their feet brushing through long grass that had refused to wilt beneath the summer sun, and Jonny saw the two trees ahead that acted as a kind of gateway. He distracted himself as they approached by trying to find the branch Coralie had tripped over. Maybe he'd take it back to her so Brendan could mount it over the mantle—the object responsible for the conception of their only son. That should make for an interesting conversation piece.

Now they were between those towering sentinels and back into the bush, though this last leg wouldn't take long. Jonny's every nerve grew taut with tension as they approached the mass that loomed ahead in the shadows, a sleeping giant with a yawning maw that swallowed everything.

Only this time, it'll have some nice wooden braces on, and that will make all the difference.

The ground opened out around them, and the trees fell away, and then they stood before the mound of rock that rose from the earth and stretched back toward the coast. Jonny felt his heart quailing in his chest, and as they walked closer it seemed ready to fly right out of his mouth.

"Wow," Sloane whispered.

Someone had repainted the white cross-within-a-love-heart sigil above the entrance. It glowed in the moonlight, fresh as the day it had first been applied.

And the mouth of the cave gaped open just the way he remembered it, unblocked, unbraced, not a single plank of wood in sight.

"Oh, no, no," he murmured, beginning to tremble.

"It's all right, baby, it's okay. It doesn't even look that bad, really. After all I'd heard, I was half-expecting a sign over the top saying *Abandon hope all ye who—*"

"This is wrong!" he insisted, cutting through Sloane's attempt at humour, turning to her with a pained expression. "Brendan told me that after I left, the townspeople boarded it up. It's supposed to be blocked, Sloane! What the hell is going on?"

She frowned and let go of his hand. "Stay here a moment."

"Don't!"

"I won't go inside, I promise. I'm just going to take a look." She crossed her heart as she backed away, then turned to face the cave as she walked closer. "Right. No sign of any boards around here. If they'd just rotted and broken apart, you'd be able to tell."

"Someone's taken them down." Jonny could see it all too well, Mr. Dogsbody's perennial grin wider than ever as he gleefully ripped the planks away with a crowbar. "And I can guess who."

Sloane stood before the cave and stared in. Maybe she caught a weird vibe beaming out from its depths, for she shuddered and hugged herself as if against a sudden chill. He was terribly disturbed by the sight of her framed by that gaping mouth, had an irrational fear that this might be the last he ever saw of her. It was all too easy to imagine a thin black tongue lashing out of the darkness, looping around her waist, jerking her in before he could even—

Get a grip!

He danced the torch around the cave mouth as Sloane stepped to one side and ran her hand up and down one of its rough gums.

"There was something here, all right. I can feel holes where the boards would've been fixed to the rock."

"That's enough. Come away from there."

Sloane sent him a reproachful look, then backed away from the cave and returned to his side. He felt immeasurably better just having her within touching distance and reached out to brush her arm.

"So, now what?" she asked. "Do we give her a yell, or what?"

Jonny shrugged, doubting the use of it but happy to delay the inevitable just a little longer. He ran his tongue over dry lips and took a long, shaky breath.

"Jessica!"

The call rang out across the clearing and into the trees, so loud in this near-silence, and Jonny pictured every living thing within a kilometre turning its head in his direction.

"Jessica Grzelak! Are you here?"

They waited while the crickets continued their endless song of need and the breeze stirred leaves to dance against leaves, and no reply came.

"I guess that would have been too easy," Sloane muttered.

"Of course it would." Jonny didn't like the edge in his voice, and by the way she flinched, she didn't either. "They've taken the planks down, opened the cave. Obviously, we're supposed to go inside."

"Do you really think she's in there, though? I mean, if it's been boarded up for so long, she couldn't have been inside the whole time. That said, I can totally see her hunched down over some rock pool like a goth Gollum, eating raw fish and—"

"Stop it!" he snapped, and Sloane cast him a hurt look. "I'm sorry, baby, but the last thing I need right now is another overactive imagination putting ideas in my head."

She conceded the point, and they stood staring at the cave in silence.

Again. Always this fucking place! Why can't I ever get away from it?

He was beginning to feel like the Chapel was the centre of his universe, the alpha and omega, the cold and inscrutable black fireball at the beginning and end of everything.

"Jonny?"

He knew what he had to do now, but he just couldn't make himself do it. His body was wiser than his brain.

"Jonny!"

He swung around to face her. "Sloane, you love me, right?"

"What? Of course I do. Yes."

"Then take my hand. And no matter what happens, remember that you love me, and that I love you even more."

Sloane slipped her fingers between his, intertwining them. "You're starting to worry me a little. It's just a cave, honey. It can't hurt us."

He kissed the back of her hand. "It's more than a cave, sweetheart. But you're right. It can't hurt us, not if our love is pure and true. And it is, isn't it?"

"I don't know if what we did back there on the bus counts as *pure*, but—"

"*Sloane.*"

"Okay, okay. Sorry. You know I have no sense of occasion."

Jonny took a deep breath, let it out. He remembered a ritual from when he was little—Mum would nag him to get out of bed, and he would call out a long, slow countdown to put off facing the new day: *threeeee…twoooooooo…onnnnnnnnne hundred…ninety-nine…*

Mum. What if she's *in there?*

Stop it. No-one's in there—except maybe Jessica, and if she is, she's just as alive as us. Now man up and get this shit over with.

Holding Sloane's hand tight, Jonny forced himself forward on leaden legs, and together they walked into the darkness.

and no more shall we part

LIKE SO MANY OTHER PLACES Jonny had revisited today, the cave looked like it had sat untouched for the past fifteen years, and he had the oddest feeling that he was stepping back into his youthful memories instead of forward into an uncertain future. He fought the impulse to flash the torch at his companion, to make sure it was Sloane's hand linked in his and not another.

"It's beautiful," she whispered, her voice dancing from wall to wall and back. Jonny didn't reply. He was too busy trying not to lose his shit.

What the hell am I doing in here again?

He darted the torchlight about, half-expecting the beam to fall across a gaunt shadow waiting for him in the darkness, its pale and all-too-familiar face cracked in two by a sinister smile. When it became clear that the chamber was deserted, he realised just how much he'd wound himself up in expectation of a horror-movie confrontation and his shoulders slumped in relief. His torch ran its light touch over the cave floor, and he could see no hint of any other tracks; he and Sloane were the first people to set foot in the cave for some considerable time. They may even have been the first to do so since the search party had come looking for clues to Jessica's disappearance.

"She's not here," he muttered.

"What was the Widow on about, then?" Sloane wanted to know. "She did say Jessica was out here, waiting for you."

That was an idea that Jonny liked less and less with every passing minute.

Because if she's not here, she must be—

He brushed that aside for now and walked carefully forward, keeping his torch on the floor to light their passage. Sloane used her free hand to lean on clammy stalagmites, her sandals proving a poor match for the swathes of slick rock that bulged out of the dirt. The cave bore absolutely no signs of human presence, and Jonny was reminded that the fifteen years since his last visit was like fifteen seconds in geological terms. He flicked his light over to the cluster of drooping straw formations that had once reminded him of a dripping maw, saw that it looked no different, and mused that each strand might just have grown a centimetre since he'd last been here.

Soon they had picked their way across to the far wall of the cave and the torchlight was shining back at them from the gullet of water, where those cocky divers had entered the narrow chute and found nothing worth their time.

"That's what the cops think we fell into."

"Really? What, did they think you took turns or something? That's ridiculous."

"Exactly." Jonny took a deep breath, moved the torch across the rear left corner of the chamber. "That's where we really went."

They stared at the lumpen wall for a moment. With all shadows blasted away by the light, it was plain that the dun-coloured surface was unbroken.

"Okay," Sloane said, her voice neutral.

"It was right there!" he insisted. "I *know* it was."

He stepped over to the corner, shining his torch up and down the wall and a few feet to either side. It made no difference. He couldn't see so much as a crack in the ancient umber rock.

"What would you say this means?" Sloane asked, picking her words carefully.

"It either means we're not in love, which I don't believe for a second, or…"

"Or…?"

He couldn't say it—simply couldn't force those words out of his recalcitrant throat. So Sloane had to do it for him.

"I'm so sorry, Jonny. It looks like the police were right. Maybe there never was a—"

He spun in protest, ready to remonstrate with this line of thinking. Sloane flinched from the sudden glare of the torch, her sandal slipping off some flowstone and shooting her foot out from under her. She fell with a yelp, and Jonny lurched forward to catch her. He managed to get his arm around her back, but her momentum brought him down, too. They collapsed together, and Jonny's heart leapt into his throat as Sloane gasped in shock as if stabbed.

"Shit, you okay?" he asked, thinking the worst. His torch hand was trapped under Sloane's back, pointing randomly at the opposite wall, and he could see next to nothing. "Sloane?"

"Oooooh, *Christ.* Yeah, I'm all right. But I'm sitting in a puddle of water that is fucking *freezing*. Get me up. Now. Now."

"I'm so sorry about that, baby."

"Yeah, yeah, later. *Up*."

Jonny left the torch on the cave floor for a moment as he gathered Sloane up in his arms and rose onto his knees. She clung to him like a scared little girl, her teeth chattering at the chill of the water that had saturated the back of her dress, and he shushed her accordingly as he gathered the fabric in his hands and wrung it out. While he did so, his eyes followed the torch beam into the rear right corner of the cave.

"Uh," he said.

"What?"

"We're getting up now, Sloane. And then you're going to turn around, okay?"

"Why? What's going on?"

"Up we go."

Jonny rose to his feet, bringing Sloane with him. He didn't take his eyes off the corner of the chamber for a second, and as soon as she freed herself from his clutches and got her feet on the ground again, she spun around to see why.

The light picked out a crevice in the wall, an impenetrable darkness that might as well have been painted on for all the luck the torch had illuminating its interior.

"That's it," he whispered, and a storm of conflicting emotions cascaded through him. Pride, that he'd been proven right; relief, that he hadn't imagined the whole thing; anger, that he'd been doubted and disbelieved by everybody, including himself…and awe, because the implications of this development were immense.

The Chapel is real.

After all these years, the validation was less gratifying than terrifying.

"Holy shit," Sloane breathed. "How did no-one see that?"

Jonny bent to pick up the torch, and the crevice didn't disappear like a momentary hallucination when the light flickered away from it.

"It's definitely there, and has been for a long, long time." Sloane turned to him, her brow furrowed. "So why did you think it was on the other side?"

Because it was.

"You must have gotten it the wrong way around. Misremembered that part."

He didn't want to think about that, so he just rolled with it for now.

"So, you believe me, then?" he asked, unable to entirely keep a surly snarl from his voice. "No-one found that passage when they looked for it, Sloane. But Jess and I saw it. *You* see it. The Chapel…it's through there."

They stared at the yawning crack for a few seconds, their breaths enlarged and imitated by the reverb of the cave. Then Jonny cut off the torch. They tensed as the blackness took them, with only a lighter shade of dark outside the mouth of the cave to reassure them they had not fallen into the abyss…and also, after the few seconds it took their eyes to adjust, a faint illumination that outlined the crevice in the far wall. When he was sure she'd seen it, Jonny flicked the torch back on.

"Do you think…" Sloane began, reluctant to finish.

"She's in there? I don't know." It didn't seem likely—only lovers could find the way, and wouldn't she be alone?—but Jonny was learning not to assume anything today. "Well, this is it. What do we do now?"

He already knew what Sloane was going to say. Like Jessica, she followed a path of reasoning that allowed no backtracking.

"Well…we can't turn away now. I can't say I like it much now that we're here, but we can't just leave it like this."

"I know," he said. "Okay, then. Hang on to me, babe."

They laced fingers, gave each other a supportive squeeze. Then they picked their way across the cave to the opening, and Jonny led them inside.

The torch went out immediately. Sloane let loose a little gasp.

"Yeah, that happened last time. Don't worry. The light will lead us through."

And like last time, that faint glow grew stronger as they shuffled through the tight passage, on and down and deeper into the rock. Jonny might have felt penned in by the close walls, claustrophobic, if not for his memory of the last time he'd traversed this path.

When it was on the other side of the cave. You realise what that means, don't you?

The passage wound a little one way, then the other, until Jonny had no idea which direction he was facing. But the trip didn't take long. Rounding one curve, he saw that the light was growing stronger, taking on a blue hue, and knew they were almost there.

"Here we go," he said to Sloane, "brace yourself," and then the two of them were stumbling out of the narrow passage and into the Chapel.

The huge chamber hadn't changed at all to his eye, but Jonny would never have expected it to; places like this counted years like humans counted seconds, and entire civilisations could rise and fall above without so much as a single notable variation below. The countless azure lights glowed on the rough ceiling above them, on the stalactites that hung from it, like the roof had been ripped off and another galaxy could be seen through the hole. The pool lay flat and still across most of the cavern floor, and the walls marched off at incoherent angles. The weird hump of rock that reminded him of a pulpit squatted on the other side, incredibly old and incredibly patient.

"Oh," Sloane sighed, the sound drawn out like a yawn. "Oh, Jonny. It's *wonderful.* It's…no, it's beyond words."

She took a few steps forward, turning on the spot to take it all in. Jonny gazed up and about with her, until he abruptly remembered what else might be in here. He cast his gaze all about the Chapel, looking for anything that appeared out of place—but he saw no menacing shadows, no sign of life other than what Jessica had assumed to be glow worms up above. Jessica herself was nowhere to be seen, unless she was folded into one of the wall's curves or lying under the water. He remembered imagining his mother beneath the pool's surface, her eyes open and staring up in cold silence, and shuddered even as he recalled there had been no sign of anyone or anything in the water last time.

Still, he had to be sure.

"Jessica?" he called, and at that volume, his voice gained a repeating echo that seemed to take forever to fade. The name rang in his ears over and over until the vocal loop diminished to silence.

Sloane pulled her gaze down to him. "I don't think she's here."

"No," he agreed, and while it opened up a new round of questions, it also came as somewhat of a relief.

"Then what's going on here, Jonny?" Sloane's voice was calm, as if the blue lights dotted overhead were soothing away her anxiety. "Why was Kassia so keen to get us out here? She must have been behind the envelopes, the planks being pulled off the cave—so why?"

And at last, he knew.

"She wants us to take the test," he said. "Of course. *That's* why. She wants to punish me for losing Jessica…by losing you, too."

Sloane's eyes widened and her voice lost its newfound serenity. "What?"

"But that's not going to happen. I swear to you, Sloane. I will never let that happen."

"No, it won't, because now we've seen this, we can leave. Just give me a moment…this is so awesome…where's my—*shit*!"

"What?"

"I left my handbag in the car. Have you got your phone?"

"Yeah, hang on."

Jonny fished it out of his pocket. According to the device, the time was now *#k:4@*, and all other recognisable text on the screen had been distorted into similar gibberish. He said nothing, just selected the camera and passed the phone to Sloane.

She took a few snaps of the azure-encrusted ceiling, then pointed at the pool and grabbed some shots of that too. Jonny marvelled at the incongruity of the scene—this was undoubtedly the first time anyone had ever photographed the Chapel. What next? His mind spun at the idea of Sloane posting an image of it on Instagram, but that would make a weird kind of sense; silicon came from sand and sand came from rock and so places like this were, in a sense, the ancestors of the device she now held. That both seemed to harbour a near-infinity of chaotic patterns that hinted at a kind of intelligence beyond human perception was entirely fitting.

"Right, that's that." Sloane handed him back his phone. "So…the Chapel's real, Jessica's not here, and we're done. Some questions you're just going to have to live with, I guess. Let's go."

She took a few steps toward him, then stopped dead and stared. She darted her eyes to either side and shook her head in denial, faster and faster. Even before he turned, Jonny was sickly certain that he knew full well what he was going to see—and what he was not.

The cave wall stood unbroken behind him.

The passage was gone.

"What…the…*fuck*." Sloane put her hands to her mouth. "That is…that is not *possible*, Jonny."

He sighed, closing his eyes. She was right, this was absurd…but so was a passage that only lovers could see, a path that moved from one side of the cave to another. Everything about the Chapel was preposterous, so this development made a strange kind of sense.

"What are we going to do? How are we going to get out? Jonny, we're trapped in here—*what are we going to do*?"

He turned and placed one hand on Sloane's arm. "It's okay, babe. There's still a way out."

"What?" She glanced wildly around the Chapel. "Where?"

"That way," he said, nodding toward the pool. "Sloane, the only way we can get out is to take the test."

She followed his gaze, then turned back. "Oh, no. *No*. This is the test you took with Jessica, right? The one you failed?"

"That's right. But this time—"

"No, there will be no *this time*!" Sloane yelled. "Jonny, you've kept the truth from me, fucking *lied* to me about your past since the day we met! And with all the shit that's come out today, I feel like I don't even know who you are anymore! And now you want me to risk my life on *faith*?"

"I'm sorry," he said, quiet and resolute. "But I told you everything, and you kept pushing, and you insisted we come here. Not me, *you*. And now this is the only way out. I'm sorry, Sloane, but we have to."

Her face was wrought, aged by the weight of his words, and for a moment she was the very image of her mother. "I don't want to do this, Jonny."

"I know. But we don't have any choice now."

Because all our choices have already been made, he thought, folding Sloane into an embrace that she clung to with a desperation born of fear. *No-one's ever forced to come here. We walked our own path. We had to see; we had to know. And now, again, we've come to the moment of truth.*

He kissed Sloane's head. "Baby, this is going to work, okay? Remember, all you have to do is focus on our love. It's as simple as that."

"But Jessica—and your *mum*—"

"That was different! When I was here with Jess…I was a different person then. A boy. It was the first time I'd been in love, and it was…complicated. I didn't know how to handle it. As for my mum…well, I guess life sucked the soul out of whatever she and Dad had together. Maybe they would've split one way or another in the end. But me and you, babe…what we've got is real, and it's strong. It's pure and true. And besides, we know people have come here before and passed the test. Remember Billy and Poppy?"

Sloane pulled back and gave him a dubious look. "And they're the best example you can come up with? The fucking Mickey and Mallory of the Copper Coast?"

"All that matters is that they loved each other so much, so deeply, that they both came out the other side. And so will we. Do you love me, Sloane Nowak?"

"I do. I do." She made a sound of stressed amusement, trying to leaven the seriousness of the situation. "And wow, those words are *not* something I figured I'd be saying any time soon."

He forced a laugh. "What better place for it than a Chapel?"

Sloane started to wince, but he kissed it away before it could take.

"Hey. Next year we'll be living in Sydney together, and everything will be even better than it was before. In years to come, we'll have dinner parties there, and our friends will ask how we've managed to stay together and be so happy, and we'll just look at each other and smile."

Her own lips turned up a little at that. "Optimism. Not one of your usual traits. I think I like it, though."

He gave her earlobe a gentle tug. "One more time, okay? I love you so much."

"I love you, too."

Jonny took Sloane's hand and led her over to the pool. At the edge, he turned to her and said, "Grit your teeth. It's a wee bit chilly."

He knew that for an understatement, but the cold of the pool's touch still took his breath away. Sloane shuddered as she followed him in, her feet swallowed by the clear water.

"Oh God, this is *insane*. What are we doing, Jonny? Seriously?"

"It's just water. Now, Sloane, I need you to do something for me. I need you to tell me about the place we're going to move into."

"But we haven't even started looking yet!"

"No, but I know you, and I know you've been thinking about this a lot. Just picture your perfect place and describe it for me."

Sloane shot him a look that said she knew what he was playing at, but she went along with it as they edged further into the pool.

"Okay, then. Well. It's a townhouse, split-level."

"Good."

"Close to the CBD, so we can walk in for dinner, and it's a cheap Uber ride when we have a night out. Easy commute for our jobs."

"I like it already."

"Downstairs is our lounge room. There's a little nook by the window where I can sit and read my manuscripts. A laundry in the back, and a lovely little bit of garden where we can hang out—somewhere I can flex my green thumb and you can grow some herbs and veggies. The kitchen's fully decked out, all mod cons, so you can really go to town when you're cooking, and there's a bar."

"Cool."

"And a cat." Sloane tossed him a defiant stare. "I'm not budging on that. Upstairs, our bedroom—we'll get a new bed, and there's a dresser I've had my eye on, too. Next door, guest bedroom-slash-storage. And a nice modern bathroom. I'm sick of white. Maybe something in blue."

Jonny smiled at her as he brought them to a halt. While she talked, they'd made it all the way across the pool. Now they stood knee-deep in chilly water and faced the odd, looming rock that never quite looked the same shape twice.

"Are they handprints?" Sloane wanted to know. "It looks like indigenous art or something. There's so *many*."

Jonny nodded. The prints were pale, almost luminous against the dark bulk of the rock, and he couldn't even begin to understand why or how these markings had been left. He looked at them now, unable to tell the eldest from the most recent, and wondered how long ago their makers had visited this place. How many impressions were from settlers, inhabitants of the town nearby, and how many from the native keepers of the land? He lifted his hand to test his readiness, eyes falling on the spot where he'd be placing it, and he saw a print there already.

Me. That's mine, from fifteen years ago.

As if completing a thought, he looked to the other side, and his eyes found a certain handprint there. The fingers contained gaps where rings had kept skin from touching the rock.

And that's Jessica.

"This is it," he said. And he barely managed that.

Sloane nodded, took a deep, shuddering breath. "I'm ready. Actually, no, I'm not."

"Just think of us, our happiness. Keep that thought in your mind. Hold on to it. Make love to it. Don't ever let it go."

His partner bit her lip, regarding him with a deep concern. Was that doubt he saw in her wide eyes? If so, her next words denied it.

"I love you, Jonny. And we're going to find that townhouse together, and we're going to be so happy it'll make people sick."

They kissed one more time, and Jonny could feel a tremor in his lover's body that was more than a reaction to the cold water. Her words were false bravado—she was terrified.

Me too. But we're in this together.

Jonny lifted his right hand, and Sloane mirrored the movement with her left. He brushed away the memory of he and Jessica doing the exact same thing fifteen years ago—tried to ignore his suspicion that, less than an hour ago, he had remembered what came next and then immediately forgotten it all over again. Together, they reached forward and carefully placed their palms on a clear part of the rock.

The pulpit was colder than ice and it burned without injury, just as Jonny remembered. He heard Sloane suck in a breath at the sensation, and then—that was it. Nothing else happened. Somewhere nearby, water dripped as it might have been doing for millennia, counting off the seconds like an unstoppable clock at the heart of the world.

Sloane turned her face toward him. "Is that—"

She cut off suddenly, sucking in a shocked gasp of air, and Jonny felt a sick sense of *déjà vu* and vertigo at the same time as he realised the floor had disappeared. He managed to grab a quick breath before they dropped like stones, and then the waters closed over his head once more.

How had he ever forgotten this? It was the most terrifying thing in the world. Jonny threshed madly but held on tight to Sloane's hand, and she dug her nails in hard. Their bodies sank like lead diving weights and Jonny tried to prise his eyes open, even though he knew there was nothing to see. Sure enough, blackness—a dark so complete it might have been the void of space before the first stars were born. He couldn't even see Sloane right next to him, though he could feel the motion in the water from her thrashing limbs. All he could see was the soft sapphire glow of the Chapel three metres above them, five metres, ten.

Sloane.

He kicked and fought without thinking, even as he tried to corral his thoughts.

Love.

His lungs ached, expressing an urgent desire to fill themselves. He kept his mouth shut and eyes open. He could see nothing—ancient leviathans could be cruising by just feet away, and he would never know. A whole new cosmos could be opening up beneath him, swallowing him into its infinite spread, and he would remain blind to its indifferent majesty.

Sloane's hand tugged at his as though something had grabbed hold of her other arm and was trying to pull her away. He tightened his grip even more and thought hard. He thought of the two of them sprawled on a functional couch in their new townhouse, arms and legs wound around each other like loving vines, a brindle-furred cat curled up against their shared warmth. He thought of them blessing the new bedroom, plunging and sweating and crying out and erupting, enacting their personal sacrament. He thought of them old and infirm and still laughing and loving, their hands still linked, because they were always and forever and nothing was going to tear them apart, nothing, not ever.

Sloane's fingers slipped from his grasp.

NO!

He groped frantically for her with both hands, but there was nothing. He tried to swim that way, fought against the downward pull and failed.

SLOANE!

No air. No time.

No point in panicking. This was how he'd fail. He had to remember what was important.

LOVE.

Jonny closed his useless eyes as he sank further and further into the illimitable depths, and pictured instead everything about her that had ever made him happy—every silly little joke, every luminous smile, her instinctive kindness, the way she sneezed, the feel of her body from the inside, the way her hands absently alighted upon him when she walked by as if to get a quick fix of touch, the smell of her perfume and the perfume of her sex, the love in every fibre of her that sometimes—too rarely—left him agape with awe at the enormity of what she'd done for him and would continue to do without even needing to be asked.

I love you. Don't leave me. Come back to me. I will never hurt you again, I will never leave you again, I will be yours forever.

Please—

Jonny's body was spasming against his efforts to hold his breath. Only seconds now until he could fight no more, until his straining lips burst open and allowed the cold dark to fill him with nothingness. All was black, but he tried to see the light.

I love you

His lips were still sealed but the blackness was inside him now, shutting him down, fading him out. The only sense he had left was touch. But as he dropped further and further, far beyond the point of no return, he knew that his love was not in vain. He knew that it was pure and true. He knew that this time he had not failed, because even as he continued to sink, even as he gave up all hope, a cold hand slipped into his and held it tight.

after the fall

THE DARKNESS EXPLODED.

Breath.

Then water again, invading, choking.

He convulsed and jack-knifed upward, coughing and spluttering as air turned his wet face to ice, his hands flinging out and grasping something firm, rough, unmoving. He hacked out the water that filled his gullet and gasped, choked, gasped. His feet found purchase beneath him and he thrust himself forward onto land.

Dazed, he had no idea how long he lay there drawing in deep, wheezing breaths, no idea how much time had passed before enough of his mind came back to him that he could make sense of the chaos. He lifted his head and stared at a world he had never expected to see again.

He was slumped over an edging of rock, his body still half-submerged in water. Weak as a newborn, he got his hands under him and somehow swayed upright on trembling legs.

Alive!

He was standing in a small pool a few metres across and four feet deep, shivering and shaking as if suffering a seizure. The chill of the water had robbed the summer night air of its warmth, had stolen any heat that remained in his body and left winter lurking in his bones. Above him, the stars gleamed down like pinholes in the dark fabric of space, and he gasped in relief to see the familiar field of white points that had watched over him his whole life, not those strange azure constellations they'd seen overhead in the Chapel—

His whole body jolted at the recollection.

Where is she?

He twitched around, barely managing to stay on his feet. The pool was surrounded by a verge of rock that gave way to humble dirt and then sloped sharply down to an army of trees, breeze hissing through their branches like indistinguishable gossip. The surface of the water was still and there was no-one else in sight.

He croaked her name again and again, his voice waterlogged and ineffectual. There was no reply. She was not here.

Maybe she got out first!

He staggered across the pool, sloshing the water with his grasping hands, hoping that at any second his fingers would catch in knots of long wet hair or folds of sodden fabric. They did not.

He was alone.

No…no!

He had to get out of the water, lest fate take back this miraculous favour. He stumbled over to the edge of the pool and dragged himself onto dry land, his muscles groaning at the Herculean effort required. But he couldn't stop now.

He muttered as he gathered his legs beneath him and rose, fell, rose again on heavy feet. He said her name over and over again like a mnemonic, a lucky charm. No reply.

Had she come up first, staggered away in shock before him?

That, or she was not here, and never had been.

His mind felt like it had slipped free of its moorings, and he knew he didn't have long before it gave in to a healing oblivion. His body and soul craved unconsciousness, but he had to hold it off a little longer—had to find her, find *anyone.* He stared wildly about the pool, saw a rocky path that led around a huge hump of rock rising from the earth. He staggered onto it, wetness dripping from his waterlogged clothes and spattering on the stone beneath him.

He walked almost without knowing it, utterly lost. The only experience that compared to this was when he'd been so drunk he could barely stand or think, and once or twice he paused to vomit water down the front of his shirt before stumbling on. The path ended in outcroppings of rock, and he had to clamber and fall over them so he could keep moving.

And now the surface was levelling out to shale, dropping down to a familiar clearing in the woods. He hit the edge and fell to his knees in the dirt, and the mammoth rocky growth alongside him was opening out into a deep, dark mouth that he dared not look at for fear it would suck him in all over again. Moaning, he shambled on across the open ground and then into the trees, bleary eyes keeping him on the narrow path. Crickets sang songs of their own concerns, ignoring his crisis.

The short trail opened out into a meadow just ahead, and someone was sitting in the grass at the edge, leaning back on their hands and looking up at the moon. A woman.

Mum.

No.

Jessica!

He opened his mouth to make some entreaty to her, and she yawned and looked away from the moon and caught sight of him. She screamed and jumped to her feet, hands flying to her mouth.

"Brendan!"

That man appeared out of the bush in a hurry, pulling up the zipper of his jeans as he raced to answer her cry. Brendan stopped beside Coralie and stared at this apparition, his eyes almost as wide as the moon.

Friends. Safe.

"Jess," he moaned one more time.

His knees buckled and the night spun tight and fast around him like a cold, dark web. But fate might finally have allowed Jonno a small mercy, for his consciousness had blinked out by the time his sodden body pitched forward and crashed face-first into the dirt.

love will tear us apart

MIDNIGHT WAS HALF AN HOUR away when Alan Trotter's wake finally wound up. The boozy, maudlin crowd either headed home to sleep off their indulgence or wandered in the direction of the Waterwich Hotel & Bar to pursue their commiserations in less salubrious surroundings. By the time Mick closed up and disappeared to mourn in private, only Jack Nichols and Brendan Swain still lingered on the footpath outside the pub. Jack handed Brendan a flask of gin to hold while he stabbed awkwardly at a mobile phone and called his wife to come pick them up. That done, he took the flask back and lit a cigarette. Brendan, who'd finally quit smoking before Mae was born, licked beer-slicked lips and almost regretted his abstinence.

"Not a bad night, all up," Jack judged, looking to the moon for agreement. "You know, considering the circumstances. I reckon Alan would've been happy with the turnout."

"I thought Jonno would've made it back by now," Brendan grumbled, more saddened than slighted. "You know, I never realised just how much I missed that bastard 'til he turned up today."

"He staying at the pub?"

"Reckon so. Mick gave him and his missus a key."

Jack grinned and raised his flask in salute. "He's done well for himself. She was a bit of all right, wasn't she?"

"Yeah. Not a patch on what I got waiting at home, but yeah."

Jack nodded in understanding. He was pushing seventy and had been in love with the same lady for over half a century. Whenever he felt cynical about modern marriage and its staying power, Brendan thought of Jack and Sally Nichols and knew that sometimes, just sometimes, love worked out the way its disciples promised it would.

"I always felt sorry for that poor bugger," Jack said. "You know how his girlfriend disappeared, oh, years ago now?"

"I was there, you old duffer."

"That's right, yeah. Anyway…as I remember, he reckoned they found that place. The one Waterwich kids have always whispered about—the Chapel. Said it was real after all, but the search party never found it."

"Yeah, he said that." Brendan winced, recalling his response to that claim. "I was on that search party, too. Just a plain old cave, mate, I can guarantee it."

Jack squinted and regarded his younger companion with an air of indecision. Brendan knew the look well—a drunk man trying to decide whether to share a confidence or not. Of course, there was only ever one outcome to that exercise.

"Thing is, Brenny, people have been talking about the Chapel for donkey's. It was an old story when I was knee-high to a grasshopper."

"When mammoths roamed the plains."

"Shut up, you. No shit, when I was in school, the girls used to sing a playground song about it. It was just one a them local myths, or so I figured. But there was this one bloke I knew who said different. He said the Chapel was real, too—even reckoned he'd been there. You know how you get told things and you just brush 'em off, assume they're bullshit, and then later something happens to make you think twice? Well, this bloke I knew…his name was Billy Ross."

Brendan coughed out a breath that had suddenly gone down the wrong way. "Bloody hell, Jack! You *knew* that guy?"

"Yeah, all through school 'til he dropped out, and a bit after that. We was never close, but we used to have a bash of cricket now and again, have a smoke and a yarn outside the town hall after they screened a flick, whatever. Anyway, not long before he and that jailbait girlfriend of his went on their killing spree, he told me they'd found the Chapel. They went in there together. He said they was tested, and they passed, and they was gonna be together the rest of their lives, no matter what."

Brendan remembered Jessica telling them this aboard the 49er on the last night anyone had seen her alive, and he shuddered a little despite the summer night air. The story had sounded like hyperbole at the time, her own dramatised re-enactment of the truth, and even reading about Billy and Poppy online years later he'd felt a certain distance from their sordid tale. Jack's words brought the whole mess back into sharp focus—the killers had walked these very streets, been at home in the heart of this town, pulsed through the same familiar veins as Brendan and his family.

"I was already dating Sally back then, and we was getting serious—hadn't done the deed yet, she wasn't ready for that, but we was pretty familiar with each other. I loved the hell outta that girl even then, and we was already talking about tying the knot. You don't see that much these days, but these was different times. We figured we'd get engaged when we was both eighteen and start saving for the big day. My point being, you couldn't have found two kids more in love than us, not even Billy bloody Ross and his psycho wench. And we was so into the romance of the whole thing, we decided we'd go to the Chapel, too."

Jack Nichols lowered himself onto a nearby bus stop bench, groaning as his knees were relieved of duty, and Brendan sat right beside him. He had a feeling this story was going somewhere he needed to be.

"From what Billy had said, it wasn't too hard to work out where the place was. So me and Sal went out down Mermaid Drive to the Hunter property, though it belonged to a bloke called Crisp back then, and we found that cave. And mate…we found the Chapel, too."

Brendan's response was reflexive. "You're shitting me."

"Nope. We went into that cave, and yeah, I know—you blokes never found no other passage, I've heard it from a dozen mouths, but *we* did. There was a way through."

Brendan stared, gauging his sincerity. He needn't have bothered—Jack Nichols was widely known as one of the most honest, no-shit blokes you'd ever meet. That meant he was telling the truth as he saw it, so either he'd somehow imagined all this, or…

Fuck off, it can't be true!

But how badly did he want to believe that for his own reasons? How tightly did he cling to what he'd always seen as the truth in order to justify what he'd done? After all, he'd thumped his best mate in the face and sent him packing, something he'd bitterly regretted ever since. If the Chapel was real, if Jonno had been telling the absolute truth that night—

"So what happened, then?"

"Never been sure, mate." Jack shook his head, staring vacantly across the road. He was young at heart, but in that moment, he wore every one of his sixty-nine years. "There *was* a test, I know that. Blue lights, that's all I can remember. Sal doesn't know exactly what happened then neither. Next thing we agree on, we was in a little pool somewhere out back of the cave, gasping for air. Scared the shit out of us, I don't mind telling you. We held hands so tight when we walked back to the Valiant that I thought Sal's nails would stick right into me bones and never come out—and it's funny, you know, 'cause they never did, in a way. We never told no-one about that night, but it stayed with us, and I reckon it's one of the things that's kept us glued together, you know? Fifty-two years, mate. Best thing that ever happened to me, no contest."

Brendan said nothing, thinking of Coralie and the kids—the best things that had ever happened to him.

"So when I heard about Jonno and his missus back then, I knew straight away what had happened. They'd taken the test, only he'd failed and lost her like the stories warned about. The poor bastard. Not only does he lose his girl—and she was a lovely one, weird and dark but lovely—but no-one believes him. No wonder he did a runner as soon as he could. That's probably what he's done tonight, too—had enough of the joint and buggered off home. Can't blame him, to be honest. The way some folk were talking about him tonight was downright mean."

Jack took a swig from his flask. Brendan scratched his hairy chin, wondering how he was going to reconcile this new account with his own experience.

"Mate, if what you're saying is true...*Jesus*." Brendan leaned back on the seat, slapped both hands to his skull. "Jonno tried to tell me about the Chapel, and you know what I did? I tried to knock his block off. I turned me back on me best mate."

"Not your fault, Brenny. I wouldn't believe it meself if I hadn't been there. Important thing is, you got the chance to be mates again. Make sure it sticks this time."

"Like shit to a blanket," Brendan assured him.

Headlamp eyes roved down the street looking for them, and they stood up to flag down their ride. Brendan hopped in the back of the Nichols sedan and greeted Sally, who had to be reminded of his address, and then they were off.

Brendan spent most of the short trip deep in thought. If he decided to believe Jack, to accept that the Chapel was real after all, he would have to rethink everything that had happened fifteen years ago...and either way, he still had a new and rather disturbing theory to consider.

Jack had suggested that Jonno and Sloane might have just driven home to the city, but judging by the way they'd been drinking at the wake, Brendan didn't think it was likely—and besides, Coralie had texted him a few hours back to say she'd bumped into them at Dino's and invited them out for drinks. No, he didn't believe that Jonno had run off without saying goodbye—not again, not with certain fences well on the way to being mended. And if he hadn't left town, and he wasn't at the Arms...

Sally Nichols pulled up outside his house, and Brendan thanked them for the lift as he stepped out into the summer night. Then, on impulse, he popped his head back into the car.

"Sally, do you ever regret going to the Chapel?"

She turned to him quickly, blinking at this unexpected question, and shot a look at Jack. He tipped her a slight nod.

"No," Sally said, "no, I don't. I don't know how much Jack told you—"

"Everything I remember, love. He needed to know. Jonno's his mate."

"Righto. Well, I'm not sure exactly what happened out there, Brenny, but I think sharing that experience—passing that test—has helped keep us together all these years, and there's not one thing I'd change about the time me and Jack have had."

"Fair enough. Thanks, guys. See you soon."

Brendan carried a heavy head into the house, trying to be quiet for the kids' sake. Not that they ever showed him such consideration; tomorrow's hangover was sure to be greeted with a racket that would make a Metallica concert seem like a whisper in the dark. He guzzled some water, began to kick off his shoes, then changed his mind. He walked up to the bedroom, where he found the lamp on and his wife reading a Serendipity Jones paperback.

"Hey, sweetie." Coralie turned her cheek up for a kiss and wrinkled her nose at his breath. "You smell like a brewery. Clean those teeth before you come to bed."

Brendan sat on the edge of the mattress, one hand resting on her leg through the summer sheet, trouble writ large on his face. "Coz…something's bothering me."

She sighed and put her book face-down on the bed. "If this is another apology for flirting with Mandrill's boobs after a couple of beers—"

"It's Jonno."

Coralie turned serious at once. "Did everything go okay? You didn't…?"

"Everything was cool, babe. But he didn't come back to the pub after you saw him and his missus at the pizza joint, even though he's supposed to be staying there tonight."

He shook his head, hefted the weight of the words, and spoke his fear aloud.

"I think he's gone *out there.*"

Sitting up straight, Coralie grasped his hand. "What? Why would he?"

Brendan shrugged. "He must've been dreaming of that place over the years. Wouldn't you? I think he needed closure. And it gets worse."

He filled Coralie in on the story Jack Nichols had just told him. By the end of it, she was kicking the sheets clear and shucking off her nightie. He watched as the love of his life dressed in the old clothes she'd been wearing that day, feeling the same rush of affection and desire her bare breasts had always awoken in him, and that was the least of his emotions where she was concerned.

"We need to go look," she said. "If he's out there…I don't like it, Brendan, not one bit."

"Me neither. The place is boarded up now, but it still gives me the creeps to think of him going out there again. If nothing else, we can't have him stumbling around pissed in the bush at night."

Coralie glanced up from lacing her shoes, and the look in her eyes told him a drunken sprained ankle was the least of her worries.

"Better make sure Jesse's awake, he'll have to babysit while we're out."

Brendan didn't entirely dig the idea of Coralie coming with him, even though he'd prefer to have her by his side no matter where he was. But he was in no fit state to drive, and besides, Jonno had been her best mate, too. He walked out into the hallway, rapped three times on the furthest door, waited a few seconds for Jesse to make himself presentable, then let himself in. His son was squinting at the door in bemusement, but he hadn't been sleeping—the glow of his phone gave him away.

"Drop your cock and grab your socks," Brendan said. "Me and Mum have to go out for a bit, so you're the man of the house."

"What's going on?"

"We gotta go look after an old mate. Don't think we'll be long. If the girls wake up, tell 'em everything's fine and put 'em back to bed."

Sometimes Jesse liked to give a sarcastic salute when told to do something, because he was fourteen and surliness came naturally at that age, but now he just nodded and hopped to it. He was a good kid, and when he came out the other side of puberty, he was going to be a good man—as long as he didn't fall in love with some dopey tart and decide to go looking for the Chapel himself.

Coralie grabbed a torch on the way out of the house, and, making a last-minute decision, the first-aid kit as well. Seeing that made Brendan's heart drop, even if they'd probably never need it. It was a declaration he didn't much care for: *shit just got real.*

They jumped in the family ute and Coralie got them moving, tense enough to flinch at the stereo and cut off her Thelma Plum CD in favour of a heavy silence. Brendan watched the house shrink in the rear-view and wondered if Mae and Tara would be waking up at the sound of the commotion, finding Jesse in charge, getting scared at the thought of Mum and Dad not coming back. They could be such drama queens. Hadn't he promised that he would always come home to them, no matter what? That was his most sacred vow, to them and to his wife, and he didn't need to test it to know its purity and truth. He had too much to lose and nothing to prove.

Coralie asked him to clarify a few points on the drive out, putting her foot down just a little harder when reminded that Sloane had spoken to Kassia Rzepka. As they swung onto Mermaid Drive in a cloud of dust and gravel, Brendan wondered if his wife was also remembering all the times they'd driven out here in his dear old LX. She'd ridden in pride of place beside him, Jonno in the back seat boisterously debating some ridiculous topic with the driver—and next to him, Jessica, quiet unless she had something meaningful to say, her deep green eyes lit from within with a kind of detached amusement. That had been her customary look, and Brendan would've sworn she was wearing it even on the night he'd fucked her on his mum's couch while Coralie and Jonno grunted and moaned nearby—the devil's advocate, triumphant once more.

That memory had always left him more queasy than pleased, and he pushed it away before he could examine it in detail. He glanced at Coralie as she spun the wheel and turned them onto Gavin Hunter's land, all business, all miracle—his wife, the mother of his children, the centre of his universe. It was so hard to imagine her with anyone else, even though he'd seen it with his own eyes; Jessica, not so much. She'd never shared more than thumbnail sketches of her life before Waterwich, but where Coralie had known only two lovers and both of them dear to her, it was easy to imagine Jess leaving a string of stricken and smitten suitors in her wake, none of them worth a backward glance as she pelted headlong into the night.

Brendan had often wondered how she had even gotten involved with them in the first place, why she'd fallen for a regular bloke like Jonno. Jessica Grzelak had seemed like the kind of girl who never fit in anywhere, who could never get comfortable enough to set down roots, and that made it almost impossible to imagine what her life might have been like had it continued. Jess with a job, a uniform? It had been hard enough to reconcile her stories of working at McDonald's with the present tense of her. Jess with a husband and a house to clean, two screaming kids and a dog, a breast pump and a chocolate craving, a *Woman's Day* subscription for the crosswords, a BABY ON BOARD sign hanging in the back window of her SUV? Fuck off.

Maybe she couldn't imagine her own future either, Brendan thought, with a flash of what he was startled to recognise as insight. Maybe that's why she'd been what she was, why she acted the way she did—she'd long since become who she wanted to be, and couldn't see any way out of it. Maybe that even explained what happened to her. Given the choice between old age and cancer or a deep black hole in the ground, which did he honestly think Jessica would choose?

The trail opened out into the first clearing, and Brendan swore in uneasy confirmation when their headlights picked out a Clubsport parked right where Jonno had used to leave his XF. Coralie pulled up alongside and they checked the car—empty, of course. Then the two of them were hurrying over to the bus that had replaced the 49er, hoping against hope that Jonno and Sloane would be sitting on the back seat and sharing a smoke and a joke or maybe just sleeping off the beers they'd drunk. But of course the new derelict was empty, and only now was Brendan considering the insidious implications of its presence in the first place.

"You idiot, Jonathan," Coralie muttered under her breath, and the two of them headed around back to where the obscure trail began.

The trip was faster than it had been fifteen years ago, as this time they had a working torch and urgency on their side. It was only a couple of minutes until they reached the meadow, and then they had to work their way around the edge to find the sentinel-marked spot that opened up into another short path. When they found it, Brendan pointed to the grass at the edge.

"Right there, Coz. Me and you, making history."

She didn't smile, too tense to reminisce. "Maybe one day we'll embarrass Jesse and put up a plaque there. Come on."

They hurried down the last stretch, the anticipation of tragedy turning their spit sour. And now the rock was looming up ahead of them, rising out of the earth like some incredibly slow giant, and Coralie played the torch over its face with a gasp of shock.

"Look!"

The boards were gone. The cave mouth gaped wide open. Brendan felt his stomach pickle, and knew it wasn't just the booze.

"Oh, what the fuck?" He crossed over to the mouth of the cave, leery of the darkness he could almost feel seeping out of it. "This wasn't Jonno—looks like the planks have been gone for a while. But why?"

"Never mind that," Coralie snapped, anxious. "Brendan, they've gone inside. They've gone looking for the Chapel. *What are we going to do*?"

They stood there undecided, Coralie flicking the torch around the cave mouth as if hoping to find a clue or a friend just inside. The beam landed on the rock above that gaping maw, where the cross-within-a-love-heart sigil Brendan remembered from fifteen years ago glowed with a fresh intensity. Whoever had re-opened the cave had rebranded it as well, and that boded ill indeed.

"I'll tell you what we're *not* doing," Brendan said. "We're not going in there. Not together, anyway. I'm not putting my family at risk over this."

"But if we don't go in together, we won't be able to find the way through to the Chapel, and you *know* that's where they've gone. So what the hell else can we do?"

Brendan shrugged. They stared at each other, lost.

And then, they heard the moan.

Their eyes widened, still locked together, and each knew what the other was thinking—what they were remembering.

More moans and sobs, coming closer. From behind the cave.

The last time they'd heard these sounds had been right after Brendan had shot Jesse and a few hundred million of his potential brothers and sisters into Coralie's reproductive system. He'd gone off into the trees for a satisfied post-shag piss, had heard his lover scream his name, had hurried back to see—

A shining figure, shambling and stumbling over the rocks, leaving behind a trail of water that ran from its clothes like blood from a mortal wound.

"Oh, no," Coralie moaned, a deep anguish stretching the second word out like an echo of itself.

The figure reached the edge of the rocky path that led around the side of the cave and then tripped over, landing on its hands and knees in the dirt of the clearing. This seemed to shock some vague sense of awareness into it, because now it started wailing, and in that sound was a loss so profound it shoved a chill blade right into Brendan's heart. Tears welled quickly in eyes that hadn't known such a thing since the birth of his last child, but these did not come in happiness.

Coralie ran to the sopping wet figure, knelt beside it, tried to soothe it—but it just kept screaming, its shock and anguish so deep that it might never stop. Coralie turned and cast a look at Brendan, and after knowing her for twenty-six years, he could read it even without the help of the torch. He turned away and fished his mobile from his pocket, checked he had a connection. Then he went through his contacts and selected MACKLIN, because that man was head cop in this town these days, and though he'd been at the wake for a while, he would still be up and sober. Sure enough, the sergeant answered after two rings.

"Mate, it's Brendan Swain. I'm out on the Hunter property. At the cave. Yeah, that's right. Yeah. It's happened again."

He listened to what Macklin said, indicated his understanding, then hung up. He glanced over to see Coralie holding the woman tight, muttering the kind of soothing things that helped the kids relax and get to sleep, but it wasn't doing much good. Knowing he could do little to help, he looked up at the stars scattered across the summer sky and was surprised to find himself remembering a sleepover he'd attended at Michael Gregson's place as a kid. Jonno had been there too, and they'd gossiped about girls they liked and teachers they didn't, all the while staring up at the random pattern of glow-in-the-dark shapes glued to the ceiling. A strange new galaxy had hung over them that night—constellations they didn't recognise, worlds they couldn't even imagine.

Eventually the screaming stopped, and Brendan and Coralie managed to get Sloane over to the car and wrapped in a blanket. They stood close to each other as they waited for the world to come, reminded of what could be lost in an instant. Brendan kissed his wife on the forehead and her hand slipped into his, a promise made and a promise kept. They held hands when the police arrived to take control of the scene, when they gave their statement to Sergeant Macklin at the station, when they returned home and cried together over their loss. They were still holding hands hours later when the sun rose and chased the last shadows of night away from their bedroom, falling asleep side by side—falling fast into the vast and depthless darkness, but never alone.

acknowledgements

Midnight in the Chapel of Love was written at Ghastly Manor in Somerton Park, with additional work done at my parents' house in Port Pirie (on Christmas night, no less), the office of their Autopro store on a lunch break, and a hotel in Collingwood, Victoria whilst on the road with Priority Orange. Editing took place at Ghastly Manor, Meg Wright's flat as I babysat her cat Juniper, the house she and I shared in Darlington, and my current home in Somerton Park (informally known as Asian Delights due to past scandals that have nothing to do with me or with my bands recording there). These books were helpful to me during the research process: *Nharangga Wargunni Bugi Buggillu: A Journey through Narungga History* by Skye Bischoff (Wakefield Press), *Great Caves of the World* by Tony Waltham (Firefly Books), and *Beneath the Surface: A Natural History of Australian Caves* by Brian Finlayson and Elery Hamilton-Smith (UNSW Press).

Warm thanks are due to the following:

Jessica Harvey put up with me babbling on about the earliest iteration of this story while we were hanging out. Eva Grzelak graciously let me borrow her name and taught me how to pronounce it. Brendan Smart became the inspiration for Jonno's best friend as soon as I gave him the same first name, and if you like the fictional man, it's because the real one is a total champ. The folks at Tandanya National Aboriginal Cultural Institute were kind enough to answer a couple of my questions on indigenous matters. Bethany Clark and the staff at the SA Writers Centre graciously tapped me to read the second chapter of this book at an author event in Adelaide's West Terrace Cemetery. Joanne Ielasi, whom I befriended whilst putting up posters in her café, read an earlier draft and was incredibly enthusiastic about its potential. Kylie @ Allen & Unwin and Anna Solding @ MidnightSun reluctantly passed on publishing this book but provided detailed notes full of praise and encouragement. Scarlett R. Algee is the reason you're holding this book in your hands right now—she took a chance on this story by picking it up for publication, and she's been nothing but supportive and enthusiastic along the way. Sean Leonard picked up on some embarrassing mistakes and provided some astute editing suggestions. Don Noble at Rooster Republic Press created the gorgeous cover art. My family, friends, and fellow writers provided support, inspiration, and brilliance, as always. And the wonderful Meg Wright offered thoughtful feedback upon reading the manuscript, helped me with the blocking out of certain scenes, accompanied me on a road trip to Naracoorte to explore the cave systems there, and lent her considerable talents to the author photograph—thank you, Pie.

And last but never least, thank *you*.

chapter title playlist

"Destruction Makes the World Burn Brighter"—Chelsea Wolfe
"From the Edge of the Deep Green Sea"—The Cure
"The Last Day of Summer"—The Cure
"Be Quiet and Drive (Far Away)"—Deftones
"A Night Like This"—The Cure
"Forgive Our Fathers"—Godflesh
"Anthem for the Year 2000"—Silverchair
"The Funeral Party"—The Cure
"I Put A Spell on You"—Marilyn Manson
"About A Girl"—Nirvana
"She's Lost Control"—Joy Division
"After All These Years"—Silverchair
"My Own Summer (Shove It)"—Deftones
"Where Boys Fear to Tread"—The Smashing Pumpkins
"The Memory Remains"—Metallica
"Came Back Haunted"—Nine Inch Nails
"Summertime Sadness"—Lana Del Rey
"Sooner or Later You're Gonna Have to Do Something About Me"—Something for Kate
"Gloomy Sunday"—Diamanda Galás
"Suspicion Bells"—Effigy
"Chapel of Love"—The Dixie Cups
"Stranger Than Kindness"—Nick Cave and the Bad Seeds
"The Great Below"—Nine Inch Nails
"The Fireball at the End of Everything"—Something for Kate
"And No More Shall We Part"—Nick Cave and the Bad Seeds
"After the Fall"—Chelsea Wolfe
"Love Will Tear Us Apart"—Joy Division

about the author

Author photo by Red Wallflower Photography

Matthew R. Davis is an Australian Shadows Awards-winning author and musician who grew up in Port Pirie, South Australia, and now lives in Adelaide. He plays bass and sings in idiosyncratic heavy rock/metal bands such as Blood Red Renaissance and icecocoon, sometimes performs spoken word shows with punk poets Paroxysm Press and has worked on short films and video clips as a composer, scriptwriter, director, editor, producer, cameraperson, grip, and even actor. His first collection of horror stories, *If Only Tonight We Could Sleep*, was published by Things in the Well in 2020. Find out more at matthewrdavisfiction.wordpress.com.

www.ingramcontent.com/pod-product-compliance
Lightning Source LLC
Chambersburg PA
CBHW030116260626
47156CB00008B/2676